All it took was one wrong decision.

Book 3, The Liquor Collection
Liquor has never been so disturbingly saucy

I had it all. Great friends, amazing job, perfect boyfriend. My life was just filled with rainbows and unicorns...until it wasn't.

Everything that defined my life disappeared within the blink of an eye, leaving me alone and desperate. Two things that can make a woman do stupid things.

After accepting an offer I couldn't refuse my life went from bad to worse—except the part where I met Logan.

He's strong and kind, and seems to be the only light in the darkest corners of my life. When I'm with him I no longer feel...empty.

But the decisions I've made in order to survive won't allow me to start over. Too many secrets lurk in the shadows waiting for the right moment to strike.

When it does...it will ruin us both.

WARNING

This book contains content this is not suitable for persons under 18. Drugs, alcohol, assault, torture, sexual content, including a threesome and non-consensual sex and lots of coarse language are included in this book.

If these subjects offend, then this book probably isn't for you.

Once again this book is set in Australia, so for my non-Aussie readers, here is a glossary of sorts to help you out with the terminology and Aussie slang.

Thongs – Flip-flops
Singlet – vest/tank
Trackies – Sweat Pants
Pushie - bicycle
Missus – Wife/Girlfriend/Partner
Arvo – Afternoon
Arv sesh – meet up at the pub and drink in the afternoon
Head job – Blowjob
Undies – Panties
Mullah – Cash/Money
Tender – Contract/Job
Ambo – Ambulance Officer
Physio – Physiotherapist
Bottle-O – Liquor store

Origin – yearly Rugby League game between Queensland and New South Wales
Brewskies – alcoholic drinks
Boot – Car trunk

The legal drinking age is Australia is 18.

THE LIQUOR CABINET SERIES

Liquor has never been so disturbingly saucy

Malt Me (Book 1)

Tequila Healing (Book 2)

Wine Not (Book 3)

The Final Shot (Book 4)

The Liquor Cabinet: Series boxset

Antecedent

Seven Nights

Titanic Tales, a charity anthology (no longer available)

Gone Coastal, a sizzling summer beach anthology

Leave Me Breathless: The Lilac Collection

To my year ten English teacher,
Mrs. Jenny Martin

You always told me if I apply myself (and shut up) that I could achieve anything, you have been a silent support to me on this journey and I thank you for all your encouragement back at school. I wish you were still here to see what I have achieved but I know that you are up there cheering me on and still telling me to shut up.

PROLOGUE

It's so good to hang out with Kenz, Jordan, and Mike again and to finally get to know Sav. I'm glad that Kenz kept pestering me to come, I think I need to spend more time with them so I don't lose myself down the rabbit hole that I'm currently stuck in. It's hard keeping it all hush-hush, but the focus is on Mike and Sav tonight so my secret will be safe...for now.

After a rough trot, things are looking up for Mike and Sav, they are extremely happy and recently bought a gorgeous cottage together, hence the housewarming party. I'm still amazed that Mike has fallen in love and with a gazillionaire. His girlfriend, Sav, is the sole owner of Blac Family Jewellers. If you had told me twelve months ago that Mike would be all domesticated and have a girlfriend, I would have told you to put down the crack pipe. Mind you, I didn't expect my life to end up the way it has either.

"So, Sarah, where have you been hiding?" Jordan asks, as he hands Kenz and me another wine.

"Ummm, work, I literally live there at the moment." *Which isn't a complete lie.* "Mmm, this wine is heaven. It's so fruity but not too sweet, really refreshing."

Kenz looks at me and smiles. "Sarah, you totally need to become a wine critic, or even better open a wine bar. I'd have a beer hubby and a wine bestie."

"You front the mullah and I'll totally do that." As I take a sip, I think of a recent conversation I had regarding this, *maybe I should take the leap*; it would get me away from 'her.' Taking another sip, I cheekily reply, "I can see it now, the bar would be broke in a week 'cause the owner's bestie drank all the stock."

"Pfft, if I haven't drunk the brewery dry yet, I doubt I could do it to your bar." Winking at me she adds, "But I'm totally up for the challenge."

"I have a better idea, me and you run the wine bar together, like we used to talk about when we were at school, and we will become wineaires."

"What the hell is a wineaire?"

"Like a billionaire, but with wine."

Kenz slings her arm over my shoulder. "And this is why I missed you so much. You take my shit and turn it into an idea that would work."

Laughing, Jordan says, "If you two ran a bar, it would be broke before the end of the first day. Nope, not gonna happen for you, Kenz." She pouts at him, so he pulls her into his side and kisses her gently head. Looking back at me, he points with his finger that's wrapped around his beer mug. "I can totally see you doing that though, Sarah."

"Naw thanks, Jordan, but I doubt anyone would give

me the capital to start it." Looking at Kenz, I poke my tongue and say, "Suck it, Kenz, your husbut likes me better than you." As I take another sip of wine, my mind drifts off to my imaginary wine bar. *I would totally love to do that, but before that can happen, I need to get my life back on track,* I think to myself.

She punches me in the arm really hard. "Pfft, what-evs, Bitch."

Magically, I don't spill a drop. "Winning!" I proudly declare fist pumping the air and lifting my leg in a slight kick to the side as I do so. Both Jordan and Kenz clap when all of a sudden my skin prickles. I freeze on the spot. I feel his presence, but it can't be him. Turning around, I scan the room, and then I see him standing over near Mike and Sav, looking ever so sexy in jeans and a button-down shirt.

My heart is racing and I swallow hard just as he turns around, our eyes lock onto one another. All that I have been hiding these past few months is all about to unravel, due to the demigod standing in front of me. I'm going to be exposed; No, No, No...Oh My God, I can't believe he's here, this can't be happening.

I'm fucked...my secret is about to be exposed.

1

———

SARAH

...Four months earlier

STANDING UP FROM MY CUBICLE, I FOLLOW THE REST of the staff into the boardroom for a last minute, urgent meeting. As I'm walking down the corridor, I start to get a sinking feeling in the pit of my stomach. I'm one of the last to arrive, so I take a seat on the windowsill and wait for the meeting to start.

My colleague, Julie, walks in and I shuffle over so she can sit next to me, both of us looking at each other curiously. Glancing my eyes around the boardroom, I see that the mangers at the front don't look happy, and that sinking feeling in my stomach magnifies.

The big boss finally walks in, slamming the door behind him; I jump in surprise, as I was lost in thought trying to figure out what's happening. Brian stands at the front clears his throat, "Thank you for coming, everyone. I know this was sudden and I appreciate you dropping everything to come to this meeting." He looks really nervous; his hands are shaking. "As you are all aware, there have been quite a few changes of late and the rumor mill has been in overdrive. I can officially confirm that, as of twelve p.m. today, the company has a new owner." Everyone in the room lets out a sigh of relief. "However, they are making some cuts." He sighs, swallows deeply, and then quietly says, "Everyone, who is in this room, is being let go. I'm sorry to say that you all no longer have a job here. This will be your last day at KDM."

The room erupts to a chorus of shouts, screams, and tears. Looking towards Brian, my heartbreaks for him. He put his heart and soul into this company and everything that he worked hard for is no longer his. Closing my eyes, I let out a big breath and shake my head, I knew times were tough but I didn't realise how tough. Snapping my eyes open again, I realise that I no longer have a job.

It isn't until Brian touches my shoulder that I realise I'm the last person sitting in the boardroom. "Sarah, are you okay?"

Looking up at him, my eyes well with tears. "I'll be fine, Brian, I'm just shocked and sad. I've been here since I finished university, what do I do now?"

"I'm so sorry, Sarah. I did everything possible to keep the doors open myself, but I just couldn't do it anymore. They didn't tell me about the cuts until the deal was done and there was nothing I could do." Patting me on the shoulder he dejectedly says, "I'm so sorry, Sarah."

"I know, Brian, I know. It's just a shock, it was the last thing I expected to hear today." Reaching up I give Brian a hug. "Thank you for everything." Rising on my tippy toes, I give him a kiss on the cheek before heading back to my desk. Sitting down in my chair, I look around at my cubicle. As I place my belongings into a box, I lower my head onto my desk and I start to cry. Once it's all packed up, I grab the box and my handbag and for the very last time, I walk out of KDM.

On the train home, I try and call Josh but I can't get hold of him. I leave a message asking him to call me when he gets a chance. On the walk home from the station, my mind starts thinking about everything and I start to cry again.

Getting to our house, I see Josh's car in the driveway and I smile, knowing that he will give me a big Josh hug, and for tonight at least, he will make me forget about this shitty day. Digging out my keys, I unlock and swing open the front door to be greeted by Josh and Sam...having sex...on my couch. Josh is on all fours his eyes closed, moaning in pleasure as Sam rams into him from behind.

The sight in front of me stops me dead in my tracks and I scream, dropping my keys on the tiles. Josh's eyes pop open, Sam stops mid-thrust, and they both stare at me open-mouthed, in shock.

Before either of them gets a chance to say anything, I turn around, slamming the front door behind me, and I run off. Putting one foot in front of the other, I run and run until I'm back at the train station. There is a train for the city sitting there, so I jump on. Taking a seat, I pull my legs up, wrap my arms around them, rest my head on my knees, and I let the tears fall. The floodgates have opened and I'm sitting there sobbing my heart out. Fellow passengers stare at me in shock, but not one of them asks if I'm okay and I'm fine with that; I wouldn't know how to answer them anyway.

Getting off in the city, I walk around in a daze, the events of today running through my mind on a continual loop: loosing my job, finding Josh and Sam screwing on my couch, and repeat. Eventually, I find myself at The Dirty Duck, our old college bar, so I head inside so I can drown my sorrows.

Taking a seat at the bar I order three tequila shots, a bottle of Pinot Grigio, and a serving of wings. The bartender returns with my drinks, and I down the shots one after the other, savoring the burn. I'm starting to feel numb so I ask for three more. "Rough day, huh?" he asks, as he pours three more shots.

Laughing, I down another shot. "You could say that."

"Wanna talk about it?"

"Well, today I lost my job, and when I got home I found my boyfriend on our couch getting fucked in the ass by his colleague, Sam." Slamming back the remaining two shots, I pour myself a glass of wine and take a big gulp.

"Wow, that sure is a shitty day." He places another shot in front of me, I look at him curiously as I didn't order another shot...I don't think. "On the house, you deserve it."

For the next few hours I sit at the bar, drink my wine, eat my wings, and chat with the bartender. He and I chat about anything and everything. I discover that Dave is studying medicine at QUT, he recently married his high school sweetheart, and they are expecting their first baby later this year. His happiness and perfect life makes me feel even shittier.

I'm pretty drunk and I start to cry again. "How did I not know my boyfriend also liked boys? I'm so stupid." Dave places a glass of water in front of me, and I drink it down in one go. He refills it and tells me it's closing time.

As I'm walking out my phone rings, and my shitty day just goes from shit to complete and utter shit.

2

LOGAN

"It's over, Logan!" Lili screams at me, throwing her arms up in the air before turning her back on me. She's having another one of her temper tantrums, and to be honest, I'm over it. She stares out the window for a few moments before spinning on her heel, she glares at me, and screeches like a banshee, "I'm done, we're done. It's done!" Pausing, she takes deep breath to compose herself. "I'm outta here." Grabbing her Gucci handbag off the dining table, she storms towards the entrance, slamming the door on her way out. I'm left standing in our, well, I guess now, my lounge room, totally flabbergasted. She was cheating on me...for our whole relationship; I'm such a schmuck...but to be honest, I'm not surprised. I haven't been happy for a while now, but I was too gutless to end it with Lili.

Sighing, I stare out the window and wish that Sav was here. She'd know exactly what to say, and then she'd whip out the tequila and all would be forgotten. I miss my best friend, I really need her right now but she gone.

She has disappeared and no one knows where she is; not even her uncle. Kelvin's reaction when I asked was shocking; he was so angry and pissed off. I know there is no love lost there, but I at least thought he'd care.

I've tasked a friend to find her but I know Sav, if she doesn't want to be found, she won't be. She was the best hiding-go-seek player in Wentworthville when we were kids, and the time she disappeared when we were eleven will go down in the history books. Mr. Blac, her dad, said no to her—for the first time ever—and she took off into the woods behind the store. She hid out for two days, evading everyone, even me. The whole town was out looking for her and she was right under our noses the whole time. She got in so much trouble...I'd give anything to go back to those times. Life was so much simpler and less complicated back then...ohh how times have changed; adulting sucks.

Turning around, I head to the bar and I grab a Malt Me Checker Plate lager, *this beer is to die for,* and I head out to the back patio. Sitting down on the lounger, I stare at the sky and watch the storm roll in. The clouds darken, the winds pick up, blowing the leaves around, causing the pool furniture to tumble over, creating chaos in its wake, much like my life at the moment.

Finishing my beer, I go inside and grab another before I head back outside to continue watching the storm. How did I not know that Lili was cheating on me? Was I just blind? Or was I too focused on my development company like she said? I know I've been busy getting DeBiers Developments off the ground, but how was I to know that I was going to get a multi-million dollar contract on my first tender and open doors that I never thought possible? Something like that never happens, especially to me, and I wasn't going to let an opportunity like that pass me by; I guess my personal life was the casualty of that.

Sighing, I sit back and watch the sky darken further, the clouds twirling and mixing together. The lightning strikes brightening the night sky, it truly is wonderful watching Mother Nature. With the next crash of thunder, the sky opens up and I'm drenched. I don't care and I don't move a muscle, well except for my beer-drinking arm. Staring at the night sky, I continue to lie there and watch, there is nothing behind this rain band and it will shortly pass, and then it will be humid as hell.

Not ten minutes later, the dark ominous clouds have passed and in its wake, we are left with a stunning sunset. The sky is bursting with colour; oranges, yellows, and reds, all mixing together as the fiery orb of the sun slowly descends behind the mountains to the west.

A chill passes over me, so I get up, grab another beer, and head to my room. Stripping off my wet clothes as I walk into the master ensuite, leaning in, I turn the shower on. Letting the steam fill the bathroom, I finish my beer before jumping under the spray and warming my body up. After drying off, I put on my trackies, grab another beer, and head into the media room for a night of drinking beer and listening to music. The last thing I remember before passing out is hearing Metallica singing about giving me fuel and fire and all that I desire.

3

VICTORIA

SLAP "Get out!" I roar. "If you ever show your face around here again there will be trouble."

"But..."

"There are not buts, missy, you knew the rules and you broke them; end of story, Crissy. The rules are there to protect us all, and you know I don't tolerate misbehavior. You have thirty minutes to get your things and leave." She begins to cry and nothing pisses me off more than crying, especially when you are to blame.

"I'm sorry, Victoria," Crissy pleads.

SLAP "Save it, time is ticking." I wave my hand at her dismissively and turn my back on her. Walking over to the bar, I pour myself a brandy before taking a seat on the lounge. Sitting down, I watch my best girl, Crissy, sulk as she walks away. As much as it killed me to do that, she broke my most sacred rule and that is unacceptable.

Ten minutes later, I look up to see her standing in the doorway. She is broken and sad, that gives me a little pleasure as I stand up to escort her out.

Taking her by the arm, we walk through the foyer towards the entry doors. "Crissy, darling, it has been a pleasure having you here." Her head snaps towards me in shock at my nice tone. "Your final payment has been wired to your account, and Simon here, will take you wherever you need to go."

"Thanks for everything, Victoria, I'm sorry to have disappointed you."

"There's no one sorrier than me right now, Crissy. You not only have disappointed me, but you broke my trust and now my business will suffer. I've lost my best girl because she couldn't follow the rules. The rules you agreed to when you came to work here." Shaking my head, I look at her angrily. "This is going to cost me."

"I'm sorry," she mumbles, as a lone tear falls down her cheek.

"Enough!" I shout, causing her to pause in her tracks. "Sorry won't fix this, Crissy." Letting go of her arm, I pause and stare at her, disdain on my face. "Now, get out of my sight."

She begins to cry harder now and pleads, "I don't have anywhere to go."

"That's of no concern to me, nor is it my problem. You should have thought of that before you defied me. Goodbye, Crissy." Turning my back on her and Simon, I walk back inside the apartment, thanking my stars that this one is leaving without incident.

As the door closes behind me, I sigh in frustration, why does this keep happening? Turning around, I look out the patio doors at the darkening night sky and wonder what I will do now. Sighing, I head over to kitchen and grab my bag off the bench. Locking the door behind me, I shoot a quick text off to the cleaners to have them prepare the now vacant apartment. As I step into the lift, I start thinking of ways to increase business and keep the girls in line. When I exit the lift, I head to the bar for a much-needed drink. Sitting in my usual seat at the bar, I once again sigh in frustration. Looking up, I see that Stephen has placed a napkin under a champagne flute and is opening a bottle of *Krug Grande*. "Thank you, Stephen, at least there is someone around here who can follow rules and do their job properly."

"My pleasure, ma'am. Is there anything else I can get you?"

"For starters, you can stop calling me ma'am, it's Victoria. And secondly, you don't know anyone who needs a job do you? I need to replace Crissy and I need to do it quickly."

"Sorry, ma'a...I mean, Victoria. I can't help you there."

"I didn't expect you to, Stephen," I say dismissively. Picking up the champagne flute, I take a sip and close my eyes; this is liquid gold and just what I needed, the bubbles instantly calming me. Opening my eyes, I look around the bar and smile at all that I've achieved. I notice that it's quiet for a Tuesday night and that makes me unhappy; I need to breathe new life into this place. "Stephen, can you please bring the bottle over to my table, I have a long night ahead of me."

"Yes, Victoria. I'll bring it right over for you after I serve these people."

Walking over to my table, I wonder what I will do. If

I don't replace Crissy quickly, he will not be happy, and if he's not happy then I could lose everything I have worked so hard for. That will not happen, I refuse to give up all of this; I will do whatever it takes to keep what's mine and him happy.

4
____

SARAH

As if things could not get any shittier in my life, Mum and Dad have lost everything, my trust included, due to a bad investment recommended by that sleaze ball investor. I never trusted him but I'm amazed that Dad made a choice like this, very out of character AND to make things worse, they were involved in a serious car accident while in Madrid. Dad broke his leg in several places and is in hospital; he won't be able to travel for a while.

Fuck. My. Life. Right. Now!!!

Seriously, did I run over a black cat? Or was I a total an utter bitch in a previous life? How can everything fall apart at precisely the same fucking time? I wish I had Kenz to talk to, but she's been through so much. She doesn't need my worries added to her already hectic life; nope, I can do this on my own...I think.

____

Two weeks later, and things have gone from bad to worse. Josh is being a total douche canoe asshole, and because he paid the deposit on our house, he is kicking me out. I have three days to find somewhere to live and get my stuff out. Like seriously, he cheats...with a dude, and I'm the one who gets fucked, and not in a good way.

Mum and Dad are going through too much for me to ask about moving back home, plus there's a chance they will loose the house too. I don't need to add to their worries at the moment. I can't ask Kenz and Jordan; they've only just gotten home from the hospital with the twins, Indi and Rory, and besides that, they have been through enough; they don't need my problems added to theirs.

I'm at the Dungeon drowning my sorrows and Sav is working, she seems shy and reserved but she knows how to mix a wicked margarita. On the weekend, that was my drink of choice to numb everything and she sure helped with that. Apparently, tequila is her drink so there's no surprise that she can mix a mean margarita. Today though, I'm drinking a lovely New Zealand Sav Blanc and chowing down on wings. Taking a sip, I sigh loudly, garnering the attention of the lady sitting a few seats over from me.

"What's a pretty girl like you doing here, drinking her sorrows away on a beautiful day like this?"

Normally I would ignore someone chatting to me, but at the moment, what more do I have to lose? Looking over at her I dejectedly say, "You wouldn't believe the shit luck I've been having lately."

"Try me," she replies, as she slides over to the seat directly next to me.

"Okay, well in one day: I lost my job, found my boyfriend cheating on me, my parents were in a serious car accident overseas, and they lost everything due to a bad investment. Now said ex-boyfriend is kicking me out of our house, and I have three days to find somewhere else to live."

"So rather than house hunting, you're drowning your sorrows in wine and wings?"

"Wine Not?" I giggle, "...and he can get fucked." Taking a big gulp, I continue, "He can get fucked in the ass by Sam again, for all I care."

"Wow, that is pretty 'shit' as you so crudely put it. Why don't I buy us a bottle and we can come up with a game plan together?" She stares directly at me, stretching out her manicured hand. "I'm Victoria, by the way."

It must be the wine talking because I take her hand in mine, shake, and confidently say, "I'm Sarah and at this point, Victoria, I'll take any and all help that I can."

"It's nice to meet you, Sarah, I think you and I are going to be great friends."

If only I knew...

5
____

VICTORIA

A FEW DAYS AFTER THE CRISSY DEBACLE, I HAVE A meeting with a possible new member; he wanted to meet at some dive bar called The Dungeon. It's not a place I would normally be seen dead in, but his financials check out and he's too good of a member to pass up.

Our meeting went very well and Jonathan is now officially a member of Elite. I'm sipping on my glass of champagne when I look up and see a sad, yet stunning, young lady sitting across the bar. She has an aurora about her, and in this moment; I know that I have found my new Crissy.

Walking around the bar, I take a seat near her and listen in to her conversation with the bar staff. Smiling at myself, as I knew I was right, she's down on her luck. Lucky for her, I'm happy to swoop in and be her fairy godmother and turn her life around; and mine.

I'm trying to work out the best approach when she sighs and that's my chance. "Rough day?" I enquire.

She looks at me but doesn't reply, so I try another

approach. "What's a pretty girl like you doing here, drinking her sorrows away on a beautiful day like this?"

She is still hesitant but she finally opens up, and her life at the moment is shittier than ever. I offer to buy us a bottle of wine and suggest that together we can come up with a plan. Without hesitating, she takes up my offer and I inwardly smile. After ordering the bottle, we take our wine and glasses and head to a corner booth. Personally, I'd rather get out of this dump and go somewhere more sophisticated but I need to play this safely. I don't want to spook her.

Sarah and I fall into comfortable conversation, well, I let her do all the talking, I want to play this to remain relaxed and surprisingly, it's not awkward with her at all. She's chatting away, and in my head, I'm pairing her up with appointments from my current client list. The dollar signs are adding up and that pleases me immensely. Alexander will be very happy too, and when he's happy, life is perfect.

Glancing at her over my wine glass, I stare and subtly watch her every move. There is a graceful poise about her, and I know that she is exactly the girl I am looking for. Tonight, she will be coming with me; I refuse to leave here without Sarah...and I always get what I want.

LOGAN

After waking up with the hangover from hell, I've decided that I'm too old for hangovers and getting shitfaced is not the answer. I'm going to throw myself into work, and that actually works out perfectly; I have a tender in for another big project in Brisbane. If, no when, I get this tender, I'll move there and see the project through myself: two birds, one stone.

Later in the week, I get confirmation that I won the tender and I'll be developing the new sports stadium for the Queensland Academy of Sports. It starts in three weeks time, but I want to be there as soon as possible. I decide a road trip is in order, plus it will allow me to let loose on the highway in my new baby, my Mercedes G-Class SUV.

My assistant, Beth, books me into a hotel in the city for ten days, and hopefully in that time, I can find myself somewhere more permanent to stay.

After three fun-filled days, I have finally arrived in Brisbane and checked into my hotel. Dumping my bags in my room, I decide to head to the hotel bar, Charlie's, for dinner and a few brewskies. It's lonely eating and drinking by myself, but when you're new in town, what are you going to do?

Over the next two days, I scope out the city to get my bearings. I find a temporary office immediately. Locating the office space was easy; finding a place to live, is another story. Everything that I have seen so far is not me at all. Looks like I'll be in this hotel for a little while longer, at least it's comfortable and the bar/restaurant downstairs is fantastic.

Returning to the hotel after I finalised the lease on the office and getting the keys, I head to the bar for a celebratory drink and an early dinner. While I'm waiting for my steak, I notice a few lovely ladies enter the bar, but after Lili, I'm not sure I want to go there again so soon. I'm still shocked that she was cheating on me, how did I not realise that she was? Was I so engrossed in my business that I became a horrible boyfriend? Surprisingly, I'm not concerned that she was cheating on me, and truth be told, I'm not really that upset that we broke up. I'm more upset that she treated me like a chump.

Before I can dwell anymore, my dinner arrives and it smells magnificent. As I start eating, my thoughts leave Lili and all her bullshit, and I start thinking about the future of LDB Developments and where I can take the company next. Winning this tender was big for the company and me; the rush was exciting, and I haven't felt like this about work for quite a while now. Maybe this move it just what I needed to refresh and reboot.

After dinner, I head back up to my hotel room. Grabbing a beer, I head out to the balcony and look over the city and ponder my future. As I stare out at the sparkling city lights, I realise that getting away from Wentworthville and moving here was the right decision; personally and professionally. *Here's to a new adventure* I think to myself as I head back inside for an early night...if only I knew the adventure that was awaiting me.

SARAH

I'm so glad that I decided to come to The Dungeon today. I met this really nice lady. She has offered me a job and place to stay; it's like my fairy godmother has stepped up to the plate, finally.

Victoria escorts me to her car; it's a navy blue Mustang convertible. "Holy shit, is this your car?"

She laughs, "Yes. Do you want to drive?"

"Are you shitting me?"

"Your language is atrocious, but no I'm not shitting you, as you so eloquently put it."

"I would love to but I've had too much to drink. Speaking of, are you okay to drive?"

"Darling, of course I am, besides you drank most of that bottle yourself. I was just enjoying the company of my new friend. Now, get in."

"Yes, ma'am." I mock salute her as I slide into the car. These seats are heaven; I think I actually moan. They wrap around you like a leather glove. I can hear her mumbling something as she climbs into the driver's seat, but I am loosing myself in the comfort of this car seat.

She floors it as we pull away, the thrust forces me back into my seat, and I squeal like a schoolgirl. I begin to laugh, this is the most fun I've had in over a week now, turning to Victoria, I smile. "Thank you, Victoria, this is the happiest I've been since everything started to fall apart."

She reaches over and squeezes my hand. "It's all up from here now, darling."

That sets me off and I start to cry; everything that I have been holding in is now flowing down my cheeks. When I look up again, I see that we are in an underground garage and Victoria is opening my door. She squats down and wraps her arms around me. "Let it all out, darling, there's nothing like a good cry."

Finally the tears stop and after that outburst I feel much lighter, almost like me again. Victoria stands up and says, "Come on, let me show you up to your apartment and around. Your roommates should be home, too."

Climbing out of the car, we silently walk to the elevators; the only sound is the clicking of Victoria's Loubitons on the cement floor. "Oh My God! I fucking love your shoes."

She sighs, "Your language is deplorable, Sarah. You swear like a trucker. If you are to live and work here, you will not swear. You will act like a lady at all times, and you will follow the rules and guidelines." Pausing, she turns to me and glares. "Are we clear?"

"Umm, yeah, ahh, sure. I can do that. Sorry."

"Glad to hear it." The lift arrives and we climb in.

We make our way up to the thirty-fifth level, the doors open and we make out way over to the apartment. She opens the door, and when I step inside my new home, my chin drops to the floor. This apartment is out of this world: the foyer has marble floors, a gorgeous ornate mirror on the wall, and a foyer table with the biggest flower arrangement I have ever seen. Straight ahead is a staircase that leads up to the bedrooms, a door next to it; I presume it's a downstairs powder room. To the right is a doorway that opens into a massive lounge room, kitchen, and doors that lead out to the balcony terrace.

"Holy fucking shit, I've died and gone to heaven." I hear Victoria scoff and I look over to see disappointment on her face. "Sorry, I'm just, umm, overwhelmed. This place is stunning."

She smiles at me and I release the breath that I was holding, I was expecting another tongue-lashing. "I'll let that one pass, it is pretty stunning the first time you see this place. Now, come with me and I'll give you a quick tour."

We spend the next twenty minutes walking from room to room, eventually ending up in what will be my room. Victoria tells me that there are two other girls who also live here, as well as our personal chef and cleaner. After leaving my bags in my room, we make our way downstairs, just as Morgan and Angel, my new room-mates, arrive home.

"Ladies, this is Sarah, she has just moved in. Sarah, this is Morgan and Angel."

We all say hi and wave to each other, Victoria escorts us all into the lounge room and Angel heads to the bar.

Popping open a bottle of *Veuve Clicquot*, the cork popping makes me jump. She hands me a glass and I quickly drink it to calm my nerves. Taking my glass she refills it and proceeds to pour a glass for Morgan and Angel. Once we each have a glass, we head out to the terrace. Stepping out the door, my eyes bug out; this balcony is bigger than Josh's and my apartment...*I guess it's not mine anymore,* I sadly think to myself.

I become sad when I think of Josh; Angel notices the change in my demeanor. Leading us over to the outdoor lounge, she sits next to me and smiles. "So, Sarah, tell me about yourself?"

Taking a deep breath, I think, I may as well get this over with so I tell her all my troubles of the past week. When I have finished, I look up to see her staring at me open-mouthed. I expected to see pity but all I see is empathy.

"I hear ya, sister, my ex did the same thing, except it was with my mum. Suffice to say, I no longer have a mum or boyfriend. Luckily for me, Victoria ran into me and saved me." Pausing, she smiles at Victoria before adding, "As they say, the rest is history."

"Wow, your mum, seriously?" She nods at me. "That's got to be rough. How did you cope?"

She replies with one word, "Victoria." Smiling, she add, "She came along at the right time and saved me, she's my fairy godmother with a kick-ass shoe collection, wardrobe, and liquor stash."

"Language, Angel. But yes, I do have a kick-ass collection of everything you mentioned and so much more. And on that note, ladies, I will leave you to it.

Angel, would you be a dear and bring Sarah by the office tomorrow at ten a.m. and we can begin?"

"Begin what?" I curiously ask.

"All will be revealed tomorrow, Sarah. Enjoy your night with the girls and I'll see you in the morning." Standing up, she heads back inside, turning around, as she closes the door she says, "Night, ladies and, Sarah, I'm glad you decided to come back with me." Spinning on her heels she waves before exiting the apartment.

When the front door closes, Morgan jumps up, grabs another bottle of *Veuve* and pops it open on her way back outside. The chef, Miguel, appears and places down the most decadent antipasto platter I've ever seen. My stomach grumbles as he walks away and we all start laughing.

We are on our third, or forth, bottle of *Veuve* when I look over at Angel and Morgan. I'm pretty pissy by this point and with my emotions all over the place. I know that tonight will be 'emotional drunk Sarah' and I giggle. Smiling I say, "I think I'm going to love it here. You guys are awesome, thank you for making me feel so at home."

They both reply at the same together, "Anytime," and giggle.

Angel stands up and comes over to me; she leans down and hugs me. "I'm glad you're here too, Sarah. Tomorrow is going to be so much fun." She pulls back and says, "'Night girls," before heading upstairs to bed.

Morgan comes over and sits next to me, topping up our glasses before she leans back into the couch and takes a sip. She moans and looks over at me and smiles. A look passes over her face as she leans forward, she places her glass on the table; she takes mine and puts it next to hers. Turning towards me, she leans over and out of the blue kisses me. Her tongue seeks access to my mouth, and it must be the bubbly, because I open up and allow her in, our tongues caressing each other. When I feel her hand cup my breast, I pull back and push away and stand up. "Umm, I'm ahh, umm, I'm going to head to bed. I'll see you in the morning, Morgan."

Turning I quickly head inside and up to my room. As I'm racing through the lounge room, I hear her say, "Night night, Sarah, sweet dreams."

Opening my bedroom door, I slip inside, close it, and flick the lock. Leaning my head against the door, I close my eyes; my breath laboured from racing up the stairs...or is it laboured from that kiss?

What the hell was that?

And why the hell did it turn me on so much?

———

What's happening to me?

The next morning, I'm sitting in the kitchen having a coffee when Morgan walks in. She smiles at me as she grabs a coffee and sits on the stool next to me. "Morning, how did you sleep?"

"Fine, that bed is to die for. How about you?"

"Like the dead." She takes another sip of coffee, before looking back over at me. "So, about last night..."

I put my hand up to stop her. "It's fine, Morgan. I'm flattered but I'm just not that way inclined, sorry."

"No, I wanted to apologise. I don't know what came

over me." Pausing, she adds, "But if you want to do it again I wouldn't say no." Morgan gets up and goes outside. As I sit there and finish my coffee, I watch her walk away from me. She takes a seat where we kissed last night and the memory of that kiss comes rushing back to me. Smiling into my coffee, I clench my legs together as the memory is invoking feelings that I've never felt before. I'm a little turned on.

A few hours later, we are on our way to the office to meet up with Victoria for my training to begin. Angel and Morgan have taken me under their wing, which gives me comfort...it feels like I have found forever friends. Staring out the car window, I start to doubt my decision to be here and myself. I'm not sure I can do this, but at this moment in time, I'm backed into a corner and have no choice.

We meet with Victoria at the office; and by office I mean a building that overlooks the river, it's decadently decorated but in a tasteful way. I'm given a brief rundown as to what it means to be one of Victoria's girls before Angel, Morgan, and I are sent to the salon for a day of pampering and a makeover.

When we arrive, we change into the softest, pale pink robes, are handed a glass of champagne, and escorted to a waiting room...then my transformation begins. I'm treated to the full works, and when I say full, I mean my whole, entire body. I don't think there is one part that hasn't been touched, poked, plucked, or pampered. First up was waxing, *OUCH!* I was waxed in spots that I never knew could be waxed. I got my first Brazilian but with a little landing strip, in the shape of a love heart, which is really cute. Being hair free down there was kind of weird to start, with but I have to say, I like the feeling, especially when I slipped my satin undies back on. I'm kind of in a perpetual state of bliss at the moment, one flick and I'll be tumbling over the orgasmic cliff, *I like it...a lot.*

After waxing the relaxing pampering began; a full-body scrub, followed by a mud wrap. Once that was washed off, I had a full-body massage and then it was off to the salon for the final stage: hair, makeup, French manicure, and a spa pedicure.

As soon as I sit down, I'm handed another glass of bubbly and I realise that for the first time in weeks, I'm relaxed and genuinely smiling. The stylist comes over and we have a fight about my hair. She wants to cut it off short but I want to keep the length. We eventually come to an agreement and I'm now rocking bangs and my hair is a rich, chocolate brown colour, which I totally love.

When we leave, looking fabulous by the way, we meet with Victoria for an early dinner at a restaurant over-looking the river. We start with cocktails before we dine on lobster, prawns, and oysters, and for the first time in my life I'm drinking *Cristal* champagne, which by the way is amazing. It was a nice relaxing night and I think I will like working for Victoria and Elite. After dinner, we say good night to Victoria, and the three of us head to Club Duex for a night of dancing and more cocktails.

The next morning I wake with the hangover from hell to banging on the front door downstairs. Stumbling down the stairs, I open to door to an irate Victoria standing there. "Morning, Vicky," I sleepily say.

SLAP "My name is Victoria, never call my anything but that. Now go get dressed. Your late for your first lesson."

Holy shit, she slapped me. My cheek is still stinging as I make my way upstairs to get changed. As I'm rounding the corner at the top, I see Morgan duck back into her room and her whisper, "fuck," as she quietly closes the door. Not wanting to piss Victoria off any further, I quickly pull on my jeans, white tank, and navy Chucks. I quickly brush my teeth, throw my hair into a ponytail, and head back downstairs to Victoria, secretly hoping she will have a coffee waiting for me, but the tingling on my cheek tells me that it probably won't happen.

When I enter the lounge room, she looks me up and down with a look of disgust on her face. "Rule number two, you will dress like a sophisticated lady at all times. This will do for now, but in the future, keep that in mind."

"I'm sorry, Victoria. Do I have time for coffee before we leave?"

"Sorry, that's all I seem to be hearing lately. Fine, but make it quick. By the looks of things, I will have my work cut out for me. Don't prove me wrong, Sarah."

Turing on her heels, she storms out the French doors, slamming it behind her. I head to the kitchen and quickly make two coffees before joining Victoria on the balcony.

Ending her call quickly, she smiles and looks at me as I place her coffee down and says, "Your first client is booked for this evening at 6:30 p.m. His file will be delivered in the next ten minutes." She takes a sip of coffee and obviously doesn't like how I made it as she has a look of disgust on her face. Staring up at me from where she is sitting, she snarls, "Sarah, I suggest you read it thoroughly and be up to speed; Mr. Akin is one of our longest serving clients. Don't screw this up, this is your one and only shot, Sarah." Without another word, she walks past me and leaves the apartment.

Grabbing my coffee, I go and sit on the lounger and mumble, "What the fuck have I done?" There's a knock at the door and I get up to answer it, but by time I get there, Angel is closing the door holding a file. She looks up at me and smiles. "Morning, Sarah. This was just delivered for you."

Reaching out, I grab the file and say, "Thanks."

Grabbing my arm, she turns around, and we walk back into the kitchen where she makes us each another coffee, and I tell her all that just went down. "No fucking way, you called her Vicky?"

Nodding my head, I quietly say, "Yep." As I take a sip of coffee I moan in delight; this tastes so much better than what I just made.

"You are game doing that."

"Well, after the slap, it won't be happening again. My cheek is still tingling." I subconsciously rub the spot.

"Well, who's your first client?"

Opening the file, I read, as I can't remember. "It's with Mr. Akin."

"Naw, I love him. He will be perfect as your first client. Do you want me to help you get ready?"

My face breaks out in a huge smile. "Oh My God! Yes, please, I'm so fucking nervous. What if I stuff this up?"

"You will be fine, Sarah. Mr. Akin is a doll, he's just a rich, lonely old man; he's harmless."

"What if he wants more? I'm not sure I can do that."

"Give it time, you will be surprised how easy it comes to you. I never thought I would, but it's quite exhilarating and exciting, to be in control like this. Just ease yourself into it and remember, you have the power, but I assure you, Mr. Akin isn't after that."

"Okay, I'm just really nervous."

"You'll be fine. Come on, go get a bikini and we will have a spa before we get you all dolled up for your first night."

"Are you sure Victoria will be okay with this?"

"Vicky will be fine with it," she smart-assly says as we both burst out laughing.

"You are evil...I like it. Come on, let's go."

As I'm getting changed I get a text from Kenz.

Kenz – *Hey bitch. Wanna meet up for coffee?*

Seeing who it's from, I start to get upset and think that maybe I should just tell her what's going on, but I don't want to admit what a screw up my life has become.

Sarah – *Flat out at work, sorry. Rain check?*

I feel bad lying, but technically I'm working, so it's not a total lie...just a huge stretch of the truth.

Kenz – *Fine but you owe me*
Sarah – *Deal. Love your face*

Throwing my phone on the bed, I quickly change into my black and orange micro bikini, and I head down to the pool area.

When I get outside, Angel and Morgan are already in the spa, sipping champagne and chatting. Angel looks up and smiles at me. "Come join us, there's a glass on the table for you."

"Thanks." I grab my glass and slip into the spa. The temperate is just right, and I moan as I slide down into the whirling, bubbly water. "This is just what I needed." Closing my eyes, I rest my head back on the edge and relax.

"So, Angel tells me you got bitch-slapped for calling Victoria, Vicky. I would have loved to have seen that, I've heard how much she hates being called that."

"Yep," I say, as I rub my cheek where her hand collided with my face.

Smiling she says, "Well, you are officially one of us now, welcome to the bitch-slap club. Getting bitch-slapped is your initiation in and you completed yours in record time."

"Thanks...I think. So, tell me what I can expect tonight?"

8

———

VICTORIA

I'm so glad that I found Sarah when I did; I think she will be Elite's saving grace, and my instincts have never let me down. I simply cannot afford to loose another girl, with Crissy leaving, that is the third girl in a matter of weeks. At least her leaving was easy to deal with, unlike the other two girls. I hate getting my hands dirty, but I will do anything and everything to keep Elite running smoothly.

Yesterday with Sarah went brilliantly, much smoother than I anticipated, she's a feisty one, that's for sure. She didn't argue too much about the makeover, and even though I wanted her hair lopped off, I have to say the bangs and colour were a great compromise. To be honest, I was sure she was going to put up more of a fight, that girl has quite the spirit. She reminds me of me at her age, maybe I have finally found our successor.

At dinner, she really impressed me, and these days it's quite hard to do so. When we stepped into the restaurant and the girls started on cocktails, I was expecting a messy, booze-filled night but surprisingly, all three of them behaved like ladies. I was very proud to be in their company. Heads turned when they walked in and I could not have been happier in that moment, actually if I had secured another client I would have been ecstatic.

The four of us had a lovely evening together, we will need to do it again. The key to success in this business is to keep the girls happy and content; maybe that's where I went wrong with the other girls. No point dwelling on the past though, it's onwards and upwards now that I have found Sarah. I'm pretty sure that when I dropped them off, they were heading out somewhere to continue the party, but after their behaviour this evening, I was happy to let them indulge...just this once.

However, as usual, it all came crashing down the next morning when she called me Vicky. I despise being called Vicky, thanks to Mother, but that chapter of my life is done and dusted, never to be thought about again. Mother will be turning in her grave at my success; I just wish she was here so I could flaunt it in her face. Finally I have made something of myself, I'm Victoria Chalmers and no one fucks with me, no one!

9

———

LOGAN

THE PAST WEEK HAS FLOWN BY, AND I'M NO CLOSER to finding somewhere permanent to live. For the first time since arriving in Brisbane, I start to think that this wasn't such a good idea after all. Heading to Charlie's for dinner, I decide to sit at the bar so I'm not so much of a loaner. I order a burger and a Malt Me beer.

While I wait, I look around and I notice that there are private apartments is this building, too. I shoot off a text to Beth and ask for her to arrange a meeting with the realtor. Not five minutes later, my ever on the ball assistant tells me that I have a meeting with the realtor in three days time.

My burger arrives and I order another beer. Taking a sip, I smile to myself, being able to get this stuff on tap is major perk of moving here; beer tastes so much better on tap rather than from a bottle or can. Striking up a conversation with the barman, I discover that the Malt Me brewery and restaurant is located nearby. Since tomorrow is Sunday, I decide to head there for the day and chilax, it sure beats hanging around here by myself.

After a late breakfast, I jump in my baby and take the scenic route to Malt Me. The owners have done a brilliant job, from the looks of the building I'd say it was an old factory that they have revamped, and they've done it well. They've kept the old school charm of the building, yet modernised it and the two mesh together perfectly, I'm impressed. Sitting in my car gazing at the building, I think that I need to get the details of their builder to add to my contractors database.

Climbing out of my car, I walk through the back courtyard, which reminds me of a beer garden that I visited at the Oktoberfest, well everything except for the sunflowers but they work well with the area. Opening the timber doors, I head inside. The first thing I notice is the floor-to-ceiling glass panel that separates the bar from the brewery, which is a neat concept; kudos on the design.

Walking over, I'm looking around and bump into a guy, he looks scary: baldhead, goatee, and vivid blue eyes. "Shit, sorry, dude."

"No worries, mate." He slaps me on the back, smiles, and heads towards the bar.

Phew, I think to myself, as I walk over to the glass wall to have a look inside the brewery. This place is bloody awesome. Along the side of the building, I notice the checker plate stairs winding up to a secondary bar area that overlooks everything. After looking around for a bit, I head to the bar, totally blown away with how awesome this place is.

Grabbing a stool at the bar, the bartender walks over. "Hey, what can I get ya?"

"Hey, umm, can I get a Checker Plate lager to start, please?"

"Coming right up."

Turning around, he grabs a beer mug and fills it up, with the perfect amount of head, placing it in front of me as I give him my credit card to set up a tab. "I'm impressed, not many people can pour a tap beer properly."

He laughs at me. "Well, I should be able to pour one properly, I'm the owner." He puts his hand forward to shake. "Jordan McRoberts."

Taking his hand and shaking, I reply, "Logan DeBiers. I really love this place. I tried your beers when you popped up in Sydney at Circular Quay earlier this year, and I've been obsessed ever since. When the hotel bar guy said the brewery was nearby, I had to come here. It truly is spectacular, Jordan, well done."

"Thanks, man. I'm lucky, I have a great team behind me and my wife and girls are very supportive."

"That's awesome. Look, I don't normally do this, but here's my card. I'm in developments and a chain of these breweries would be awesome."

He takes my card and looks it over, before he places it in his back pocket. "Thanks, Logan, but I'm not looking at expanding to that scale just yet, but I will definitely keep your details and be in touch if that changes."

"That's fine. In the meantime, can I get another Checker Plate and a serve of the cheeseburger sliders please?"

"Coming right up. I suggest adding the chili fries too, they go really well with the burgers."

"Okay, add that too," I say, as I finish my beer.

Sitting here, I sip on my beer and wish that Sav was here, she'd love this place; I hope my guy finds her soon. I really miss her.

I've just finished my meal, which was amazeballs. I spin around on my stool, my eyes darting around the room around and smile. I'm determined to get Jordan and Malt Me on my development schedule and to come here with Sav when I find her.

10

SARAH

Waking early the next morning, I groan and stretch out in this magnificent bed. Seriously it's like sleeping on a cloud and these sheets are to die for. *Kenzie would be so jealous, being the sheet snob that she is*, I think to myself, as I climb out and head into the ensuite.

Looking into the vanity mirror, I smile. I feel happy, content and that everything will be okay; and it's all due to meeting Victoria. To be honest, I was worried about doing all of this, but my first assignment with Mr. Akin was really easy and relaxed. I'm pretty sure that I can do this.

Turning around, I turn on the shower and let it steam up. Stripping off my satin nightie and pulling down my undies, I flick them to the side and step under the shower spay. This rainhead has just the right amount of pressure and I moan; it feels like heaven. I'm soaping up my body and I run my fingers over my now bare cleft, and I start to tingle deep inside. Closing my eyes, I gently slide my finger up and down, the water cascading over my fingers as I work myself over. Lifting my leg, I place my foot on the shower seat and I begin to rub my clit in circles, my breathing picks up, a tiny moan escapes my lips. Just as I'm at my peak, about to tumble over the edge, there's a knock on the door, scaring the shit out of me. "Yeah, what?" I manage to squeak out.

"Victoria just called, she will be here in thirty minutes and you need to be dressed and ready for a last minute assignment!" Morgan shouts.

"Okay, I'm just in the shower. Give me five minutes and I'll be down and ready."

"Cool, I'll put the coffee on," she says, closing the door behind her, thankfully I'm in the shower and she couldn't see anything...I hope.

"Thanks!" I shout back, as I lower my leg and grumble; *I was so close.* Sighing, I quickly get washed, step out, and dry myself before lathering my body in mosituriser and doing my makeup quickly, luckily I'm just a mascara and lippy girl.

Walking into the closet, I grab a navy and white Victoria Secret bra and undies set before slipping on a yellow and white spotted sundress; perfect for a Sunday lunch. Pairing it with white, strappy wedge sandals from Nine West, I smile at myself. I grab my handbag, ready and excited for my second appointment.

I'm walking down the stairs when the front door opens and in strolls Victoria; she looks up at me and pauses, she looks stunned. "Well, the morning won't be as hectic as I thought. You do know how to dress appropriately," she dismissively says, as she walks into the kitchen, not saying anything else to me.

My face breaks into a smile because I just shocked Victoria. I think that will be my new hobby, finding different ways to shock and piss off Victoria. Giggling to myself, I walk into the kitchen, both Angel and Morgan look up and whistle. Morgan says, "How the hell do you look that good at this time of the morning?"

Walking towards to coffeepot, I just shrug my shoulders and say, "Good morning, Victoria." Pouring her and myself a coffee before taking a seat next to Angel.

"You didn't make this did you?" Victoria asks.

"You're safe... for today anyway."

"Thank God for that. That drivel you served me the other day was revolting, thankfully coffee making isn't a skill that you require. Now, come along, I want to run through a few things with you at the office before your client picks you up later today."

"Yeah, sure, okay. Just let me grab my stuff."

"We really need to work on your vocabulary, Sarah. You sound so bogan and uneducated. Women like us need to speak eloquently and refined at all times."

"Yes, Victoria," I snidely say, as I skip past to grab my things that I left in the foyer.

As I'm walking away, I hear Victoria say, "Why must you girls test my patience?"

Twenty minutes later, we are pulling up at her office and just like the last time I was here, I'm amazed at the beauty of this building. We both get out of the car and make our way silently towards the lift. The silence is kind of awkward but I'm too nervous to say anything. I'm not sure if I'm nervous to be around Victoria, or for my next assignment. My first was easy but I'm pretty sure they all won't be like Mr. Akin. Seriously, who pays this much money just to spend time with someone, and not want anything? As the lift takes us up to her office, I think to myself that I'm not sure I could do that, that would make me a hooker, escort I can do but hooker, nope.

"Sarah, today you are having lunch with Xander C. He is taking you out on his yacht, depending on how the afternoon progresses, it could turn into an overnighter. This is your one chance to shine, Sarah, don't let me down."

"Overnight? Like sleeping over?" Lowering my voice, I add, "Sex?"

"Yes, Sarah, you will do whatever he requests of you, as long as it's within the law, but I suggest you keep him happy." She turns towards me and says, "Whatever. He. Wants. Sarah."

"How is whoring myself within the law?"

"Whoring yourself, as you so crudely put it, is not what we do here. We provide companionship and if that leads to a sexual encounter, that's on you and not us. I would strongly suggest, however, if anything sexual comes up that you seriously consider it, your place here could be jeopardised if our clients are not happy."

As I follow Victoria into her office, I think, *Holy fucking shit, what have I got myself into?* Taking a seat, I stare at Victoria, open-mouthed, totally shocked. "Victoria, I'm not sure I can do that. I'm happy to provide companionship, but I don't think I can just sleep with someone, I'm not a whore."

"I never said you were a whore, darling. I just said I advise you to sleep with him if the situation arises, think of it as a random hook up." Pausing she defiantly looks at me. "Especially, if you want to keep your job here at Elite."

"Umm, o...o...okay, I'll do my best to not disappoint you." Why do I care so much if I disappoint her?

"And stop stuttering and stammering, it's unbecoming of a lady."

"I'm sorry, Victoria." Swallowing hard, I ask, "Do you have any information on Xander that will help me out?"

"That's more like it. His file is in the next office; go over it, thoroughly. Xander is very dear to me and you will do whatever he wants. I'll send Simon in to collect you when it's time to go." As she talks about Xander, I notice a look wash over her face; it intrigues me.

"Yes, Victoria." Standing up, I head to the office next door and I keep repeating to myself, "*You can do this, you can do this.*"

An hour later, Simon gently knocks on the door and tells me it's time to go. Taking a deep breath, I stand up, nervously smooth down my dress, and politely say with a smile, "Let's do this." Following him out to the waiting car, he gives off a creepy vibe and I internally call him 'Sleazy Simon.'

The car trip to the marina was quick, too quick, but we pull up and I notice all the yachts and motor cruisers, it houses some of the biggest yachts I have ever seen. Walking towards us is a ruggedly handsome older man, and by older, I mean like George Clooney old. Thankfully, he's not a creepy, old, bald, greying man; he's quite attractive and that puts me at ease.

Simon opens my door, and I take his hand, as I climb

out of the white limo. The marina precinct is full but no one takes notice of me or what I'm about to do. Before I know it, I'm standing in front of Xander; I'm so nervous that I stand there and stare at him like a fool.

"My God, you are even more beautiful than Victoria said. I'm Xander C., it's a pleasure to meet you, Sarah," he says in a deep gravely voice.

"Hhh...hi!" I stammer.

He takes my elbow and leads me towards the marina slips. "Don't be nervous, love, I don't bite." Pausing he looks down at me, he is at least four inches taller than me. "Unless you want me to." He winks as he says that and laughs, totally putting me at ease.

"Well, let's save the biting for another time, shall we?" I wink back at him, wondering to myself where this confidence has all of a sudden come from.

"I like you already, Sarah. Come, the yacht is all prepared and I really want to set sail."

"Lead the way, captain." I quickly step ahead of him, smiling to myself; I start swinging my hips seductively from side to side as I make my way down the walkway. I'm just about to turn around and ask which yacht is his when he wolf whistles. Spinning around, I pause, placing my hand on my hip, look up at him, and give him my megawatt happy smile, which I'm not faking by the way, "So, which of these babies is yours?"

He points towards the third yacht from the end, my eyes bug out of my head. "Holy shit, that's a Seahawk from *Perini Navi's* 60m series?"

"I'm impressed, how do you know that?"

"My dad and I attend the boat show each year, he'd

kill for one of these babies, I can't wait to tell him that I've..." I stop speaking mid-sentence, as I know I can never tell Daddy about this. He would be ashamed to know that this is what I'm now doing, all the joy I felt earlier has vanished. Staring sadly at the stunning yacht in front of me, I'm startled when Xander places his hand on my shoulder. "Are you okay? Where did you go just now?"

Lying I say, "Just missing Daddy. He and Mum are in Europe at the moment and were in a car accident. Dad broke his leg so they are delayed until he can travel again."

"I'm sorry about your dad, Sarah." He reaches over and places his fingers under my chin and tilts my head up, he's grinning at me and his smile again puts me at ease. "Let's turn that frown upside down and head out. The fresh air will do you good; there's nothing more freeing than being out at sea. What do you say?"

"I say, lead the way and thank you."

"Why are you thanking me?"

"Well, you're paying me to keep you company and here you are cheering me up, that's not entirely fair to you."

"Babe, the day is still young. Now let's get going, I can't wait to get you alone."

With that one statement, my undies dampen and I'm entirely at his mercy. *I'm such a whore*, I giggle to myself as we make our way to the yacht.

"What's so funny?"

"Nothing, I'm just really happy to be here." Surprising myself with my honest answer.

"I'm happy you're here, too. I was disappointed to hear that Crissy was no longer working for Victoria, but I'm no longer upset about that." Pausing, his eyes rake over my body and I can feel his gaze burning my skin, hunger radiating from him. When his eyes land on mine, he takes my hand, squeezes, and says, "Sarah, you and I are going to have so much fun together."

Xander climbs aboard first and turns around, offering me his hand as I step up. I lose my footing and fall into his arms. Looking up into his dark chocolate eyes, I smile. He places me back on my feet and before I know it, he is kissing me deeply. Wrapping my arms around his neck, I return his kiss. Our lips are tightly pressed together, my tongue seeks access to his mouth and our kiss intensifies, until someone clearing their throat interrupts us.

Looking over, I see the deckhand, standing there awkwardly looking at us. "What is it, Davey?" Xander says, still staring intently at me.

"Umm, sir, we are all ready to set sail."

"Thanks, Davey, that will be all. I don't need you to come with us today."

"Very well, sir. When do you want me back here to clean her down?"

Dismissively he says, "I'll text you."

"Yes, sir." With that, he leaves, and a few moments later he is off the yacht and heading towards to car park.

Xander releases me from his grip, places a quick kiss on the tip of my nose, and says, "There's GH Mumm in the galley, why don't you pour yourself a glass, make yourself at home, and I'll join you shortly."

"Sounds good to me. Would you like a drink or anything?"

"I can't really drink where I want to drink from with all these people around, but as soon as it's just you and me and the open seas, I will be feasting on you. Rest up, Sarah, your in for one hell of a sail." He turns around and heads towards the cabin, leaving me standing there, open-mouthed, shocked, and dare I say, a little turned on.

I make my way to the top deck where I find the champagne and some cheese and crackers. Kicking off my shoes, I pour a glass and take a seat. Digging in my bag, I pull out my Ray Ban Aviators, slipping them on. Relaxing back into the lounge, I sigh and take in the scenery as we depart the harbour.

By time Xander comes back to join me, we are cruising the open seas and I'm totally relaxed; three glasses of bubbly and fresh sea air will do that to you.

"The open seas agree with you, Sarah, you look relaxed."

"I feel relaxed."

He smiles at me, as he grabs another flute, pours himself a glass, and tops mine up.

"Are you trying to get me drunk?"

"Maybe." He winks at me before raising his glass. "A toast, to the start of a beautiful arrangement."

His words cause my smile to fade when I remember that he is paying me. I quickly shake away the doubts and smile. "Cheers to that." We clink glasses and both take a sip. I close my eyes and moan, savoring the flavour of the bubbles as they slide down my throat, tingling as they make their way down.

"Fuck, Sarah, if you moan like that when drinking champagne, I can't wait to hear you moan when you are coming."

My cheeks turn pink and I look towards the horizon, embarrassed at what Xander just said. Wanting to change the subject, I stand up. Placing my glass on the table, I walk to the back of the deck and lean on the railing. "So, where are we off to today?"

He shrugs his shoulders at me. "No set destination, I just wanted to get away."

"Well, I'm happy to accompany you. The water is magnificent, I'd love to dive in from up top here, it's a shame I didn't bring a bikini with me," I reply, as I lean on the railing and stare out to sea.

Xander stands up and walks over to me, cocooning me in his arms he leans down and whispers into my ear, "There's no one around except me, no need for clothes." He nibbles on my ear and again I moan, it must be the fresh air mixed with the bubbly because I spin around and pull Xander towards me and kiss him.

Our tongues meshing together, you can't tell where I end and he begins. Our bodies press tightly together, our hands exploring each other's bodies. I feel his cock pressing into my stomach, without thinking, I drop to my knees and undo his cargos, freeing his engorged cock. The slit dripping with precum, I dart my tongue out and lick the tip before taking his cock deep into my throat and sucking.

"Holy shit, Sarah. Suck me harder, baby."

Xander runs his fingers through my hair, shoving my face further onto his cock. My head bobbing up and down as I suck and nip his cock in and out of my mouth. Reaching up, I begin massaging his balls and I hear him groan. His balls tighten in my hand just as I feel the first burst of cum hit the back of my throat. "Fuuuuck!" he shouts as I continue to suck him dry.

Once he has finished, I kneel back, look up at Xander, and smile, wiping the sides of my mouth before dragging my fingers across my bottom lip, slipping my finger in my mouth and sucking. Standing up, I turn around, walk over to the table, grab my bubbly, and take a sip, looking over my shoulder at Xander I seductively whisper, "Mmmmmm, would you like a top up?"

"Fuck me, Sarah. That was unexpected and totally amazing and yes, please, top me up."

Grabbing the bottle of bubbly from the ice bucket, I walk over and fill his glass before filling mine, but I only get a few drops, as the bottle is empty. "Bugger," I say and look at Xander with sad, puppy dog eyes.

"I have more, no need to cry. I'll be right back."

He walks down the stairs and I'm left alone, again. Leaning on the railing I look out at sea, and wonder to myself where my inner porn star just came from. I have never, ever done anything like that before in my life; I'm shocked and proud of my self. Completely lost in thought, I don't here Xander come back until I feel his arms wrap around my waist. He's grinding his cock into my ass; I circle my hips and rub back. Looking over my shoulder, I grin. "Hey you." He kisses me while continuing to grind against my ass; his arm slides down my stomach, lifting the hem of my dress before pulling it over my head.

Our lips only breaking to let the material of my dress pass by. I'm standing there in my navy and white bra and undies set, extremely turned on, wrapped in the arms of a man who is paying me to be here. I start to feel bad about this, but that thought evaporates when I feel his fingers at the edge of my now soaked undies. He grips them and literally rips them off my body. Breaking our kiss I say, "Hey, they were one of my favourites."

"I'll buy you another." Before I can reply, he is kissing me again and sinking his finger deep inside of me before pulling out and thrusting two more in. Moaning, I thrust my pussy against his hand as he increases his pace, I feel my pussy walls tighten and I shout, "I'm coming. Fuck, I'm coming!" My legs giving way as my body explodes, my juices coating his fingers as I continue to ride out this pleasure explosion.

He withdraws his fingers and sucks my juices off, winking at me as he does this. Leaning forward, I place my palms on his cheeks and I crash my mouth against his and kiss him deeply, moaning, as I taste myself mixed with bubbly. "Mmmmmm," I say, as I pull back and look into his eyes. "Wow, that was, just wow."

He smiles at me before bending down to pick up my now shredded undies and dress. He hands me my dress and shoves what's left of my undies into his pocket, smiling at me before turning around and heading towards the stairs. "Guess we better head back."

I'm left standing there only in my bra, my undies now in Xander's pocket, holding my dress when it hits me; I'm a hooker, a fucking hooker. The floodgates open as I slip my dress back on. Picking up the bubbly, I drink from the bottle before pouring myself a glass and sitting down.

Staring out at the horizon, I feel used and abused but also content and happy; I'm so confused right now. I know I signed up for this, but emotionally; this is much harder than I thought.

After getting back to land, it was awkward to say that least. I thought for sure I was going to get raked over the coals when I got back, but waiting for me at the apartment was a huge bunch of pink tulips with a note from Victoria.

Congrats on a great first weekend
Welcome to the family
Regards, Victoria

The note puts me at ease but it has also garnered hostility from the girls in the apartment next door, apparently Saskia wanted to be paired with Xander now that Crissy is no longer here, but thankfully Angel and Morgan have my back. I would be lost without those two girls; I'm ever grateful that they are my roommates.

To celebrate my first weekend on the job, Angel, Morgan, and I decide to make a jug of margaritas, and spend Sunday arvo lounging by the pool, listening to music. I'm in my room, changing into my orange micro bikini when I start to feel guilty over what I did today. *Where did that come from?* It's so not me. I don't think I can sleep with people randomly. I'm not a slut. I've never been a sleep with a guy on the first date girl. Staring at myself in the mirror, I feel disappointed in myself but I really don't have any choice, do I?

My thoughts are interrupted by Morgan telling me to hurry up, I throw on my cover-up and decide that I will stay, but no more sexual encounters. Well I guess I will have to, if I get paired with Xander again, as I have already started that, but nope, no more sex for me...at least while I'm working here.

The girls and I have a fantabolous evening filled with margaritas, swimming, and takeaway Chinese from Kung Fu Palace. I'm feeling relaxed and happy with my decision to stay. Angel and Morgan both put me at ease and make me feel like I can do this. I keep my no sex decision to myself, but I'm happy with the decision I have made. I keep telling myself, Victoria said it's up to me if I do anything sexual with a client. I just won't do it again, that's just not me.

I'm feeling slightly buzzed and happy as I'm climbing into bed, I sigh when I snuggle down, it's like I'm sleeping on a cloud. Grabbing my phone, I realise that I have a missed call and voice message from Kenz. Seeing that, all the guilt and shame comes rushing back and I burst into tears. I'm hiding so much from my friends and family... I'm such a bitch.

11

LOGAN

THE HESITATION OVER MOVING HERE HAS FINALLY passed and I think it's all due to my positive attitude. The hurdles I was facing with the new project have passed and all is going well; we should be finished by the completion date, if not sooner. Secondly, I managed to find an apartment and not just any apartment. Beth found me the most amazing penthouse apartment that overlooks the river and towards the bridge...right here in the hotel I have been staying at.

When I first walked in, I knew it was for me and the first person I wanted to call and tell was Sav; man I miss her. It breaks my heart that she took off like that, but I guess I can understand. It's kind of what I'm doing; I couldn't stand being in Wentworthville after what happened with Lili. I can only imagine what it would be like living in the same place where you lost your family.

I'm pretty sure that her store manager at home, Sierra, knows something but she's keeping tight-lipped. When I left, I told Sierra to contact me if Sav needed anything, her reply confirmed my suspicion, but I left it alone. I would do anything for her, she's my best friend, and she's my family. When I lost Dad, I would have fallen apart if it hadn't been for her. Luckily, Mr. and Mrs. Blac were happy to help me out from time to time. Don't get me wrong, Grandma did her best but she was too old to be looking after a teenager.

I've ordered room service for dinner tonight, and while I'm waiting, I start thinking about Mum. I haven't thought about her for years now. She ran off when I was five, with Dad's best friend, but truth be told, it was the best thing that could have happened to Dad and me.

There's a knock at the door and my dinner is here. They leave and I sit down and to enjoy my steak when my phone rings, and I see that it's Beth. "You have impeccable timing, Beth, I'm just about to hoe into a juicy steak."

"Well, give me three minutes and then you will be celebrating."

"Do tell, Bethy."

"You know I hate it when you call me Bethy. Anyway, the realtor has just faxed through everything for your penthouse sale and settlement will be in twenty-one days." Pausing she then adds, "I have also extended your stay where you are for four more weeks, the extra week is to allow you time to work and get settled in your new place."

"Beth, you are my hero. Get everything filled out, courier them to me, and I can drop them off later this week."

"Can do, boss, enjoy your steak."

"Ohh, I plan on it. Have a good night, Bethy."

I can hear her say, "Asshole," as I'm hanging up; she makes me laugh. I'd be lost without her. Finally things are looking up for me and I have a feeling things will continue to improve.

12

VICTORIA

To say I'm impressed with how Sarah has taken to being one of my girls is an understatement. When I sent her on the date with Xander, it was a little test. From the report I got back from Xander, she far exceeded any expectation that I had, and it was a total shock. She is an exceptional young lady. Sarah continues to surprise me and it's hard to surprise me; maybe I have found a new Crissy.

I'm still disappointed that she screwed me over the way she did, but the girls know the rules. I'm just glad she left with her head held high, unlike Megan. It was unfortunate the demise that came to her but as usual, my hands are clean and everything continues as normal.

Word seems to have spread that there is a new girl in town and I have been getting requests left, right, and center for my Sarah. This makes me happier than a Cartier sale. Due to her popularity, I can charge a premium and the additional income is heaven. The poor girl will be run off her feet, but the dollars she'll bring in will make things much easier. Times have been tough of late and if I lose any more girls, I won't be happy, but hopefully Sarah is my saving grace.

In between appointments on Tuesday, I call Sarah in for tea. She looks magnificent when she waltzes into my office and I inwardly smile. I can't let on that I'm happy; rule number one, always keep them on their toes.

Smiling, I stand up from my desk and walk towards her with my arms open. "Darling, you looking exquisite." Leaning forward I air kiss her cheeks, before taking her hand, and leading her out to my terrace.

"Thanks, Victoria. You look stunning, as always."

We both take a seat and I could not be more proud of how Sarah is handling herself. We sit staring at each other, I love making the girls squirm. It's a joy of mine with the newbies, but Sarah isn't squirming and that doesn't sit well with me. After a few moments of awkward silence, I ask, "Would you like some tea, Sarah?"

"Actually, I'd love a coffee. I've been so busy today that I need a caffeine hit."

Asserting my authority, I say, "Coffee is for the morning darling, tea it is." Leaning forward, I pour us both a tea but Sarah doesn't touch hers, she is quite stubborn. I need to pull her into line quickly so I get straight to the point. "How has your week been so far?"

"Umm, it's been crazy busy but I think I'm doing well." She looks over at me hesitantly. "Have I been doing well?"

"Darling, there is nothing the matter, if anything, you

have far exceeded any expectation that I had for you. You have surprised me."

"T…Thank you, Victoria," she stammers.

This is the part I love, making them squirm and guess why they are here. "You really need to stop with the stuttering, Sarah, it is unladylike." Pausing, I look down at her tea, then back at her, willing her with my eyes to drink. Leaning forward, she adds sugar to her tea and takes a sip; I give myself in inwards high five. "The reason I called you here today, was to see how you are getting on, just a catch up." Taking a sip of my tea, I stare at her. "Do you have any questions or concerns?'

"No, none at all. The girls have been really helpful and have made the transition that much easier for me. Victoria, thank you for everything. I was at rock bottom when I met you," Pausing, she looks at me before adding, "You really are my fairy godmother."

"No, darling, I was just in the right place at the right time. Fate has a funny way of guiding us when we least expect it."

"Tell me about it, I was starting to feel like I had no way out, and then you came along when I needed a boost. Hopefully, I'll be back on my feet in no time and I can get back to my life."

"You want to leave?"

"Not now I don't, but I can't do this forever, Victoria."

We will see about that. "Hmmm, well if that's how you feel." I don't say anything further because if I have my way, Sarah will be here for a long time to come. She is a money-spinner and I will not be letting her go so easily.

"Well, I must be going, I need to go and get changed for the fundraiser I am attending tonight. I will see you later, Victoria."

With that she stands up, comes over, kisses my cheek, and leaves me sitting on the patio, open-mouthed and shocked. *No one tells me they are leaving; I always dismiss them.*

Sarah continues to shock me, she is an enigma that I am yet to figure out, and it's unsettling to say the least.

13

SARAH

WORD SEEMS TO HAVE TRAVELLED THAT THERE'S A new girl on the block, and I've been an extremely busy girl this past week, seeing at least one appointment each day. Thankfully, none have been sexual, except for the one with Xander, and if I'm honest, I'm a little sad about that, which totally surprises me. I do however think that I will keep those ones to a minimum, I don't really want to whore myself out, but it was pretty exhilarating.

Today I have back-to-back appointments, which I have never done before and I'm a little nervous. I have a luncheon to attend to with Victoria and then an evening one. After our afternoon meeting the other day, I'm now super nervous to go out with her. Victoria is very intimidating at times and to be out in public with her will be quite daunting. My last appointment is with Xander; this will be the first time I have seen him since our boat encounter. I'm really nervous, yet excited to see him again, wondering if it will become sexual again.

The luncheon with Victoria was uneventful, extremely long and boring; watching paint dry would have being more exciting. It was hard to remain happy and stoic. But I was thankful that it was an easy afternoon with her, my apprehension was for nothing. At least there was yummy food and amazing cocktails.

After rushing to get ready because the afternoon luncheon with Victoria ran overtime, I'm nearly ready for my date, if you'd call it that, with Xander. I'm putting the finishing touches to my outfit and I feel like a princess. I'm wearing a knee-length, figure-hugging, backless plum dress with a modest 'V' neckline and two inch, black strappy heels. Due to the backless dress, I'm not wearing a bra and my undies are microscopic. It's pretty daring for me but I feel confident that I can do this; the old me, no way...even though I'm freaking out that one of the girls will pop out in the middle of dinner.

I've just done up the strap on my shoe when Morgan comes into my room, she stops midstep. "Holy fuck, you look hot, Sarah. Xander won't be able to keep his hands off you." My cheeks turn pink at what she says and I smile. "Give us a twirl." She spins her pointer around indicating a spin.

Smiling as I stand up, I spread out my arms and I spin around and around, like Maria in *The Sound of Music*. Due to my heels and the long dress, I lose my balance, but Morgan steps forward and catches me before I fall over; our eyes lock, she pulls me closer, and kisses me.

Closing my eyes, I open my mouth and let her tongue

invade my mouth. She wraps her arms around me and I lose myself in the kiss. A throat clearing interrupts us, pulling apart I see Angel standing in the doorway, holding up a necklace for me with a smirk on her face. "I, um, thought this might go well with the dress you are wearing." Pausing, she declares, "You look fucking hot, Sarah."

Morgan pipes in, "She sure does, Xander won't know what hit him." She smacks me on the ass and says, "Have fun, don't do anything that I wouldn't do."

Angel scoffs, "There's not much that you wouldn't do, Morgan, so, Sarah, in that case you're in for a fabulous night."

"Bitch!" Morgan yells, before adding, "But yeah, you're right. Have fun, Sarah." Morgan winks at me as she heads across out of my room.

Angel walks over to me, holding up the necklace, I lift up my hair, which I straightened and left down, so she can put it on. Turning towards the full-length mirror, I look at my reflection. I don't recognise the person staring back at me. For the first time in a longtime, I see a confident girl looking back at me. My eyes well with tears, I realise that I'm happy...being a hooker.

"What's wrong, babe?" Angel asks as she rubs my arm, just like Kenz does when I'm upset and she's worried, that thought makes me start to cry harder. **SNIFF** "I miss my friend." **SNIFF** "But I can't tell her about this, or anything that's happened." **SNIFF** "I'm a whore." **SNIFF**

Angel wraps her arms around me and holds me tight,

I cry onto her shoulder. "Shhhh, it's okay, Sarah. It will all be okay and you're not a whore." I don't say anything; I just hug her and continue to cry.

When I can cry no more, I look up and see that my face is all red and splotchy. "Shit, I look a mess and Xander will be here soon."

Pushing me towards the bathroom, Angel says. "Watch and learn, sweetcheeks, watch and learn."

Five minutes later, my makeup has been reapplied and you can't tell that I was blubbering mess a few moments ago. "Holy shit, you're a magician, Angel, thank you so much."

"You're welcome, Sarah. Now let's go downstairs and have a glass of bubbly before you have to go, it will help calm you."

"Best idea ever, I don't know why I'm so nervous tonight. I've been out with Xander before, it should be a walk in the park." Angel just shrugs at me, takes my arm, and leads us out.

We are halfway down the stairs when there is a knock at the door; Angel jumps down the remaining few steps and swings it open. Xander is standing there looking drop-dead gorgeous. He's wearing black slacks, a charcoal grey, long-sleeved, dress shirt with the top three buttons undone, and a black sports coat hangs loosely off his shoulders. My pussy begins to throb and my undies dampen at the sight of the man standing before me. Clenching my thighs together, I make my way down the remaining stairs and over to him, placing a kiss on his cheek before saying, "Hi, you're early." Stepping aside, I usher him inside the apartment.

"Fuck me, Sarah. You are stunning."

My cheeks turn pink and I look to the floor bashfully, he lifts my chin so I'm looking directly into his eyes. "Don't be shy, I'm just saying it how I see things."

"Thank you, Xander," I shyly say. "Should we get going or would you like a drink before we head out?"

"If we stay here, we won't be leaving your room and I want to show you off. You will be the hottest chick at the restaurant."

"Okay then, let me just grab my purse." Turning on my heel, I walk into the lounge room to grab my purse, the only sound is my heels clicking across the marble floor.

Bending down, I grab my purse when I feel someone standing directly behind me. Standing up, I turn around and I'm now face-to-face with Morgan. Before I have a chance to say anything, she kisses me on the lips, but this time I don't kiss her back. I'm too stunned because out of the corner of my eye I see Xander and Angel watching us.

"You ready, babe?" Xander says, in a deep gravelly voice that sends shockwaves through me.

"Yep, I'm coming."

"You will be soon." I hear Morgan murmur as I step around her and make my way back towards the foyer.

Putting my hand around Xander's bicep, I pull him towards the door and say, "Let's go." Over my shoulder, I say, "Later, ladies." As I close the door behind us, I hear a chorus of "Bye" and "Have fun."

Once, we are in the lift, Xander turns to me and says, "That was fucking hot, I think I'm going to need to arrange another date." I start to feel dejected when he adds, "Would you be up for a threesome?"

My head snaps towards him, "I...um...ah, I've never considered it before. Up until last week I had never kissed a girl."

"Then I would love to be your first threesome. Let's discuss it some more over dinner."

"Okay," I hesitantly reply, as we make our way through the foyer to the waiting limo out the front. *Tonight certainly has taken an unexpected turn*, I think to myself as I climb into the limo.

Xander wines and dines me, and I realise when we are in the limo on our way home that again I had a great night with him. Looking over at Xander, the streetlights flashing by reflecting on his face, he is deep in though as I rub my hand up his thigh, "Thank you for a lovely night, Xander." Licking my lips, I lean forward and kiss him.

He kisses me back, pushing me back into the seat as his body crushes me. His hands skimming over my breasts, I moan when he squeezes them, he deepens our kiss before nipping and sucking his way down my body, as his other hand pushes my dress up slowly. Lifting my ass, he shoves my dress to my waist and groans when all he feels is bare flesh. "Fuck, you're not wearing any undies."

"I slipped them into my purse before we left the restaurant," I pant, my heart beating erratically in my chest.

"You dirty fucking girl." Before I can register what's happening, he grabs the hem of my dress and lifts it over my head. I'm sitting in the back on a limo in nothing but black strappy heels...and I have never felt sexier. Xander's eyes heat with lust when I start to skim the tip of my finger over my chest, squeezing my nipples before tracing a path down to my pussy. Running my finger down my slit, I look at Xander and whisper, "Like what you see?"

"Fuck yes," he replies. Leaning forward, he sucks on my clit before slipping a finger deep inside of me, hooking it around and flicking that magic button deep within.

"Yes, that's the spot," I moan. He continues to suck my clit and flick his fingers until I'm tumbling over the edge; my whole body shudders as my orgasm rips through me like a tidal wave. "I'm coming," I breathlessly shout as I ride his fingers until my body tremors stop.

He looks up at me through hooded eyes and growls, "I need to fuck you now and it's going to be hard and fast. You okay with that?"

I'm still blissed out from my previous orgasm that I just nod, in one swift motion, he flicks open his button, shoves his pants down to free his cock, and thrusts into me until he is balls deep inside. His cock fills my pussy perfectly, and I clench around his length as he continues to assault my pussy.

He wasn't wrong when he said hard and fast. He pounds into me over and over, grunting with each thrust; my teeth shuddering together each time he slams into me. A few thrusts later, I feel his cock harden and he explodes, just as another orgasm ruptures through me, wave after wave rippling over me. We both cry out in ecstasy as our bodies thrum with pleasure.

He climbs off, and sits back next to me; we are both breathless, panting as if we have just run the Gold Coast

Marathon. Feeling self-conscious, I lean forward and grab my dress, pulling it over my head and shimmy it down over my hips.

The air smells like sex but it is also really awkward, it's similar to what happened on the yacht the other day after we got busy on the deck. I couldn't say slept together because there was no sex that time.

Looking over at Xander, I'm hesitant to say anything, I'm just about to say something and I realise that we are back at the apartment. He quickly pulls his pants back up, tucking away his now flaccid cock when the driver opens my door. It doesn't seem like he is going to move, so I lean over kiss him on the cheek and murmur, "Thanks for a lovely night, Xander." Turning around, I take the driver's hand and climb out.

Before the limo has pulled away, the tears are flowing down my face. Slipping off my heels, I run inside and wait for the lift. The doors finally open after what feels like eternity, and I push the button for our floor. Sliding down the wall, I sit on the floor and cry, sobs rack through my body. The lift doors open but I don't get out; I just sit there, crying like a baby.

I'm still sitting in the lift, sobbing, when I hear an apartment door open. I'm too upset to look up, but before I know it, Angel is wrapping her arms around me. "Shhhh, it will be okay, Sarah. I know exactly what you feel. Xander can be an ass, don't take it to heart."

"I thought he really liked me."

"I know, it's hard to separate your feelings in this job but I promise, it does get easier. Just try have fun, eat and drink things that you have never heard of before and have fan-fucking-tabolous sex when the opportunity arises."

"I'm doing things I never thought I would, ugh, what am I becoming? I feel like a whore."

"Everclear?"

"Not in this instance, I mean literally." **SNIFF** "I just got paid for out of this world sex." **SNIFF** "I'm a hooker, a prostitute, a skanky ho slutbag. This isn't what my life was meant to be."

"None of us want this life, but sometimes you have to do what's needed to survive. Sarah, you are none of those things, you are a survivor. Albeit surviving in a non-traditional way but YOU are still getting on with your life. So it's taken a little detour, big fucking whoop." Emphasising the word 'you.' "You have food and shelter, a new kick-ass wardrobe and might I add, new kick-ass friends." She smirks as she says the last bit.

"I guess you're right. I just never expected to end up here."

"Neither did I, neither did I. Now, let's get inside, put on trackies, and break out the Hagen-Daas and Netflix."

"Do we have any Ben and Jerry's?"

"Since you moved in we do, so come on. Let's go inside."

Standing up, I wrap my arms around her in a tight embrace. "Thank you, Angel, I'm so glad I ended up in your apartment and not with Saskia."

"I'm glad too, Sarah. No one deserves to live with that psycho bitch."

Just as we are exiting the lift, she devil herself, Saskia,

saunters out of her apartment dressed to the nines. She's obviously been called for a late night hook up. She looks at me in tears and snickers as she enters the lift. "I knew you couldn't handle him, just pack up and go home."

Angel bites back, "Fuck off, Saskia, you're just jealous that he didn't choose you but I don't blame him, your nothing bu..."

"Stop!" I interrupt, "She's not worth it." Turning around I stare her in the eye add, "Jealousy really doesn't suit you, Sass, besides, Xander isn't into washed up, two-bit whores. He has class and his class is currently dripping down my leg. Now if you excuse us, go fuck yourself."

As the lift doors are closing, Saskia is standing there open-mouthed and fuming. Angel is pissing herself laughing as we walk through the door; Morgan comes into the foyer. "What's so funny?"

"Sarah here just tore Sass a new one."

"You called her, Sass? She hates that as much, if not more, than Victoria being called Vicky. Man, I wish I could have seen that."

"Oh it gets better, our girl here said, and I quote 'Xander isn't into washed up, two-bit whores. He has class and his class is currently dripping down my leg. Now if you excuse us, go fuck yourself'"

"No fucking way?"

"Yes, fucking way," I say. "Now, I'm going to clean up and then we can Netflix it up."

Angel and Morgan head into the lounge, talking about my Saskawhore takedown, and I head upstairs. When I enter my room, I strip off my dress and quickly have a shower, washing away the filthiness of tonight. Slipping on my trackies and a singlet, I head downstairs to find Angel and Morgan on the couch eating ice cream, and I notice a bottle of tequila on the coffee table. "You two read my mind, so what shit are we going to watch?"

———

Jumping onto the couch in between them, we settle in and have a night of eating ice cream, drinking tequila, and watching *The Ranch*. Ashton Kutcher is so hot, just what the doctor ordered. Tonight reminds me of Kenz and me, I miss her so I decide that tomorrow I'll give her a call.

The sun is shining and I'm up way too early, especially considering today is my day off. I've been flat out this week and I'm looking forward to a day lounging by the pool, drinking wine, and chillaxing. After my mini breakdown last night, I'm feeling refreshed and this morning I feel like I could conquer the world. Chillaxing today is the perfect way to celebrate my newfound happiness.

Heading to the kitchen, I turn the coffee maker on and while I'm waiting, I text Kenz.

Sarah – *Hey bitch. Just saying hi. Work is crazy busy. Hope you and my lil princesses are fabulous. Catch up soon Xo*

Placing my phone back on the bench, I reach up and grab a mug. My phone starts playing *Bad Things* by Jace

Everett and I smile, Kenz is calling me. Putting my mug down and I answer straight away.

"Morning, bitch. What are you doing up so early?"

"Um, kids, more to the point, why are you up so early?"

"Couldn't sleep. How have you been? It's been forever since I have seen you." Feeling a tad guilty when I say this because the not seeing one another is because of me. How do you tell your best friend that you are hiding because you're an escort, living it up in an apartment, because your ex-boyfriend kicked you out? Ohh and by the way, he's gay.

"I'm tired but good. The girls keep my busy and Malt Me is doing really well. Speaking of, we are having a tasting this weekend. Do you think you can make it?"

"That sounds awesome, I'll check my schedule and let you know. We are a few peeps down at the moment so I've been flat out." *Technically not lying, just not working where I used to.*

"Okay, keep me posted. How's Josh?"

Fuck, but luckily there is a knock at the door and I'm literally saved by the bell. "Hey, Kenz, there's someone at the door. I'll hopefully see you this weekend."

"You better, bitch, love your face."

"Love you face too, bitch."

Hanging up, I place my phone back on the bench and lovingly look at the coffee pot, when there is another knock at the door. Sighing, I walk to the door, yelling, "Coming."

Swinging open the door, I'm greeted by a fuming

Victoria. "Good morning, Victoria." She pushes past me and heads towards the kitchen, without saying a word.

Following her back into the kitchen, I grab another coffee mug; she glares at me as I pour two coffees. "There is nothing good about this morning, Sarah. Saskia is no longer with us and the schedule is now in a shambles. You have a last minute appointment and then tonight you're also working. I need you to bring in a new client, numbers are dwindling and this is unacceptable; both client and staff wise."

So much for a quiet day I think, then it hits me, she said Saskia is gone. "What do you mean Saskia is gone? I saw her heading out last night. But more so, how do I bring in new clients? That's not what I'm here for."

"Never mind where the little tramp is, she's gone. End of story. As for bringing in new clients, you will do as I say or you can join Saskia."

I'm shocked by what I'm hearing and also little intimidated. How am I going to bring in new clients? A last minute appointment, this must be paying a fortune, especially if Victoria is here this early in the morning arranging it. "So what and whom am I seeing on such short notice today?"

"Thank you, I was sure that you were going to fight me on this since it's your day off. It's with Xander, last night must have gone extremely well if he's requesting you again so soon and wanting this on such short notice, too."

Fuck, Xander, Mr. Mindfuck himself. Plastering on a fake smile, I say, "Sure, that's fine. Are we going out on his boat again?"

"No, to his house. The driver will be here to pick you up at 11:30 a.m. and then I'll be by tonight to pick you up at 8:00 p.m. and I will take you to the local hotel, where we seem to be having luck acquiring new clients."

"That's fine, Victoria." Taking a sip of my coffee I add, "Will I be back in time to get ready to meet you, my visits with Xander generally run late."

"Yes, there will be plenty of time. He is aware of your schedule for this evening and has promised to have you back in plenty of time. Don't frown, it's not good for your face." She looks at her watch and states, "I have to get going. I have a whole schedule to rearrange due to Saskia's departure. I'll see you tonight. And, Sarah, don't disappoint me, I'm not in the mood to be let down again."

With that she turns on her heels and storms off, slamming the front door behind her. I'm left sitting there stunned. *She really needs to get laid*, I think to myself as I drink my coffee. Taking a seat at the breakfast bar, I lose myself in my morning coffee, swinging myself side to side and I sigh, Xander, really? I'm not sure I want to see him again. Hearing feet shuffling through the lounge room, I look up and see Morgan, looking like shite.

"Morning, lovely, you look like shite."

"I feel like shite but I got a call from Bitchtoria. Looks like you and I have an appointment together today."

"What? She never mentioned that when she was here."

"So that's who was slamming doors this early. I thought it might have been next-door trying to piss us off since you gave her a tongue-lashing, and not the good kind, last night, and she was still pissy about it. So wish I could have seen that."

"Ha, well, apparently, she's no longer with us."

Morgan's head snaps up and she's wide-awake now. "What do you mean no longer with us?" she says, as she pours a coffee for herself, sitting on the stool next to me.

"That's all I know, hence why Bitchtoria is in a pissy mood at the ass crack of dawn. She has to redo the appointments. Isn't she like the forth girl to leave in the last two weeks?"

"Five, no six, there were a few girls just before you got here. Wow, wonder what's happening?"

"Beats me. But tonight, I'm on scouting duty with Victoria."

"Fuck me, times are hard if she's using us to get newbies."

"Huh?"

"Well, it's normally a let them approach us system, but times must be tough if we are bringing them in. It's going to get crazy busy in that case."

"Great, like I'm not already shattered."

"Welcome to the glamorous life that is working for Victoria Chalmers. Anyways, what's up with the double appointment?"

Looking over at Morgan, I bite my lip. "Umm, Xander saw our kiss last night before he and I left." Pausing, I quickly add, "And he wants to have a threesome with us."

"Okay, cool."

Just like that, she's okay with this. I'm in shock but

also turned on by the thought of a threesome. "Really, just like that you're okay with it?"

"Yep, it's the nature of the job, darl." Looking over at me, she enquires, "Have you ever had a threesome?"

Shaking my head from side to side, I bite on my lip and whisper, "Nope. I'm kinda nervous."

She slides up beside me and squeezes my hand. "Did you like kissing me?" Shyly, I nod my head up and down as I look towards Morgan and smile. She grins back at me and somehow it relaxes me. "Then just follow my lead and prepare to be mind blown." She leans over, grabs my cheeks, and kisses me, the stool spins towards her and I spread my legs to let her in. Sliding my arms around her waist, I deepen the kiss and moan into her mouth. My heart rate increases, I've never been kissed like this before. She gently cups my breast and massages, that tingly feeling deep in my belly starts fluttering when Angel entering the kitchen interrupts us. "Don't stop on my account, ladies."

Morgan pulls away and winks at me, before turning to Angel. "Guess what?"

"It's too early to play guessing games."

"You'll love this." Morgan pauses for effect. "Saskawhore is no longer with us and our newbie here is about to have her first threesome...with Xander and me."

Angel closes her eyes and sighs. "I remember my first ménage with you." She takes sip of my coffee before spitting it out. "What the what? Saskawhore's gone, what? How? Why? Spill."

Morgan and I both laugh, and I say, "Yep, Vicky popped by this morning and told me."

"Come on, spill?"

"That's all I know. She told me 'End. Of. Story' in her snotty voice and then stormed off. A few minutes later, Morgan came down to tell me about today's new adventure."

"No fucking way, that totally blows me away. I thought for sure Saskawhore would be here till her vagina was old, wrinkly, and about to fall off. Man she was a whore, so glad she's not here anymore, morale will definitely improve next-door then."

Morgan pipes in, "Yeah but now, the rest of us have to deal with the freaky fucked up appointments that she used to keep to herself."

Angel shudders. "Damn, didn't think of that. So how did today's ménage à trois come about?"

"Xander saw Morgan kiss me last night and mentioned that he'd want that with us, I didn't think he'd be serious...or arrange it so quickly."

"Sarah, he's a male. He would have been thinking about that all night long, even when he was balls deep inside of you. Wonder if we can entice him to make it a foursome?"

"Umm, let me try this first and then we can go from there."

"Seriously?" she eagerly asks.

"I guess so, why the hell not?" They both nod at me as I say this. I think I shocked them with my reply, especially after last night's meltdown.

Finishing my coffee, I say, "And on that note, ladies, I need to go get ready." Turning towards Morgan, I shyly ask, "Umm, Morgan, what do I wear?"

She finishes her coffee, places our mugs in the sink, throws her arm over my shoulder, and we head up stairs together to get ready. "You're in good hands, babe, leave it to me. Today will be a day that you will never forget."

...And it sure is one that will go down in the history books.

14

VICTORIA

FINALLY, SOMEONE WHO JUST SAYS, "YES, VICTORIA," without complaining or wanting anything in return. I knew I could count on Sarah to help me out. At least this clusterfuck has so far been easy to repair, but something is going on and I don't like it. Another girl has screwed me over, and that is unacceptable. This one makes four in the last two weeks and seven in recent times. What shocks me most is that it is was Saskia this time, I didn't want to forcibly remove her but the situation required it. At lease Crissy went peacefully and I didn't need to get my hands dirty, but Saskia, she was a wild one, not surprising really. In the beginning that's what I liked about her, but I gave her too much free rein, I've learned my lesson, it's time for a change.

It's time to bring the girls inline and reiterate to them that no one fucks with me, no one. An intervention with the girls is needed, and it needs to happen soon, I can't afford to lose another girl. Thankfully, I found Sarah when I did, never thought I would thank a client but him wanting to meet in that dump led me to her.

She is a diamond in the rough, that's for sure. Her language is appalling but she has this aurora that sucks you in. She's taken to the job like a pro. With a bit more refining, she will be the best girl that has ever worked for Elite. With the guidance from Morgan, Angel, and myself, I can turn her in a cash cow, even bigger than Crissy was.

Pouring myself a brandy, I sit on my leather couch. I keep thinking about what's happening with the girls at the moment. This situation is really grating on me, why all of a sudden is this happening? Is someone trying to sabotage me? I hope not, after all, I'm Victoria Chalmers; no one fucks with me!

15

SARAH

If you had told me five weeks ago that this was going to be my life, I would have laughed in your face and told you to take another toke because you were smoking crack. It's amazing how in the blink of an eye everything can change, and then when you are at rock bottom, an opportunity of a lifetime comes along and completely turns your life around. Without Victoria and Elite, I would have been alone, jobless, and homeless. This isn't what I envisioned my life would be, but surprisingly I'm really enjoying this, and to be honest, trying to snag a new client seems exciting.

A few hours later, Morgan and I arrive at Xander's. His house was over the top, exactly what I pictured for him. He opened the door and I was sure I was going to pass out, a rush of endorphins ran through my body as I realised I was about to partake in my first threesome. He invited us in and led us out to the patio. He went back inside and returned with three mojitos: alcohol, just what I needed to calm my nerves.

As I suspected there was very little small talk, the air was thick with lust, confusion, and excitement. Before I knew it, Xander was leading us upstairs towards the bedroom. Xander and Morgan ran the show, and for the most part, I was just a bystander, and truth be told, I was fine with that, not that I knew what I was doing anyway.

I have to say it was quite arousing watching two people go at it in person; it's way different to watching porn. When they both turned their attention to me, holy shitballs, Batman. I'd never experienced pleasure like that before; I didn't know where to concentrate. Four hands roaming my body, two mouths sucking and nibbling simultaneously, it was mind-blowing.

In typical Xander style, once it was over, he left, without a word, leaving Morgan and I lying in his bed. Looking to Morgan, I noticed that she didn't seem fazed. She just stood up, grabbed my hand, and led me into the ensuite to shower and get freshened up. Leaning in, she turned the shower on, and once the water was warm, pulled me into the most heavenly shower I have ever had. The shower stall was big enough to fit several people, there were eight wall jets and an overhead rainwater tap thingy; it was pure bliss. The water temperature was perfect and just what my body needed.

Morgan and I showered in silence before she started to wash and soap up my body. I had never had a girl touch me like that before, but after what we had just done together, a shower was nothing. We soaped each other up, kissing and indulging in a little more fun before hopping out—I quite enjoyed the girl on girl action. I think because girls know what they like, they know how to evoke the pleasure just right. Once we were dressed, we headed downstairs to the waiting limo. When we got home, Morgan and I didn't have time to chat, as I had to get ready to go out with Victoria.

I'm lying in the tub, relaxing my body, as it's sore from earlier. I never knew that a threesome could be so physically draining. Closing my eyes, I remember the events from earlier today and I can't help but smile, it was exciting and so not what I thought it would be. The books make them look so sexy and erotic, don't get me wrong, I had fun, but I can't say I'll be rushing out to have another one. I'm more a twosome type of girl; sorry Angel there will be no foursome either.

Stepping out of the bath, I dry off and lather my body with moisturiser and spritz on my perfume. Walking into the closet naked, I put on a fire engine red strapless bra and undies set. Turning to the dresses hanging up, I can't choose between the red knee-length strapless or the midnight blue, floor-length, one shoulder dress. I'm standing there staring at both when Morgan comes in and whistles at me. Laughing, I smile and turn around. "Hey, which should I wear?" Lifting up each dress to show her.

"Umm, the blue. It will make your eyes pop. Save the red for the first date with whomever you snag."

"Thanks. Did you need me for anything?"

"I just wanted to check and see how you were doing, you were pretty quiet when we got back from Xander's earlier."

"I'm fine, Morgan, just tired and worn out. The soak in the bath reinvigorated me and now I'm ready to go." Slipping the dress over my head, I do a spin. The material feels amazing against my body and when I look in the mirror, I feel and look like a princess. Turning towards Morgan I ask, "What do you think?"

"Whomever you choose tonight, will be eating our of your hands. You are fucking gorgeous, Sarah, I'm a little envious of you."

"Envious of me, please."

"Seriously, Sarah. You have taken to this job like a duck to water, no wonder you are the fav."

"Pfft, I'm not the fav."

"Yeah, you are, but you know what? You deserve it. You've been to hell and back and now the sky is the limit. I'm so happy for you, Sarah. You are a pro at this, and not in the hooker for sex slash blowjob kind of way. You are gorgeous, fun, bubbly, free-spirited, and sexually adventurous; the perfect mix for this job."

"I don't know about all of that."

"I do, I've been doing this for a few years now and everyone loves you, everyone. Listen, I've been involved in my fair share of ménages, but Sarah, I've never enjoyed myself as much as I did with you today. If you ever want another, I would happily oblige."

"Umm, I don't know, Morgan. Don't get me wrong, I enjoyed it, and this, but I can't see myself doing this forever."

"Victoria will have something to say in that, you are her cash cow at the moment, Sarah. There is no way in hell that she will be letting you go anytime soon." With that she turns on her heel and exits the wardrobe; leaving me to ponder what she said...am I really going to be stuck here forever?

I'm finally ready and as I'm heading downstairs my phone pings with a text.

Kenz – *yo, bitch! What time you getting here for Origin 2nite?*

Fuck, fuck, fuck, I think to myself. Turning around, I head back to my room. If I don't call, Kenz is going to call me, so I quickly dial her number and she picks up in the second ring.

"Yo, bitch, how far away are you?"

"Umm, that's why I'm calling. I can't make it tonight. I have to work."

"Noooo, it's Origin, Sarah. You have to be here."

"I know but something at work has come up. I have to go, we will catch up soon."

"Yeah, sure, okay. If you get off before the game ends, pop over."

"I'll see what I can do. Love you, bitch."

"Love you too, laters."

Phew, I think to myself as I slip my phone into my bag and head off to meet Victoria. As I climb into the limo, I realise that I'm still smiling, and dare I say it, glowing; guess that happens when you have a threesome with multiple orgasms.

Half an hour later, we've picked up Victoria and I'm sitting next to her in the limo; all of a sudden, I'm nervous as all hell. My palms are sweating and my heart rate is accelerating the closer we get to the bar. I'm more anxious about tonight, and bringing in a new client, than I was this morning when I was faced with a threesome with Xander and Morgan. My nerves kick up a notch as the limo approaches the bar and before we climb out, she turns to me and gives me her intimidating stare. "Sarah, tonight is very important. Don't screw it up; a lot is riding on this. Failure is not an option."

No pressure, I think to myself as I climb out of the limo.

Victoria leads me to a table near the front windows. She orders a bottle of *Krug* and we scope out the bar. It's still early so the place is pretty empty; Victoria takes this time to educate me on how to pick up a man and the dos and don'ts of procurement. I'm not really paying attention as I see a drop-dead gorgeous guy walk in, and I know he's the one. I'm half-heartedly listening to her, my eyes and mind keep wandering to the guy sitting at the bar. Finally, she tells me to go explore; there's no exploring needed, I know exactly whom I want to chat to.

Finishing off my glass of champagne, I look to Victoria and say, "Wish me luck."

Surprising me, she replies, "Go get 'em, tiger."

To make it not so obvious, I wander the long way to the bar, casually glancing around. After a few moments, I decided it's now or never and I make a beeline for the guy from earlier. He's sitting at the bar all alone, and I think this is a sign, taking a deep breath I strut over to him repeating to myself, "You can do this, you can do this." *I seem to be saying that a lot lately.*

Taking a seat next to the gentleman, I turn towards him, notice no ring, and smile...here goes nothing.

16

LOGAN

It's Origin day but after a long day of meetings and number crunching for a new tender, I'm shattered. I head to the hotel bar for a burger and beer; my standard dinner at the moment. I've just ordered when someone takes the stool next to me, glancing over I see an attractive brunette sitting there. I smile to be polite and she takes this as an opening to engage in conversation. "Hi, I'm Sarah, Sarah Bryant."

"Hi, Logan DeBiers. Nice to meet you."

She leans in closer, flashing her cleavage in my face, and I get a good look down her dress. She notices me staring at her chest and she smiles seductively at me. "Would you like to join me for dinner, Logan DeBiers?"

"Umm, not tonight, I've just finished the day from hell and tomorrow, I'm heading out of town for a business meeting. As soon as I finish my burger, I'll be heading back to my room 'cause I'm shattered."

She looks dejected but smiles, "Okay, have a great night then, Logan DeBiers." She leans over, gently kisses my cheek, and slides a card next to my hand. When she removes her lips, I swear my cheek tingled and I was sad at the loss of contact. She turns around and walks away from me, swishing her ass from side to side as she exits the bar. I'm mesmerised as I watch the material of her dress hug her curves, she turns and blows a kiss towards me before she leaves. I can't help but smile as I watch her saunter away.

The bartender returns with my burger, I order another beer and forget all about Sarah. It isn't until I'm about to leave that I notice the card she left me, picking it up I shove it in my pocket and head up to my room. Once inside, I throw everything on the kitchen bench and head to the bedroom. Stripping off, I change into my navy basketball shorts, grab another beer, and watch some television before crawling into bed and turning out the light.

Just as I'm about to fall asleep, an image of Sarah appears, her eyes boring into me, hiding behind her bangs before she smiles, and I smile. As I'm remembering her beauty, the card she gave me pops into my mind. Rolling to my side, I try to get to sleep but it starts to bug me. Turning on the light, I head to the other room and pick it up. It's an ivory thick card, with just a number on it in heavy gold block writing; on the backside of it is an embossed gold dove. "That's weird," I say, chucking it back on the bench, I head back to bed but I can't sleep. I lay there staring at the ceiling and I can't stop thinking about Sarah or that card; it's intriguing.

My curiosity gets the better of me so I hop up again, grab the card, and dial the number; it goes straight to an answering service. I leave my details and jump back into bed. The last thing I remember before falling to sleep is Sarah's beaming smile and hypnotic eyes.

The next morning, I have a final meeting with my realtor about the penthouse to sign all the documents, officially making it mine before I head to the airport. I've just left the office when Beth calls to say the meeting later today has been postponed, and she has rebooked my flights for next week. *Beth is a gem,* I think to myself as I realise that I have a free afternoon and I'm pretty excited. Deciding to grab a coffee, I head to the Java Lava café. I've just placed my order and while I'm waiting, my phone rings, I don't recognise the number. "Hello."

"Is this Logan DeBiers?"

"Yes, who is this?"

"Yes, sorry, my name is Victoria, you met one of my girls last night and left a message. Is this a good time to chat?"

"Huh? One of your girls, no I met a Sarah in a bar."

"Yes, she's one of my girls. I much prefer to do business face–to-face, Mr. DeBiers, are you free for lunch?"

"Umm, yeah, business, what I'm confused?" My coffee order is called; grabbing my coffee I head to the nearest table and take a seat.

"All in good time, Mr. DeBiers. Now what do you say we meet at *Cha Cha Cha* at 1:00 p.m. and I can give you all the information?"

Now the old Logan would have said no immediately but I'm trying to be spontaneous and different, prove she-bitch wrong, so I decided why not? I need to eat anyway. "Okay, Victoria, that sounds great. I will see you then."

"Excellent, Mr. DeBiers, I look forward to meeting

you later today."

———

After hanging up from Victoria, I drink my coffee and wonder to myself what in the hell I have gotten myself into.

After getting lost, I finally find the restaurant, I'm ten minutes late and I hate being late. Walking inside, I ask the maitre'd for Victoria, thankfully they know whom I'm referring to as I didn't get her last name. I'm escorted over to her table in the back of the restaurant and she stands to greet me. "Mr. DeBiers, it's nice to meet you; I'm Victoria Chalmers."

"Mrs. Chalmers, it's lovely to meet you. I apologise for being late but I got lost, my sense of direction is shocking and I'm new to town."

"It's Ms., Mr. DeBiers but please, call me Victoria."

"Okay, I'll call you Victoria if you call me Logan."

"It's a deal, Logan." She winks as she says this and takes her seat.

Our waiter comes to the table. "Can I get you a drink, sir?"

"Yes please, can I get a beer, whatever you have on tap will be fine."

"Certainly, sir." Turning to Victoria, he asks, "Can I get you another glass, Ms. Chalmers?"

"Thank you, Toby, that would be wonderful." Turning her attention back to me, she leans her elbows on the table and gets right down to business. "So, Mr. DeBiers, you're interested in my Sarah?"

17

VICTORIA

"So, Mr. DeBiers, you're interested in my Sarah?" Looking over, I see confusion on his face.

"What do you mean 'my Sarah'?" He air quotes 'my Sarah.'

"Well, Mr. DeBiers. Sarah is one of my girls and from the chemistry I saw between the two of you last night, and your subsequent phone call, I put two and two together."

"I...I don't understand. I met a girl at a bar and called her, but instead of speaking to her I'm speaking to you. Is she a hooker?" He leans forward and whispers the last part, pulling back when Toby returns with our drinks.

"Thank you, Toby."

"Are you ready to order?" he replies.

"Can we please have a few more moments? I'm not sure I will be staying," Logan replies. Toby nods his head and returns to the bar.

"Mr. DeBiers, what's not to understand?"

"What and who are you?" He looks completely confused.

"My name is Victoria Chalmers, owner and proprietor of Elite. Sarah is one of my girls, and if you'd like to see her again, I can arrange that."

"What exactly does that mean?"

"Sarah works at Elite. We are the best agency in town. She would be available to attend functions, spend time with you..."

"She's a hooker?"

This gets me laughing every time I meet up with a new client, and I can't help but cackle. "Mr. DeBiers, no I do not employ hookers. I supply and employ escorts, which according to the Oxford dictionary means 'A person who may be hired to accompany someone to a social event.' Not a hooker by definition. Should said social encounter fall into a sexual nature that is between you and her." Letting him digest that, I then add, "The price will vary depending on the social activity, duration, and notice given."

"I...umm...I...I don't know what to say. I've never done this before."

Laughing, I say, "There's a first time for everything, Mr. DeBiers. Why not give it a go, what do you have to lose?"

"Well, apart from money, my dignity, and my reputation. What if this gets out?"

"I assure you, at Elite everything is confidential and discreet. You'd be surprised whom I have on my books. I'm not here to judge, I'm here to provide companionship and a good time. Nothing more, nothing less."

"I'm just not sure." Pausing, he then mumbles to himself, "I've never done anything like this."

"Mr. DeBiers, we only live once. Why not give it a go and then see where it leads from there?"

"I'm still not sure, it just doesn't feel right."

"Stop, you're beating around the bush, I don't have time for what ifs and it doesn't feel right. I will give you some time to think about it." Handing another card to him, I state, "This is my card, it has my direct number on it. When you have made up your mind, give me a call. I don't have all day."

"Umm, Okay, thanks."

"Your welcome. Now, I must run, I have another meeting across town to get to. I hope to hear from you soon, Mr. DeBiers."

Before he has a chance to respond, I'm heading out the door...*he'll call, they always do*, I think to myself as I head towards my waiting car.

18

LOGAN

Victoria has just left and I'm sitting here stunned. Hiring an escort, can I really do this? The old me would not have even called in the first place, the new me is actually considering this, because Sarah is stunning and I'm intrigued by her. Silky chocolate brown hair, beautiful eyes that suck you in, and a body with curves in all the right places; she's every man's dream girl. As I sit here and stare into my beer, I seriously start considering doing this. There is something about Sarah and I want to get to know her. We may have only said ten words to each other last night, but I'm drawn to her...I need to have her in my life.

Fuck, where are you, Sav?? I really need you right now, I think to myself as I sit here, staring out the window at the river, contemplating all of this. I'm playing out every different scenario in my head, but it all comes back to Sarah, what harm could it do? *It's just talking, I'm not paying for sex, and it will be okay...right?*

The staff here are looking at me curiously as I'm

mumbling to myself, when I notice the looks I decide it's time to leave. After settling the bill, I decide to walk along the riverfront, the long way to the hotel, soon to be my home; I'm still amazed that I got the penthouse.

Before heading to my room, I head to the bar, have a Malt Me beer, and pick up my phone. My nerves kick up when it starts to ring, it's Beth letting me know that some time-sensitive documents have been delivered, and I need to sign them immediately. I tell her I will sign tonight and post them off tomorrow morning for her. After hanging up, I make my decision and dial Victoria's direct line. I'm ready to hang up but the call connects; I pause and don't say anything.

"Mr. DeBiers, I was expecting your call."

"Good evening, Victoria."

"Have you come to a decision, Mr. DeBiers?"

"I have, yes." Pausing, I swallow hard and then quickly say, "I'd like to meet with Sarah."

"Marvelous, I knew you would. When you would you like to arrange the first meeting?"

"Umm, I hadn't really thought about that."

"Typical man," she scoffs. "Well, let me help you out. Sarah is available any evening this week, but if you'd prefer a daytime visit, I'm sure I can shuffle things around for you."

"No, no, don't disrupt her schedule. How about tomorrow night?"

"That will work. The first meeting will be at my bar, Equinox. What time would best suit you?"

"I should be done by 7:00 p.m., will that work?"

"Perfect, Mr. DeBiers. I will see you tomorrow night

at 7:00 p.m. and Sarah will join you at 7:30 p.m., once we have everything finalised and you've wired the first payment to me. Welcome to Elite, Mr. DeBiers," she says in a chipper tone, which is disturbing to say the least.

"Thank you, Victoria, and please, call me Logan."

"Goodnight, Logan."

As I disconnect the call, I start to regret my decision, but then I close my eyes and a vision of Sarah appears. Any qualms I had disappear; I cannot wait to get to know this woman.

19

VICTORIA

My lunch with Mr. DeBiers went extremely well...eventually. For a moment there, I feared I was going to lose him, but thankfully luck was on my side. After storming off and leaving him sitting there, he called me back later that evening, and he is now the latest member of Elite.

He is very interested in Sarah and they will be meeting tomorrow night here at our bar. I want to watch over her and see how she does; I've yet to see her in action. She has not yet let me down and I hope it continues; I've had enough to deal with of late. The girls really need to fall into line, or I will be forced to intervene... again...like I did, with Saskia recently.

I'm not happy when I need to specifically get involved, but no one, and I mean no one, messes with me...or there are consequences to be paid.

Today has been hectic and I'm just packing up for the evening when Simon walks in with an envelope for me. He places it on my desk and says he will be back after dropping Sarah and Logan off to dinner, and when he returns, he will wait in the bar until I'm ready to head home for the evening. Nonchalantly I wave him off. *You don't tell me what the plan is,* I think to myself as I reach for the envelope.

Reaching into my desk draw, I grab my letter opener and slide it along the envelope edge. Replacing it and closing the draw, I turn my attention back to the envelope in my hands. As I'm pulling the letter out, a feeling of unease washes over me. Reading the letter I gasp, there in block letters is my greatest fear...someone knows.

Staring back at me are five words, five words that I never wanted to see.

I Know What You Did

My heart is racing, if this gets out we'll be ruined, but if it does, I refuse to go down alone. I'll take him with me and anyone else who gets in my way.

Picking up my phone, I make the phone call that I hoped I never would have to make. They pick up on the first ring.

"Yes," they curtly reply.

Swallowing hard, I quickly say, "Someone knows."

"Fix it." That's all they say before hanging up.

As if my night could not get any worse, Simon walks back in. "Sorry to bother you but we've lost another."

"What do you mean, we've lost another?"

"Ma'am, Angel is no longer with us. As I was leaving to get the girls, I ran into her outside. She handed in her apartment key, business credit card, and phone and left."

My blood starts to boil, this cannot be happening. I'm losing girls left, right, and center and now the threat. "Thank you, Simon, place her things on the lounge, I'll deal with them later. Looks like I'll be here for a while."

"As you wish." He turns, placing the items on the lounge and leaves me alone in my office. Pondering what step to take next, a genius idea starts to develop. It's not going to be a pretty one...not for her anyway.

20

———

SARAH

I'm lazing in bed, still overwhelmed with the happenings of the past few days. They are a few days that I will never forget: I had my first threesome and I tried to secure my first client. Both were equally exciting but in completely different ways, but as soon as my eyes locked on whom I now know as Logan, all nerves I had vanished and a sense of calm euphoria washed over me.

We only spoke for a few moments, but I must have left just as much of an impression on him as he did with me. He immediately joined Elite and now tomorrow night I'll be having dinner and drinks with him.

Waking the next morning refreshed, which I haven't done in week now, I'm excited for the day ahead of me. Thankfully, my luncheon was cancelled last minute; therefore I now have the afternoon to pamper myself. I'm so nervous about tonight, I haven't had butterflies like this since my first date with Josh. Just as I'm about to jump into the shower, my phone beeps with a text from the asshat himself.

Josh – *Why does Kenz think we are still dating?*
Sarah – *Haven't told her*
Josh – *Well I did. Come get you shit*
Sarah – *Soon*
Josh – *Now. Or I chuck it*
Sarah – *Busy at work now. I'll get when I can*

After that final text, I shut off my phone, I refuse to let him ruin tonight for me. It only seems fitting that the asshole that caused all this, makes contact when I'm finally starting to feel happy again. Guess that's the world letting me know that Sarah Bryant doesn't deserve happiness.

After a long hot shower, I'm starting to feel like me again, when there is a knock at my door. Before I can shout 'come in,' it opens and both Morgan and Angel enter.

"Why, please come in, girls?" I say like a smart-ass with a smirk and a smile.

"Well, I guess us and the bubbly will turn back around then." Pausing, Morgan lifts the bubbly. "Please can we stay, pretty sure you want some bubbles," Morgan replies cheekily.

"Come on, Morgan, we can take this to the patio, she obviously doesn't want any bubbly," Angel says, smirking at me but her eyes don't light up as usual. She pops open the bubbly and pours three glasses, handing one to Morgan, holding mine hostage.

"You two are so funny. Now, Angel, please pass me my bubbles, I'm really nervous about tonight."

Morgan laughs, "If you're nervous about dinner and drinks, I wonder how nervous you were the other day before our threesome?"

"Hardy har har, but surprisingly, I'm more nervous about tonight. You guys, this Logan dude is beyond fucking hot. I'm getting wet just thinking about him."

"Oh My God! You've got it bad for this guy. Don't let Vicky get wind of this. She will pull you off his list quicker than Saskawhore can suck a cock." Angel clicks her fingers as she says the last part.

We all laugh. "Believe it or not, I miss Saskawhore and just talking about her cock sucking skills has put me at ease. Who would have thought that was possible?"

Morgan goes to grab my bubbly. "No more bubbles for you, clearly you are drunk, you're thanking Saskawhore."

Before she can grab my glass, I chug it back and hand her the empty. "Why yes, I would love another glass to calm my nerves."

"Lucky I love your face." Morgan takes my glass and tops it up.

We spend the rest of the afternoon giving each other makeovers and laughing, but Angel isn't herself. When I asked if she was okay, she snapped at me. Apart from Angel's outburst, this afternoon reminded me of my college days when Kenz and I used to do this, a pang of sadness washes over me, but then an image of Logan appears and mood instantly brightens.

It's just on 7:30 p.m. when the limo pulls up at the office, as I'm walking up the stairs, my nerves kick up a notch. When I walk into Equinox, my eyes find Logan sitting at the bar, all traces of my nerves vanish, and I'm flooded with butterflies and excitement.

Logan must feel my presence because he turns around and gazes directly at me, our eyes meet across the bar. It's like a scene from the movies, everything around us fades away except for Frank playing in the background, it's just the two of us, it's magical.

Standing up, he walks towards me, leaning forward, he snakes his arm around my waist, pulling me in close before placing the softest of kisses on my cheek. When he removes his lips, I can still feel the heat from where they touched my cheek, I miss the connection. Looking up, I see him staring intently at me, I can feel his stare deep within my soul; I've never felt someone's eyes bore into me like that before. "Good evening, Ms. Bryant. You look absolutely ravishing tonight." I completely melt at what he says. My cheeks heat with embarrassment and I can't help but grin back at him.

"Mr. DeBiers, you look pretty goodly yourself." I manage to stutter in reply.

"You do realise that goodly means of large size?"

Giggling, I push my hair behind my ear, "Yes, I'm aware but I think it works much better this way. In Sarahland, it means better than good, amazing, just wow, fantabolous."

"That's quite a definition. Well, I'm happy to be goodly in your eyes. Would you like to have a drink at the bar before we head out to dinner? I made 8:30 p.m. reservations at *Moo Moo*."

"Wow, I've always wanted to eat there. And yes, a drink would be lovely."

"I picked goodly then," he cheekily says, winking at me, before ushering me towards to bar and an awaiting Victoria, I hadn't even noticed her sitting there. She is beaming her fake smile at us and I find it hard to not roll my eyes at her.

"Good evening, Victoria," I say, as I lean forward and we air kiss.

"Good evening, Sarah. You look lovely tonight."

"She looks amazing," Logan says, snapping my attention away from Victoria and back towards him.

"Well, I'll leave you two to your evening. Welcome to Elite, Mr. DeBiers." She out stretches her hand to him; he shakes it before turning his attention back to me. "Sarah, I'll see you tomorrow morning at the weekly meeting."

"I'll see you tomorrow, Victoria." Turning my attention back to Logan, completely dismissing Victoria, I'm sure I will hear about doing that tomorrow but at the moment, Logan is all that I care about and can concentrate on.

"Good night, have fun," Victoria says and she stands up to leave.

In unison, Logan and I say, "Bye, Victoria." He and I burst out laughing, garnering attention from other patrons. Victoria shakes her head as she heads towards her office.

Our drinks are delivered, I hadn't even realised that a round of drinks had been ordered. Picking up my glass, I look towards Logan. "A toast, to a night we will never forget."

Raising his glass, he replies, "I'll certainly drink to that."

Before we both take a sip, we clink our glasses together before. Over the top of my champagne flute, I take Logan in; he is absolutely gorgeous, his dark hair is neatly styled, his chiseled jaw is clean-shaven, and his eyes are dark and dangerous. To be honest, I'm a little intimidated in his presence but most of all, excited for what lies ahead for us.

We fall into comfortable conversation, it feels like we have known each other for years, before I know it, it's time to head to the restaurant for dinner. Any intimidation that I felt earlier has evaporated and it's replaced with excitement and wonder.

As we are making our way to the waiting limo, I think to myself that this is a great first date. When I see 'Sleazy Simon' I shudder and it hits me that this isn't a date, Logan has paid to be with me. As I climb in into the car ahead of Logan, all my prior happiness evaporates when I remember that I'm an escort, and this will never go anywhere...or could it?

21

LOGAN

Watching Sarah's ass as we walk to the awaiting limo, I can't help but smile, my cock agrees too, he's been twitching ever since she walked into Equinox earlier. This evening has been amazing so far, Sarah and I get along like a house on fire; it feels like we have known each other for years. For the first time since Lili, I find myself genuinely smiling.

Sitting next to Sarah, I look over and notice that her demeanor has changed in the time it took us to walk from the bar to the car. Reaching over, I grab her hand and entwine our fingers, rubbing the back of her hand with my thumb. "You really are beautiful, Sarah, inside and out. I know we have only just met, but I'm drawn to you. I can't explain it and after only being with you for an hour, I know that I want to explore this further."

"Logan, I feel all of that too, but..." Pausing, she then dejectedly adds, while shaking her head, "Nothing, it's nothing."

"No, don't stop, tell me what you are thinking. Don't be afraid to be honest with me."

She looks over at me with sad eyes. "Logan, I'm an escort, you've paid to go out with me."

"So, I'll stop paying then, I'll do anything to be able to see you. Sarah, I want to be with you and I will do it any way that I can. If it means paying, then I'll pay."

"Logan, no, I can't let you do that."

"Sarah, be honest." Grabbing her hand and squeezing tightly, I gaze into her eyes. "Do you feel what I'm feeling?"

She doesn't say anything for what feel like light-years, but very quietly I hear her say, "I am," as she nods her head slightly.

Reaching my hand up, I gently lift her chin so she is looking at me. "Sarah, we will work it out."

The conversation comes to an end as we have arrived at the restaurant. I get out first and turn around to help Sarah out; when she places her hand in mine I feel a zing. I know in this moment that I will do everything in my power to keep Sarah in my life.

We have an amazing dinner together, and just like at the bar, conversation flowed like we were lifelong friends catching up after an extended absence. After I've settled the bill, I don't want to evening to end, so I ask Sarah if she'd like to come back to my place for a nightcap. There is no hesitation whatsoever and she immediately says yes.

We grab a cab and ten minutes later, we are back at my place. The air in the elevator to the top floor is electric, it's taking everything in my power to not press her against the lift wall and kiss her senseless. The elevator dings and I thank the interruption because my will around this girl is fading...and fast.

Unlocking the front door, I step aside to allow Sarah in first, and to check out her ass again. She pauses midstep and I bump into her. "Holy fucking shit, you seriously live here?" She turns around to look at me and her face is lit up like a Christmas tree. She quickly says, "Sorry, that wasn't very ladylike."

Laughing, I say, "It's fine, I'm pretty sure that is what I said that first time I walked in here, too. The view alone pretty much sold me on this place."

Walking further into the penthouse, I'm mesermised watching Sarah take it all in. Eventually she turns towards me. "Logan, this place is stunning."

"Thanks, but I'm pretty sure the view I have right now is much better." The sparkling city lights behind Sarah only magnify her beauty.

She walks over to the French doors and puts her hand on the handle, looking at me over her shoulder she asks, "Do you mind if I go outside?"

"That's fine. I'll get us some drinks, is bourbon okay with you?"

"Are we talking Jim or Jack?"

"Neither, Mark." She looks at me with a confused expression. "Maker's Mark," I clarify.

"Never had it before but I'm game." Winking at me, she turns back to the doors and heads outside.

I'm left standing there, completely enthralled with this woman. I pour us each a drink, and I'm excited to see where this leads, but I'm also worried that if it gets out that I met Sarah through an escort agency what it could do to my reputation. Looking out the doors, I see Sarah and I find myself smiling and happy. As I'm walking out to the balcony, Doe Zantama's quote, ***"Don't let the fear of what could happen make nothing happen,"*** pops into my mind, and in this moment I decide to go for it, consequences be damned.

Sarah turns when she hears me approaching and smiles. "Logan, the view from out here is even more amazing than from inside. I can see why you fell in love with this place."

"Yeah, it is pretty amazing. I was lucky to get this place. Here you go." Handing her the tumbler of amber liquid, she smiles at me. Our fingers graze in the handover, that same spark from before zaps us again.

She looks up at me and I know that she felt it too.

She raises her tumbler and says, "Cheers." Bringing it to her lips she breathes in the rich, fruity, spiced honey aroma and then takes a sip. I watch as she closes her eyes and savours the flavour, my eyes locked on her slim, gorgeous neck as she swallows. A slight moan releases from her mouth as she opens her eyes. Holy shit, I have never been turned on watching someone drink Maker's Mark before.

"And..." I enquire.

"Holy shit, that's so smooth and it doesn't have the burn that Jim and Jack have."

"Yeah, that's 'cause it's made with red winter wheat rather than rye. It's the rye that causes the burning sensation."

"Hmmpf, well I learned something new today and I

think I have a new fav drink." Pausing, she looks directly at me. "And a new friend, too."

Hearing her add that last bit brightens my smile. Raising my tumbler, I say, "I'll drink to that." Clinking our tumblers, we both stare intently at each other as we sip our nightcap. Reaching over, I grab her glass and place it on the railing. Turning back to Sarah I pull her closer, wrapping my arms around her waist; our eyes lock on each other. Huskily, I say, "Sarah, I really want to kiss you right now."

Swallowing hard, she faintly says, "I really want you to kiss me right now."

That's all the invitation I need, I lift one hand and cup the back of her neck; with the other still around her waist, I tug her closer. Slowly, I bend down and gently place my lips on hers, applying a slight amount of pressure. She wraps her arms around my lower back, pulling me in tight. She opens her mouth, inviting me in. Licking across her lips, I gently slip my tongue into her mouth. Our lips caress, our tongues dance, our hands explore. The taste of Maker's Mark mixed with Sarah is exquisite; *my new favourite flavour.*

This is one heck of a first kiss.

Pulling back, I rest my forehead on hers. Both of us panting; out of breath; hearts erratically beating. "Wow," we both say in unison before our lips crash together again, this kiss is ferocious and full of passion.

Lifting Sarah up, she wraps her legs around me as I make my way over to the outdoor lounge. Sitting down, Sarah straddles me as we continue to kiss. Kissing Sarah has been bumped up to my new favourite thing to do.

Just before midnight, I escort Sarah downstairs to the waiting limo to take her home. "Sarah, I had an amazing time tonight."

Shyly, she looks up at me, her eyes sparkling in the moonlight. "I had a great night, too." Biting her lips she asks, "Umm, I'd love to see you again?"

"I'd like that, too," I eagerly reply. "I guess, I'll call Victoria and arrange it."

She looks kind of sad when I mention Victoria. "Um, yeah, that would be great." She steps closer to me and gently places a kiss on my cheek, just skimming my lips. "Good night, Logan." Turning her back on me, she climbs into the limo and I close the door, giving her a smile before I do.

Standing on the sidewalk, I watch the limo drive away. Once it has turned the corner, I make my way back inside and up to my penthouse; feeling happy and over-whelmed with how quickly I'm falling for Sarah.

When I get back to the penthouse, I pour myself another Maker's Mark; smiling as I do so when I remember Sarah taking her first sip. I get hard just thinking about her. Grabbing my phone, I head outside before texting Sarah.

Logan – *Thank you for an amazing nite. I look forward to see you again soon*

Immediately a reply comes through.

Sarah – **I** *did too, thank you. I can still taste the Maker's Mark and you on my lips. Sweet dreams*

Her reply is exactly what I was hoping for. My cock hardens and throbs as I remember all of the details of tonight. Placing my tumbler on the arm of the chair, I unzip my fly, lower my boxer briefs and take out my cock. Closing my eyes, I grip it tight and stroke, imagining that it's Sarah's delicate fingers wrapped tightly around me. My strokes get faster and faster, my breathing and heart rate accelerate, and it doesn't take long before I'm coming all over my hand and dress shirt.

Using my shirt, which is already a mess, as a cloth, I wipe up and head inside. Jumping into the shower, I clean up and climb into bed. Closing my eyes, I'm met with visions of Sarah and I happily together. With a smile on my face, I drift off to sleep and dream of a happy life with Sarah.

22

SARAH

When I wake up the next morning, the first person I think of is Logan. I find myself grinning from ear to ear, giving the Luna Park clown a run for its money in the smile department. Sliding my slippers and silk robe on, I skip happily across the hall to Angel's room to tell her all about my night. When I open her door, I find that her room is empty. All of her belongings are gone, the sheets and doona are neatly folded and sitting on the end of her bed. Turning on my heel, I cross the hall to see Morgan.

Knocking gently, I wait and eventually I hear. "Come in." Opening her door I enter her room.

"Umm, where's Angel?"

"I guess she would be sleeping. After all it is..." Grabbing her phone she looks at the time. "8:00 a.m. in the God damn morning."

"Nope, she's not and her room is empty."

"Maybe she went out for a run."

"No, empty, empty. All her things are gone and the sheets and bed crap are neatly folded on the end."

She sits bolt up right in bed. "Did you say folded and neat on the end of the bed?"

"Yep, why?"

"That means she's gone. Like gone gone, Saskawhore gone."

"What? How? What?" I ask all confused.

"Beats me. Last night after you left, she went out, I presumed she was meeting up with friends and didn't think anything of it. I was just excited to have a night alone."

"Give her a call, I can't believe she'd take off like that without saying goodbye, especially to you."

Morgan grabs her phone and dials Angel and puts it on speaker. It goes straight to a recorded message. "The call could not be connected, please check and number and try again."

"What the hell?" we both say in unison.

Before we can talk further, there's a knock at the door. "I'll get it, but we need to discuss this further and find Angel."

"Agreed," she says, as I head downstairs to answer the door.

Opening the door, there's a delivery guy standing there with the biggest bunch of tulips I have ever seen. "Morning, I have a delivery for Sarah Bryant?"

"That's me." He hands me the flowers and leaves. "Thanks," I say, as I close the door and head into the kitchen to find a vase.

Morgan skips into the kitchen and as she turns on the

coffee maker she notices the flowers and says, "Holy shit-balls, that's a beautiful bunch of tulips. Who are they from?"

"Umm, I haven't looked at the card yet."

Before I can grab the card, Morgan snatches it up and opens it.

"Sarah, thanks for a lovely evening," she says. "It's not signed, who did you go out with last night?"

"The guy I brought in the other night, Logan."

"Well, someone is smitten..." Before she can continue the front door opens and Victoria waltzes in.

"Thankfully, one of my girls can do their job without issues. Angel is no longer with us. Morgan you will take on her clients and Sarah will help out when she can, but her schedule is booked solid for the next two weeks. Between Logan, Xander, Chow, and Mr. Akin she will have very little time." Pausing, she looks at the flowers. "Tulips, how boring. Ohh, and Xander has requested the two of you again today, guess he's besotted with the two of you but Sarah, you're not going. Morgan, you will see Xander by yourself, he won't be happy but pay..." She pauses before quickly saying, "Logan is new and we need to keep the newbies appeased."

Before either of us can reply, she is heading back out again, slamming the door behind her.

Morgan looks at me, "Angel wouldn't just leave like that, something's not right."

"When are things ever right with Vicky, and why does Xander get special treatment all the time?"

"He's always had special treatment but since you started here, he says jump and Vicky says 'how high?'"

Which totally isn't like her, maybe he has compromising pictures of Vicky, like in trackies, Uggs, and a singlet or depraved sexual ones."

"Who cares about her and him? I'm worried about Angel. She wouldn't just leave like that."

"I know, but what can we do?" Morgan asks.

"Nothing right now, seems we both have dates on our day off. Will you be able to handle Xander when he realises that I'm not there?"

———

"I'll be fine, he doesn't scare me," she says, as she pours us a coffee each. Sitting at the island bench, we each drink our coffee in silence. My mind is all over the place; I can't stop thinking about Angel and Logan. Just thinking of Logan, I get butterflies and my skin prickles with excitement. I'm really excited to see him again.

Over the next two weeks Logan and I see each other just about everyday; sometimes he books through Victoria but most of the time not. I manage to see him in between Elite clients. If we don't see each other, we chat on the phone or text one other.

I'm really starting to fall for Logan DeBiers.

———

It's hard hiding this from Victoria and Morgan, but I'm drawn to Logan like a moth to a flame; I can't stay away from him. I know deep within my soul that Logan is my soul mate, I know it's crazy, considering we've only known each other a few weeks, but my mum and dad met and married within three months; maybe I'm destined for the same.

I'm dying for a decent coffee, but I also need a run, so to kill two birds with one stone; I put on my running gear and joggers, slip a twenty into my sports bra and off I go. Running in the middle of the day probably isn't the best idea I've ever had, but the weather outside is gorgeous today and not too hot. Taking the scenic route, I run through the botanic gardens, along the river, and past the train station. By time I get to Java Lava, sweat is dripping off me, but I'm feeling goodly...nothing is better than getting those endorphins pumping.

Grabbing the door handle, I swing it open and enter when I come face to face with Kenz and Mike's new girlfriend. "Ohh, hey, Kenz."

"Hey, bitch, how are you? Haven't seen or heard from you in a while."

"Yeah, umm, I've been busy." *Fuck I hate lying to her but I just can't tell her, not yet anyway.*

Kenz turns to her friend. "Sav, can we take a shopping rain check?"

"Yeah, sure, that's fine. You two have fun. Catch ya's later." Sav turns and heads out the door, leaving Kenz and me standing in the doorway. For the first time in our relationship, the silence is awkward. She grabs my arm and leads us to the counter to order our coffees.

Once we have our coffees, we head to the table that is unofficially ours and we sit down. At the same time, we both say, "So, what's up?" We both burst out laughing and just like that, we fall back into the Kenzie and Sarah rhythm.

"So, what's been happening with you? We missed you at Origin the other week and our latest tasting."

"Umm, yeah, sorry about that, work has been crazy busy." *Sorry, but I was getting paid to have sex with a guy who owns a yacht, but I'm not a hooker. It's just companionship and if it leads to sex so be it*, I think to myself. "Speaking of, what a series?"

"Don't try and change the subject, what's going on, Sarah?"

"Josh and I broke up." *Yeah, I'll go with that, she will know I'm upset over that.*

"Yeah, I know and what hurts is that I heard it from him and not you. What happened?"

"I came home from work early one day and I found him and Sam on the couch together."

"Isn't Sam a dude?"

"Mmhmm," I reply, nodding my head. "Yep, Josh is gay."

Kenz spits out her coffee. "Holy fucking shit, I so did not see that coming."

"You and me both. And to top it off, he kicked me out, claiming that he paid the deposit and all that shit so it's rightfully his."

"Are you serious?"

"Yep." Taking a sip of my coffee I moan. "I miss this place, we should catch up here more often."

"Hold up a minute, where are you living then?"

Fuck, shit, fuck, I didn't mean to let that slip. "Umm,

some girls from work had a spare room so I moved in with them." *Not entirely a lie.*

"Why didn't you tell me, Sarah?"

"I was ashamed, Kenz. How did I now know that my boyfriend was gay? We'd been together for so long. I...I just, ugh. I've missed you, Kenz."

"I've missed you, too."

Thankfully the limelight gets taken off of me and we chat about Kenz, the girls, Malt Me, and the recent drama with Mike, Sav, and her crazy uncle. I'm so happy for her, last year was pretty full on for all of us, especially Kenz. To see my friend sitting across from me stronger than ever, it gives me hope that I can get through all of this, too. Kenz is telling me a story about a number three-poop explosion when I get a text, thankful for the distraction because that shit is just wrong, literally.

Grabbing my phone, I see that I have a text from Logan.

Logan – *Hey gorgeous. You free this evening?*

Smiling as I read his message, I quickly reply.

Sarah – *Just catching up with Kenz. Wanna meet up for a late lunch? I'm working tonight*
Logan – *It's a date. I'll text you where when I book*
Sarah – *Awesome. Can't wait*

After placing my phone back in my bag I notice Kenz

staring at me with a ridiculously goofy grin on her face, "What?" I enquire.

"Who was that? And don't say no one 'cause I know you, Sarah. That's your 'I'm in love' grin."

"Pfft, I'm not in love but I have met someone."

She leans forward in her chair. "Do tell and give me all the juicy, kinky details."

"Kenz, he's wonderful. New to town, in development and he's a total gentleman."

"So, where did you meet?"

Shit, shit shit, I start to panic. "Umm, at a bar. I was meeting up with someone from work and I met him. The rest is history, but it's all new so I don't want to jinx anything." *Phew, that was a good cover, kinda the truth but a little was left out...like the fact that he pays to spend time with me.* "Sorry to cut this short, but I have to get going. How about we arrange to catch up soon?"

"Sounds good. Why don't you come for dinner one night and you can see Jor and the girls, too. Bring Mr. Sarah too, so I can give him the Kenzie seal of approval. And I'll make sure my gaydar is on, too."

"Oh, you're so not funny, bitch, but dinner with you guys sounds great. Not sure about Logan yet. I kinda want to keep him to myself for now...if you know what I mean."

"Fine, you big spoilsport. But it was great to catch up with you, I've missed you."

"Me too, Kenz. Sorry for being a shitty friend."

"Your not a shitty friend, I'm a shitty friend."

"How so?"

"Well, I didn't reach out to you when I knew about

you and Josh breaking up, I should've reached out. Hell, I didn't even know you had moved."

"I'm sorry, Kenz, it all happened so quickly and I was embarrassed. I know I have nothing to be embarrassed about with you, but this one was tough to take."

"Fair enough but no more hiding stuff, deal?"

"Deal." *Even though I'm hiding a doozy of a secret.*

Standing up, we both head outside and say our good-byes. I walk Kenz to her car. After waving her off, I head back towards the river to finish my run. Twenty minutes later, I decide that's enough and I head home.

As I'm entering the building, Victoria is huffing out. "Morning, Vicky...toria. How are you?" Leaning in for our customary air kisses and fake hug.

"Ugh, you're all sweaty." She pushes me away. "I'm glad I caught you, Kristy is no longer with us so I need to you take her 3:00 p.m. appointment today with Mr. Chow, so I've cancelled your evening appointment as this thing with Chow could run late."

"Umm, I have plans with Logan this afternoon."

"I don't have it down on the books."

"Umm, he texted me this morning."

Grabbing me roughly by the arm she drags me to the side of the foyer and pushes me up against the pole. "All appointments are to go through me, Sarah. You of all people know this."

"This isn't an appointment, it's just friends."

"No!" she shouts, "All meetings with clients are appointments, they must be paid for."

"But..."

"No buts, Sarah. This is unacceptable behavior." She

rubs her temples "I don't have time for this. You will be ready for Mr. Chow at 3:00 p.m., no arguments."

"Fine," I huff, and turn away from her to go upstairs and get ready for a boring afternoon looking at dumb paintings. I'm only a few steps away from Victoria when she forcefully grabs my arm, spins me around, slapping me hard across the face, the crack echoing through the foyer; garnering us a few looks from the people nearby. Rubbing my cheek, I stand there in shock, staring at her in disbelief.

"You will not speak to me like that and walk away, remember who I am, Sarah. I can make all of this disappear in an instant." She waves her hand around and snapping her fingers. "Don't push me, Sarah. You don't know what I'm capable of." She turns on her heel and climbs into her waiting limo.

Standing there in shock, staring as the limo pulls into traffic, I grab my phone and call Logan. It goes to voicemail. "Hey, Logan, it's Sarah. I have to cancel lunch; I have a last minute work thing at some gallery this arvo. I'll text you tomorrow and maybe we can catch up then. Bye." I hang up just as the lift doors open and I head upstairs to get ready for my appointment, upset that I won't be seeing Logan this afternoon.

I'm just getting out of the shower when Morgan comes running in, tears pouring down her face. Racing over to her, I wrap my arms around her tightly. "Morgan, what's wrong?"

"It's...It's..." She's so upset that she can't speak. Leading her to the window seat, we sit, and I wait for her to calm down. She looks up at me and I know what she's about to tell me isn't going to be good. "She's dead."

I'm stunned, "Who's dead?"

"Angel."

My mouth drops open, I'm in shock. "Whaaaat?" I manage to ask, as the tears well in my eyes.

"She was on the news just now, a breaking bulletin. Her body was found this morning." Pausing, she looks at me. "She was murdered, Sarah."

I'm speechless.

"Sarah, she's dead," Morgan whispers, before she bursts into tears again.

Hearing that for a second time is enough to set me off too, and I start sobbing. We sit there holding each other when there is a knock at the door downstairs. Neither of us moves; we just sit there, holding each other as the tears continue to fall.

The knocking gets louder and quicker, they obviously aren't giving up. Letting go of Morgan, I quickly pull off my towel and slip on my robe and head downstairs. Opening the door, I find Simon standing there; he looks me up and down and with disdain in his voice to says. "Umm, you are meant to be ready to meet Mr. Chow."

"Ohh, Simon," I say, as I wrap my arms around him. Pulling back when I realise I'm hugging 'Sleazy Simon' I tearfully say, "Umm, Angel is dead, she was murdered. Morgan just saw it on the telly."

"Fuck. I better call Victoria and give her a heads up. Please go and get ready."

"Simon, I can't work. Did you hear what I said? Angel was murdered."

He doesn't say anything; he pushes past me into the lounge room, his phone to his ear. Heading back upstairs, I find that Morgan has moved from the window seat to the bed, she has finally stopped crying but she's clearly upset. Before I can comfort her, my phone rings and it's the alarm sound, Victoria's tone. Picking it up, I answer, "Hi, Victoria."

"Simon tells me you're not ready. You have ten minutes to get organised and downstairs."

"Victoria, Angel was murdered. I can't work this afternoon."

"You can and you will. It's of no concern to us that she was murdered. These things happen."

"Victoria, that's a tad harsh."

"Call it what you will. She left, she obviously had issues that we knew nothing about. Now, forget her. You have nine minutes now, Sarah." Pausing, she sighs before adding, "Don't disappoint me, young lady." And she hangs up on me.

Throwing my phone back on the side table, I take a seat and rub Morgan's arm. "Morgan, sweetie, are you going to be okay?" She just stares vacantly at me. "That was Vicky, I still have to work this afternoon and I don't want to piss her off. She's already in a shitty mood and I don't want to anger the beast within." Morgan smirks at this. "It's just a gallery thing with Chow, I'll be back by six. Will you be okay until then?"

"Yeah, I'll be fine. It was just a shock. She left so suddenly and then now this. Something isn't right, Sarah. I can feel it in my bones."

"I know what you mean." Standing up, I reluctantly

start getting ready. "Listen, you and I will chat tonight. We will get to the bottom of this, we owe Angel that much."

"Okay, you better go before the beast, as you called her, comes here. I can't deal with her in person right now. Thank God I'm not working today or tonight, I can't, I just can't."

Stepping out of the closet, I look to Morgan. "Do I look okay?"

Morgan's face breaks out in the biggest smile. This is the first time I've seen her show any emotion that's not sadness since she entered my room. "Yes, you are fucking stunning, Sarah. Wish I could get ready that quickly."

We hear Simon yelling from below to hurry up. "Coming!" I yell, leaning down, I kiss Morgan on the forehead. "Back as soon as I can."

Turning, I grab my bag and shoes and head out the door, as I'm closing it, I hear Morgan quietly say, "Have fun." There is no emotion in her voice at all; she is broken at the moment.

Skipping down the stairs, I sit on the bottom step and slip on my ballet flats. Just as I stand up, Simon walks into the foyer. I smile at him, "Let's go."

If only I knew what was going to happen this afternoon.

23

LOGAN

I'VE JUST STEPPED OUT OF THE SHOWER WHEN I HEAR my phone beep, indicating a voice message. Picking up my phone, I see that I have a missed call from Sarah; I dial my message bank and listen to her message. I'm sad that she had to cancel our lunch date, but I'm also kind of relieved, I was going to have to call and cancel on her. Beth slipped a last minute, afternoon cocktail thingy into my calendar and had the reminder not gone off, I would have missed it. One of my contractors scored an invite and apparently it's a who's who gallery function, and as I'm new in town, he thought it would be a good way to network. Networking I'm all for, but art I don't give a flying fuck about it.

I'm in the lift heading to the waiting limo when my phone rings. Digging it out of my pocket, I notice it's Victoria. I'm not in the mood for her right now so I silence the call and let it go to voicemail.

The car pulls up in front of a gallery in the Valley and I climb out. Looking up, I see that this is a pretty big affair; they've gone all out with this gallery opening. Walking along the green carpet, I make my way to the door. Giving my name to the doorman, I'm ushered inside. When I enter I'm greeted by the owner and handed a glass of bubbly and given a rundown of the artist and her works. I totally tune out, it's all abstract art that reminds of art that Sav and I used to do when we were younger, not art at all in my eyes.

Excusing myself, I walk around, deciding that I'll do one lap and then find the bar. Rounding a corner near the back, I stop dead in my tracks and stare. Standing in front of me, looking absolutely stunning in black slacks and a purple, silky button-up blouse is Sarah. She is chatting with five other ladies but none of them compare to her beauty. She must sense my presence as she looks up and finds my eyes locked on her. Her eyes bug out of her head in shock when she notices me, she gives me a slight smile, but I immediately notice that she's upset, faking her happiness with the group.

She excuses herself and walks over to me, I'm mesmerised by her beauty. The rest of the room fades away and when all of a sudden; she's standing in front of me. "Mr. DeBiers, this is a nice surprise." Leaning forward, she kisses me on the cheek and whispers, "I'm so glad you're here, meet me by the restrooms in five minutes."

"Ms. Bryant, lovely to see you again but I must be going." Nodding at her, I walk away towards the bar. Grabbing two champagnes, I head towards the restrooms, in a roundabout way. There's a half decent painting on the wall near the restrooms, so I pretend to be interested in it.

As I'm looking at the painting, a tingling sensation runs from head to toe and I know she's nearby. Looking to my left, I see Sarah standing next to me. Grabbing my elbow, she leads me to the foyer of the restrooms. There are couches off to the side before the hall leads to the unisex bathrooms; Sarah and I take a seat on the corner lounge. Placing the bubbly on the coffee table, I look over and see tears welling in her eyes. "Sarah, what's wrong?"

"Ohh, Logan," she says, before bursting into tears.

Lifting her onto my lap, I wrap my arms around her and she snuggles into my shoulder and continues to cry. Rubbing her back gently, I let her cry, whispering, "Shh... It will be okay," repeatedly to her.

She pulls back, looks at me, and gives me a slight smile, she is so upset, and grief is all over her face. Lifting my hand, with the pad of my thumb I gently wipe away the wetness from under her eyes, even all red-rimmed from crying her eyes are still spectacular. She is still the most gorgeous girl in the world. "Sarah, what's wrong?" I gently ask when her tears have subsided. Before she can reply, a Chinese man walks in and heads straight to the restrooms, not noticing us sitting here, but Sarah notices him and she quickly jumps up.

"Logan, I'm working. I'll...I'll, call you later."

I'm about to reply when she walks away quickly and heads back to into the gallery. I'm left sitting there stunned, all I want to do is run out into the gallery, wrap my arms around her, and whisk her away from here and comfort her; she is clearly upset over something. Grabbing my phone, I text her.

Logan – *Call me as soon as you get home. I'm worried about you.*

Immediately the three little dots appearing, indicating she is tying a reply. Finally my phone vibrates and as her reply comes through.

Sarah – *Promise XO*

Smiling at her reply, I pocket my phone and head back into the gallery. After one more lap, I decide that I've been here long enough, finding the owner, I buy the painting by the bathrooms for the penthouse, say my goodbyes, and head home. It's nice being able to say home again and I'm actually excited to hang my new artwork; Beth and Sav will flip when I tell them I bought a painting.

The car service drops me off and Charlie's is calling my name; this having a great bar where I live is awesome. Stopping in, I grab a quick beer when my phone rings. Looking down, I smile it's Sav. My PI managed to find her when she and boyfriend, Mike, were involved in an altercation with Kelvin. I never trusted that smug bastard and I'm so happy that he is currently rotting in jail. It's so good to have her back in my life and in the same town. Amazingly, we are both in Brisbane. Swiping the screen I answer, "Savannah, run away lately?"

"You're never going to let me forget that, are you, Loges?"

"Not anytime soon, Savvy, not anytime soon. To what do I owe the pleasure of this call?"

"Well, I'm calling to invite you to our housewarming party next weekend. Mike and I picked up our keys today."

"Okay, maybe that will make me forgive you. You sound so happy again, almost like before..." Drifting off, I don't finish that sentence. It's still raw finding out the Kelvin was behind the accident that killed the rest of her family.

"I'm happy, Loges. Extremely happy and it's all to do with Mike. Maybe you can bring the new lady friend that you mentioned."

"I'll see if she's free but it's all still pretty new, meeting the friends is a big step."

"Logan, if this mess has taught me anything, it's that, you need to jump head first into life. Life is too short. To quote a wise man 'I'm here for a goodtime, not a longtime.'"

In the background I hear Mike yell, "More like fucking awesome man." We both laugh and I realise that I do want Sarah to come with me and meet Sav and Mike.

Still laughing I say, "Tell Mike hi and yes, I'll be there next weekend, possibly with Sar..."

But I'm cut off to hear giggles and Mike yelling, "Laters, Logan." Followed by more giggling, which in turn makes me laugh. *Mike is perfect for Sav*, I think to myself as I finish my beer and head upstairs.

The lift doors open and in the foyer, sitting by my door, is Sarah. She looks up and when she sees me, she jumps up, throws herself into my arms, and starts to cry. Within seconds, I wrap my arms around her, lifting her up; I cradle her in my arms and unlock the front door.

24

SARAH

After I leave the gallery, I get Simon to drop me back at the apartment but rather than going inside, I aimlessly walk around the city. Eventually, I find myself at Logan's place so I head inside. The lift takes me up to his floor, my hands become clammy, butterflies appear in my tummy and I'm nervous, really nervous. I haven't ever felt like this about anyone, not even Josh. Today when my eyes found him at the gallery, I was so excited. All I wanted to do was run and jump into his arms, but unfortunately that's not possible...for now.

The lift reaches the top floor, the doors open, and I head over to this door. Knocking, I wait but there's no answer. My feet are rooted to the floor; I don't want to leave. I need to see Logan, like I need my next breath. Sliding down the timber door, I rest my forehead on my knees and get comfortable.

A few moments later, I hear the ding of the lift. Looking up, I see Logan stepping out; the sight of him instantly calms me. He's absolutely stunning in his jeans and black dress shirt. He notices me sitting there and smiles, immediately I jump up and throw my arms around him and break down in tears. I cry for Angel, I cry for what my life has become, I cry for not being able to freely be with him. I cry to let it all out.

Carrying me inside, we end up in the lounge room. With me still in his arms, he sits down on the couch and continues to embrace me tightly as my sobs increase. Looking up at him, through my tears I whisper, "She's gone, Logan."

"Who's gone?"

"Angel, they found her body this morning. She...she was murdered. That explains why I haven't been able to reach her since she left."

"Ohh, Sarah, I'm so sorry."

We both fall silent but it's not uncomfortable. Sitting here in Logan's arms feels right; it's where I'm meant to be. He breaks the silence, "Sarah, have you had dinner yet?"

"No, I'm not hungry."

"Well, that's too bad. I'm going to order Chinese and we will head out on the patio, eat so much Chinese that we will turn Chinese, and drink beer until we can't stand up. I'm going to give you the Logan treatment."

For the first time since I heard the new this morning, I smile. "I will only eat Chinese if it comes from Kung Fu Palace, but you can drink beer and I'll drink wine."

"After my friend took me to Kung Fu Palace last week, there is nowhere else I would get it from. As for wine, I actually have your fav in my wine fridge, I might even join you on the wine."

"You have my wine?"

"Yep, I was hoping we could do this one night and it looks today is my lucky day. I'll call the Palace while you get our drinks. Meet you on the patio in five minutes."

Standing up, I head towards to kitchen but I turn on my heel and wrap my arms around Logan. "Thank you," I whisper. "This is just what I needed."

"It's my pleasure, Sarah, now wine me up, baby."

I giggle at his reply. "You did not just say that did you?"

"Wine yes I did."

By now we are both pissing ourselves laughing. "Dude, you are so corny."

"Don't you mean corky?"

Again, I burst out laughing and this time a Kenzie snort breaks free and my giggle increase. "Oh My God! Stop, I'm going to pee my pants."

"Okay, Okay, I'll stop. Five minutes, Sarah."

"Yes, boss," I say, as I head towards the kitchen.

Reaching into the wine chiller, I grab the bottle of Tulloch Verdelho and place it on the island bench. Turning, I grab the stemless wine glasses and wine bucket out of the cabinet. Picking up the bucket, I place a few ice cubes in before opening the wine saying to myself, "Viva Verdelho" from their advertising campaign last year before, gently resting it in the bucket.

Heading out to the patio, I balance the two glasses in one hand, the bucket in the other, and I somehow manage to open the door without dropping anything. Sitting the bucket on the high-top table, I reach for the bottle and pour us each a glass.

Taking a sip as I walk to the railing, I place Logan's and my glass down and look out at the sky. It's just on dusk and there seems to be a storm in the west that is slowly making its way towards the city. The black clouds mix with the setting sun, and even though the clouds are gloomy, the vividness of the sunset makes the night sky magical.

I'm lost in the night sky and don't hear Logan come out. He wraps his arms around my waist and pulls me close, my back to his front; it's perfect. Resting my glass on the railing, I wrap my arms around his; closing my eyes, I snuggle into his neck. He places a gentle kiss on my temple, and rests his chin against my shoulder.

Spinning around, I wrap my arms around his neck and kiss him. Our lips fuse as one as we tenderly rub each other's back. His tongue seeks access to my mouth and I willingly open, letting him in. Our tongues mesh together, pulling back I suck his bottom lip into my mouth, letting it pop away. Resting my forehead against his, I close my eyes and enjoy the moment, finally feeling content. Opening my eyes, I look deep into his and smile. "Thank you," I whisper, wrapping my arms tighter around his waist, before resting my head on his shoulder.

He hugs me tighter, whispering, "I'd do anything for you Sarah, anything." The apartment buzzer interrupts the moment. "That must be dinner, I'll be right back." He kisses my forehead before heading inside to answer the door. Grabbing our glasses, I sit them on the table before heading to the kitchen to get plates and cutlery.

When I get back outside, Logan has unpacked the

food and he is staring at me intently. "What?" I say, as I sit down at the table across from him.

"I just realised that I'm happy and I think it's all to do with you, Sarah. I was lonely and just plodding along, and then I met you, and now I find that when you aren't around I deflate, but as soon I'm with you, I feel happy and alive again."

"I know exactly what you mean, Logan." She leans forward and squeezes his hand and happily smiles at him. "Now let's eat, this smells amazing and I'm actually hungry now."

We each pile our plates with food and dig in. As usual the conversation flows, it's all going well until Logan asks me a question that knocks me for six. "Where do you see yourself in five years?"

His questions stuns me, I always knew that working for Victoria wasn't a lifetime gig. "Umm, I'm not sure. I mean, I don't want to work for Victoria for the rest of my life."

"Well, I knew that. You did what you had to do to survive, there's no judgments here, please don't think that. What you did took guts and I admire you for taking the risk. Think about it, what do you ultimately want to do with your life?"

Without hesitation, I reply. "I want to open a wine bar. Kenz and I used to joke about it years ago, but then both our lives took different paths."

"Why don't you do it?"

"What? Open a wine bar? In my dreams, Logan. For starters, I'm currently a hooker, have no permanent place to live, and then there's the start up capital that I'd need."

"I'd be happy to front the money, Sarah."

"Fuck me, are you seriously that loaded?"

"LDB is doing very well, Sarah. I made a few brilliant choices and now I can pretty much do what I want." Pausing, he adds, "Within reason, of course."

"Thank you for the offer, but before I take on a venture like that, I need to get my life back on track." Taking a sip of wine, followed by a deep breath, I smile and look at Logan. "Logan, I think that's what I want to do with my life, I'm going to open a wine bar. Maybe this job came along because it would allow me to save the money that I need to start it. I just have to do it for a little while longer and then I'm going to do it."

"Why not leave now, let me help you?"

"Thanks for the offer but this is something that I need to do on my own. For once in my life, I'm not mooching off Mum and Dad, not that they have anything left after Dad's last investment failure. This is all me, albeit it's not conventional but it's all me, Logan. It's kind of freeing."

"That's very honourable, Sarah. You really are a magnificent woman."

"You're not so bad yourself, Mr. DeBiers." I stare at him intently as I say this, smiling seductively at him.

We place our glasses on the table, stand up and reach for one another. Our lips crash together as we hold each other tightly for the most intense kiss of my life. Jumping up, I wrap my legs around Logan, pulling him closer.

Our kiss becomes frenzied as Logan walks over to the lounge where we had out first kiss a few weeks ago. He gently lays me down, lowering himself over me, cocooning me under him. He continues to kiss me before nipping and sucking along my chin and down my neck. Gently he bites my nipple through my top, reaching down, I grab the hem and not so sexily, I manage to get it over my head, so I'm left in my daggy white bra. *It always looks sexy in the movies*, I think to myself as I lie back down and stare at Logan.

Logan pulls back and takes in the sight of me lying there; cheeks flushed, chest heaving. "Fuck me, Sarah. You are beautiful."

"Pfft, I think you need you eyes checked. This is the daggiest bra that I own. Had I known this was going to happen, earlier I would have dressed in my sexy stuff."

"Sarah, you are sexy no matter what you wear, but right now, I want to strip you naked and devour your body."

My cheeks darken, my heart rate accelerates with excitement; licking my lips I sit up slightly and unclasp my bra, flicking it aside. Reaching down to remove my pants, I hear Logan groan. My eyes dart towards him and I see that he has taken off his shirt; I'm frozen on the spot. His chest is magnificent, I pant with lust as my eyes roam over his chest, gazing upon indent after indent. He has the most amazing eight-pack I have ever seen and then I see the Holy Grail: those side muscles that form a 'V'. Lifting my hand, I trace his abs before running my finger along his 'V' pack. "Fuck me, Logan. You're ripped."

"As are you. You're smokin' hot, Sarah." Leaning down he kisses me again. Pulling back, he says, "Naked, now."

We both get to work, stripping off our pants and underwear. Lying back down, I expect Logan to kiss me again but he squats down next to my throbbing pussy. Staring directly at me, he spreads my folds, sliding his finger up and down before squeezing my clit and rubbing circles with his thumb. Lifting my hands, I begin to massage my breasts, squeezing and rolling my nipples between my fingers. Moaning as the tingling sensation deep in my belly intensifies. My eyes are closed and I lose myself when I feel his breath on the inside of my thighs. He dips his tongue deep inside of me before sucking on my clit. Inserting another finger, with a flick of his wrist he pushes inside of me, thrusting in and out as he continues to suck and nibble my clit. My hand reaches down and I shove his head further into my pussy, grinding myself shamelessly against his face, "Ohh, Logan," I cry out. Suddenly my body erupts with pleasure and I'm tingling from head to toe as my orgasm takes over my body.

When my body shudders have stopped, he lifts his head from between my thighs and kisses his way up my stomach. Stopping to suck and fondle my breasts before kissing and licking his way up my neck. He tenderly holds my cheeks and lowers his lips to mine to kiss me. This kiss is slow and sensual; I wrap my arms around him and pull him closer. Gently he lowers himself on top of me; I can feel his hardness at my entrance, rolling my hips, inviting him in. In one swift motion, he sinks himself balls deep inside of me, just as the rain starts to gently fall. We are both so lost in the pleasure that we don't care about the rain. Logan continues to thrust in and out of me, leaning up on his elbows he stares intently at me as we rock back and forth together. Leaning down again, he kisses me as I feel the first wave of my orgasm begin to build. Moaning into his mouth, he begins to circle his hips, which rubs my clit. My legs tighten, my toes curl, and my orgasm rips through me. I groan in ecstasy as my body shudders with the most intense and amazing orgasm of my life. Opening my eyes, I see Logan tense before his own release overtakes his body.

He collapses on top of me as the heavens open, pulling back he kisses me deeply before whispering, "I think we should go inside before we catch pneumonia. We can have a shower to warm up and maybe go for round two."

"That's sounds great, Logan, but I don't think I can move. I'm spent, that was amazing."

Without warning, Logan scoops me up and we head inside. Entering his ensuite, he flicks on the lights, and the black granite sparkles in the glow. I spot a massive tub in the corner and smile. "Can we have a bath instead?" I ask, as he sits me on the vanity.

"We can do whatever you want, Sarah."

Turning his back on me, he puts the plug in and begins to fill the tub. Pouring in some jasmine and lavender bubble bath, he swishes it around before putting his hand out towards me. Jumping off the counter, I take his hand and he helps me step into the tub before slipping in behind me. Wrapping his arms tightly around me, I relax back into him and sigh.

After soaking in the bath, I slip on one of Logan's light blue dress shirts; it's long enough to look like a t-shirt dress. My clothes are soaked from the rain, so I place them in a plastic bag. Turning to find Logan staring at me, I cheekily ask, "Like what you see?" and I lift my eyebrows at him.

"Fuck yes, I do. You look better in that shirt than I do."

"Pfft. I highly doubt that but thank you for the compliment." Pausing, I look to the floor before looking back up at Logan. He looks gorgeous in his trackies and navy Chesty Bonds singlet. "Umm, I think I better get going. I'm sure you have an early morning."

He takes two strides towards me and gently places his hands on my cheeks and looks deep into my soul; his stare burning a path deep inside of me, invoking feelings that I haven't felt in a long time. "Sarah, I'd happily be tired tomorrow if it means I get to spend extra time with you. You are more than welcome to stay, but it's entirely up to you."

Lifting my palm, I caress his hand that's holding my cheek, and lean into it. "As much as I'd love to stay, I think I should go."

Getting up on my tippy toes, I place a quick kiss on his ever so soft lips. Dropping the bag of wet clothes, I wrap my arms around his neck and deepen the kiss. Closing my eyes, I lose myself in all that is Logan. I pull back and gaze into his eyes. "I better go before things go too much further."

He laughs and looks towards his crotch, I can see his erection tenting his trackies. "Umm, I'm already there."

Giggling, I look back up at him. "Sorry, Logan, but if I fix your current situation, I won't leave and I really need to get home. We need to keep this on the down low. If Victoria finds out about us, I can loose everything. You could loose everything." Pausing, I add, "And who knows what she'll do to you. I won't risk that. Give me time to come up with a plan." Swallowing deeply, I gently run my palm over his cheek before adding, "Logan, I want a future with you."

"I want that too, Sarah. I will wait but not too long. I haven't felt this happy and content in a longtime. Besides, you are worth waiting for."

Bending down, I grab the bag of wet cloths, slip on my ballet flats and head towards to door. Logan opens it for me and places his hand on my lower back, escorting me to the elevator. "While you're in the lift, I'll call down and get them to hail a cab for you."

"I'm happy to walk, Logan."

"You are not walking at." He looks at his watch. "One in the morning...dressed like that."

"Wow, I didn't realise how late it is. Yes, a cab would be great."

"Glad you agree. Sarah, I care deeply for you. I'd hate for something to happen to you."

"Logan, I know exactly how you feel. I promise to be safe. When will I see you next?"

"I'm pretty busy with this new contract this week. Do you think you'd be able to sneak over late one night?"

"I'll do my best. Will all depend on what appointments that I have booked."

His demeanor changes when I mention possible appointments and it sucks donkey balls that I'm stuck in this situation at the moment. "Logan, I will do everything in my power to get out of this. I just need time."

"I know, Sarah, I know. I just want you all to myself...

now." Pausing, he shuffles on his feet as the lift arrives. "Sarah, you're not sleeping with anyone else are you?"

"Not anymore I won't be. But I was only sleeping with one other client, the rest were all companionship, the true definition of an escort."

He smiles at me. "That makes me happy. Now get in that lift before I throw you over my shoulder and take you back inside, where I'll ravish your body from head to toe."

Swallowing deeply, I reply, "You don't play fair, Logan. I'll chat to you tomorrow. Night."

Stepping into the lift, I turn around and push the ground floor button. Before the lift closes, Logan puts his hand in to stop it and gives me a quick kiss before stepping back out. "Good night, Sarah. Sweet dreams."

The elevator doors close and the last thing I see is Logan smiling at me. Lifting my fingers to my lips, I kiss them and blow the kiss towards Logan. He lifts his hand and pretends to catch it and place it gently on his cheek. Once on the ground floor, the doors open and the concierge is there is escort me to the awaiting cab out front.

Climbing in, I give the driver the address of the apartment and I sit back in my seat. Closing my eyes, I smile to myself. I'm over the moon happy and finally things are looking up for me...or so I thought.

25

VICTORIA

SARAH IS STILL MANAGING TO ASTOUND ME; I haven't found a girl like her in a long time. Not only did she come along at the right time, but she also was Elite's saving grace and it has kept 'him' happy, very happy indeed. It's nice to know that after all of these years, I haven't lost my touch.

Everything would be perfect if the girls would stop disobeying me and it's troubling that my saving grace is starting to slip into that category; to say it's disappointing is an understatement. Why must they disobey? It's simple, follow the rules and everyone is happy. What frustrates me the most is that when they are brought to account, they beg, plead, and cry. Why won't they just leave without incident? Their heads held high? If they did, it would all be perfect.

Luckily for me, I have people on hand to help me when things don't go smoothly. I snap my fingers and they jump into action. They've been working overtime of late. Actually, it all started to go downhill just before

Sarah came aboard. I'm really hoping it's all just a coincidence but I don't believe in coincidences. My gut is telling me she is somehow involved. If I find out that she has betrayed me, I will not be held responsible for my actions, and she will suffer the consequences, just like the others did.

My thoughts are interrupted when my phone rings, Simon's name flashes on my screen. He should be picking up Sarah for the gallery gala with Chow right now. "Simon!" I sharply say, as I answer the phone.

"Umm, Victoria, we have a problem."

Rubbing my temple in frustration, I snap, "Unless someone is dead, I don't want to hear about it. Just get Sarah to the gallery...now!"

"Well, someone is dead. Angel Hurley was found murdered this morning."

"What did you just say?"

"Angel is dead, her body washed up on the banks of the river this morning."

Shit, shit shit! I think to myself, "She no longer works at Elite, how is that any concern to us?"

"Both Sarah and Morgan are quite upset. Sarah is refusing to go."

"I don't think so. Put her on the phone."

"Yes, ma'am." I can hear him talking to Sarah and then there's a shuffling down the line.

"Victoria," Sarah sniffles, "Angel was murdered."

"Sarah, that is unfortunate. But she no longer works here, how is her death anything to do with us?"

"She was our friend."

"That is of no consequence to me. You have a 3:00

p.m. appointment with Mr. Chow. If you want to keep your job here at Elite, I suggest you get there in the next ten minutes." Pausing, I sternly add, "Am I understood?"

"Yes, Victoria."

"Good, now hand the phone back to Simon and go get ready."

Oh My God! How did this happen? I need to fix this immediately. I'm thinking when Simon takes the phone back.

"Victoria, I'm back. Is there anything else?"

"Simon, make sure that Sarah gets to the gallery on time. I'll call Chow and tell him she's running late. After you drop her off, get back here as quickly as possible. I think I'm going to need your help."

"Yes, Miss. I'll see you within the hour."

"Thank you, Simon."

Hanging up, I quickly dial Alexander. He answers on the first ring. "Yes."

"We have a problem?"

"We do not have a problem, you have a problem. You assured me that Angel would not be an issue, yet that situation is now splashed all over the news. Fix it."

He hangs up before I have a chance to reply.

Walking over to the office minibar, I pour myself a brandy and quickly drink it. Pouring myself another, I pick up my glass, and make my way over to my desk. *Why do these problems keep coming up?*

An hour later, Simon knocks on my office door and in that time, I have come up with a plan. "Simon, please do come in. I have a special job that needs the utmost discretion."

"Anything, what do you need?"

"I want you to follow Sarah Bryant. Things have been going off course lately and I bet my *Prada* collection that it's all to do with her, if not, I know she's hiding something."

"Yes, ma'am. I will do my best."

"I know you will, Simon, I know you will."

Simon leaves my office and I'm agitated and antsy, I'm not one for unanswered questions. To try and take my mind off everything, I decide that an afternoon at the spa is in order. When it hits me, Morgan is off and she's close to Sarah, I will invite her to the spa with me and do some of my own detective work.

———

Morgan reluctantly agreed to join me at the spa for the afternoon; she is really broken up over Angel, not my problem. I told her that a driver will be by to pick her up in thirty minutes and that I will meet her there.

An afternoon of pampering was just what I needed to reinvigorate the soul and recharge my batteries. Unfortunately, Morgan didn't know anything in relation to Sarah. If anything, she kept gushing about her. If she wasn't fangirling over Sarah, she was crying over Angel; it was quite annoying and not at all rejuvenating.

After dropping Morgan off at the apartment, I headed back to the office. These days I seem to be living there, trying to fix all the problems that my once great girls have caused. The business hasn't been the same since Megan, Tanya, Crissy, Saskia, Cassy, Tish, Kristy,

Alyssa and Angel were relieved of their employment, willingly or otherwise. Luckily for me, I did not have to personally get involved; I hate getting my hands dirty, that's what my henchmen are for.

My thoughts are interrupted by a call from Simon. "Simon," I sternly answer.

"I have news on Sarah. I dropped her off at the apartment after the gallery thing with Chow but she didn't head inside. She aimlessly walked around the city and then ended up at Charlie's Bar; if I'm not mistaken, it's located within the building where Mr. DeBiers recently purchased a residence."

"It could be coincidence, as I know the girls like that bar, but I don't believe in coincidences." Biting my lip in frustration, I add, "Simon, stay there. The bar closes at 1:00 a.m. if she doesn't leave around then or earlier, she's with DeBiers. Thanks for the update."

"My pleasure, ma'am."

Just after 1:00 a.m. I get a text from Simon.

Simon – *She left just after 1 am...alone. No sign of DeBiers.*
Victoria – *That's a relief*

Even though she wasn't seen with Mr. DeBiers, doesn't mean she wasn't with him; I'm still skeptical. My Spidey senses are on high alert and Sarah Bryant is the cause...what is she up to?

26

SARAH

THE LAST FEW DAYS HAVE BEEN WONDERFUL, AND it's all to do with a six-foot tall demigod named Logan. We have spoken on the phone every day, sometimes twice, text each other constantly and tonight, once Morgan is asleep, I'm going to sneak over to his place.

Since the passing of Angel, Morgan has become a hermit and has withdrawn into herself; even a spa afternoon with she-devil didn't pull her out of her funk, but that could have been due to the company. At the moment she only leaves the apartment for appointments, and then when she's home, she locks herself in her room. I'm worried about her. I really want to be there for her, but tonight is the only night this week that I can see Logan.

Putting on my running gear, I lace up my sneakers, say bye to Morgan, and I head out. She doesn't seem to notice but if I make it look like I'm running, it's easier to cover up if I somehow get caught.

Thirteen minutes later, I'm jogging up the stairs of

Logan's building and I can't wait to see him. Pausing, I look around as I have a feeling someone is watching me, but there is no one who looks out of place on the street; I guess my mind is playing tricks on me. I've felt this way ever since we found out about Angel.

Waving to the desk clerk, I make my way to the elevators and push the call button. Luck is on my side as the door opens immediately; I press the button for Logan's floor. When the doors open, Logan is waiting for me, leaning against the wall with his left leg bent at the knee and foot resting on the wall. He's wearing dark jeans and a plain black t-shirt.

"Hey, how did you know I was here? I wanted to surprise you 'cause I'm earlier than I thought."

"Grant." I look at him dumbfounded, *Who the hell is Grant?* "The desk clerk. I slipped him a twenty to give me a heads-up when you arrived."

"Sneaky, sneaky," I say. Stepping into his space, I throw my arms around his neck and kiss him. It quickly turns heated and he grabs my bum, lifting me up. Wrapping my legs around him, he walks us inside and directly to his bedroom.

Within one minute, we are both naked and Logan sinks his throbbing cock inside of me. We fall into a steady rhythm before he flips us over so I'm straddling him, managing not to slip out in the process. Rocking back and forth, I throw my head back as the tingly sensation begins to develop deep in my belly. My hands make their way to my breasts, I begin to massage and fondle my nipples, while Logan reaches between us and begins to rub my clit in circles. His touch on my clit is the spark needed to light me on fire and I explode. I see fireworks behind my closed eyes as the tremors pass over my body. As I'm coming back to earth, I feel Logan tense underneath me. Increasing my thrusts, I clench my walls tighter and milk his orgasm until I feel his hips jolt; he erupts inside of me with a growl.

When he has finished, I fall forward and rest my head on his chest. We lay like this until our breathing returns to normal. Lifting my head, I look deep into his eyes and I realise that I'm falling in love with Logan and I smile. It's totally crazy, we've only known each other for a few weeks, but the feelings I have for and with Logan are like nothing that I have ever experienced before. He lifts his hand and pushes a strand of my hair behind my ear. "What are you smiling about?"

"Nothing in particular. I just realised that for the first time in months, I'm happy. Deliriously happy and that's all because of you." Climbing up his body, I rest on my elbows and I kiss him, this kiss feels different. There is so much emotion behind it, I don't want it to end but we are interrupted by Logan's phone ringing.

We ignore it but they immediately call back. "Guess you better answer that." Climbing off the bed I head into the bathroom, over my shoulder I huskily say, "Come join me after your call."

Smiling, he picks up his phone and the expression on his face changes as he answers. Turning on my heel, I head into the ensuite and turn on the shower. Once the water is warm, I climb in and let the hot water fall over my body—*whoever invented the rainwater head is a godsend*. I've just lathered my body with his body wash, when Logan climbs in. His shoulders are tight and he looks tense. "Is everything okay?"

"Yeah, it's fine. Nothing for you to worry about." He closes his eyes and steps under the water, ignoring me. Whoever was on the other end of the call has really upset him. I want him to relax so I pump more body wash into my hands and begin to massage his back and shoulders. He moans and immediately relaxes, slipping my hands around; I begin to soap his pecs and abs, garnering a growl this time. Sliding my hands down further, I grip his cock tightly in my fist and begin to stoke.

He flips around, pinning my hands above my head and kisses me, snaking his hand down my stomach, he begins fondling my slit. Moaning into his mouth, I pull my hand free and reach down to his and resume stroking his cock. We continue to kiss and caress each other intimately, until we both tumble over the orgasmic cliff, murmuring each other's name as the pleasure rockets through our bodies.

Untangling from each other, we silently wash ourselves before hopping out. Logan puts on satin boxers and I get back into my workout gear. We head to the lounge room and enjoy the wine and cheese that he set out for us before I arrived. After finishing the wine and chatting for hours, I get up to head back home. Lacing our fingers together as we walk to the door, I whisper, "I don't want go."

He nuzzles my ear and whispers back, "Then don't, stay."

Shaking my head, I say, "I can't, but soon you won't be able to get rid of me."

"I'll never want to get rid of you, Sarah, I think I'm falling in love with you."

My head snaps towards him in shock, my mouth open. "Logan, I feel the same way." Jumping towards him, he catches me, our lips colliding in another heat-filled kiss; I swear each kiss is hotter than the last. Breaking away, I rest my forehead on his and proclaim, "I really, really need to go or we will get caught. I'll text you tomorrow." He lowers me down and opens the door. He goes to escort me to the elevator and I put a hand against his chest. "You need to stay here, otherwise we will kiss again, and it will be another thirty minutes before I leave."

"And the problem with that is?" he smart-assly replies.

"You are a bad influence on sweet, innocent, little me."

"Sweet, yes. Innocent, hell no. But I'll happily stay here 'cause I can watch you sexy ass as you walk away."

"You're a fiend, Logan DeBiers. I'll see you soon." I place a quick kiss on his cheek and head towards the elevator. Swishing my hips from side to side, Logan wolf whistles at me and I blow a kiss over my shoulder. The lift arrives and I climb in, giving a gentle wave as the doors close. Leaning back against the railing, I sigh, I'm over the moon happy right now.

Climbing into the waiting cab, I head back to my apartment and that feeling of being watched is back, again I look around but like before, I don't see anyone.

Unbeknownst to me, there is someone lurking in the night, watching my every move and reporting back to the one person who has the power to destroy everything.

27

SARAH

...Present day

IT'S THE WEEKEND, FINALLY AND I'M OFF...FOR THE first time since Wednesday; Victoria has booked me solid every-single-day. I've had back-to-back appointments and no downtime at all. I feel like I'm being punished for something but I have no idea what. Due to this, Logan and I haven't had any time together, he's been so busy too that he couldn't even 'book' time with me. We won't be able to see each other until tomorrow, as we both are busy catching up with friends this evening, and neither one of us wanted to let our mates down.

I'm climbing out of the shower and my phone beeps with a text...again. Wrapping my fluffy pink towel around me, I pick it up and see yet another message from Kenz, reconfirming, again, that I am coming tonight.

Kenz – *Don't forget it starts at 6*

Sarah – *For the millionth time today I WILL BE THERE*

Kenz – *Wow, you used shouty caps, I believe you now*

Kenz – *See you at 6pm*

Sarah – *Yes Mum, I'll be there*

Today is Mike and Sav's housewarming and Kenz has guilted me into coming. I'm excited to see everyone, but I would much rather spend the evening with Logan. Slipping on my deep plum halter dress and Nine West wedges, I'm ready to go.

Victoria is in a great mood and has given me Simon as a driver for the evening; he seems pissy as he opens the car door for me. Twenty minutes later, we will pull up to the party. He drops me off and I'm only ten minutes late. I hate being late but traffic was a bitch. As I walk up the driveway of Mike and Sav's cottage, I feel sad. They have this gorgeous house and I'm living in an apartment and working as an escort. *I really need to quit so I can have all of this*, I think to myself as I head inside behind another couple.

Once inside, I find Mike and Sav to offer my congratulations and say how awesome the house is. Just as I'm walking up to Mike, he's deep in conversation with Sav and Jordan when he says, "If you fart and no ones around, did you really fart?"

"What?" Sav asks with a confused look on her face.

"You know, like that tree forest thingy, but with farts?"

"Dude, you need to stop smoking crack." Jordan pauses, "Hey, Sarah." Mike and Sav turn and grin at me as Jordan hugs me. He leaves me with the hosts and goes off to find Kenz.

"Dude, she'll be at the bar." The three of them laugh at my statement as Jordan heads towards the makeshift bar and his beautiful wife. Turning my attention back to them, I say, "Mike, this place is awesome. Hi, Sav. I'm Sarah, it's nice to officially meet you." I stretch out my hand.

"Nice to meet you officially, too." She shakes mine and smiles, making me feel at ease and that I can do this, and have fun; while keeping my secret safe in the process. I chat with Mike and Sav for a bit when I hear Kenz laugh, turning around, I see her with Jordan. No surprises, near the bar, I tell Mike and Sav that I'll catch up with them later, and I make my way towards my bestie and her hubby.

Walking over to Kenz and Jordan, Kenz smiles when she sees me and smacks Jordan in the chest. "Well, well, well, look, Jor, it's Sarah. You remember her? My bestie, who seems to have disappeared off the face of the earth."

Hugging Jordan again, I say, "Hardy har har, bitch." Before embracing Kenz tightly, *It's good to see her again*, I think to myself. Pulling back, but still gripping her tightly, I give my best puppy dog eyes. "It's good to see you guys and, Kenz, I know I've been such a shitty friend, but I promise, I'll explain everything...soon."

"You know I can't resist your puppy dog eyes, so I'll give you a pass...for now, but you and I will be talking; soon."

"I know, I know, and I promise that I will but for tonight, I'm going to get rip-roaring drunk with my besties and have a winetabolous time." Taking the glass of wine from Kenz, I yell, "Cheers bitches!" and clink glasses with her, followed by Jordan.

From over where I just was, we hear Mike yell. "Back at ya, lady!"

Kenz, Jordan, and I fall into easy conversation; just like old times. About an hour later a chill comes over me and then I hear him. His voice is embedded in my brain and when I turn I around, I see him standing on the other side of the room. He has his back to me and is chatting to Mike and Sav, all my fears and secrets are standing not five meters away from me. I'm scared but at the same time, so happy that he's here...but how?

Suddenly, he turns around and pauses midstep when his eyes lock on me. He stares at me open-mouthed, my face mirroring his. A force takes over my body and I find myself walking towards to him, his pull is too strong to ignore. Before I know it, I'm standing directly in front of him. He reaches out and grabs my hand, squeezing it gently. "Sarah?" His sexy baritone voice completely melts me. "What are you doing here?"

The room is dead silent; all eyes are focused on Logan and me. I'm frozen, staring at him, my face pales and I feel like I'm going to throw up. Not quite believing that he is standing in front in me, in the middle of Mike and Sav's living room. The music playing fades away and all I see is Logan, he and I are the only ones there. We are absorbed in one another; the air around us is filled with lust, sexual tension, and confusion.

I'm snapped back to reality when I hear Logan say my name again and he gently rubs my arm. Shaking my head, I stammer. "LLL...Logan, what are you doing here?"

"The friend that has just come back into my life is Sav. What are you doing here?"

I'm shocked, all words leave my brain; I'm stunned to see Logan standing in front of me. Looking around, I see everyone staring intently at us. Everything I have been hiding is about to unravel, and the biggest secret of all is standing right in front of me. All six foot two inches of gorgeousness. "I...I...I have to go."

Turning away from Logan and my friends, I race towards to front entrance. Vaguely I hear Kenz and Jordan calling out to me, but I put one foot in front of the other and I get out of there. Once outside, I slam the door behind me, struggling to breathe as a panic attack sets in. Leaning against it, I stand there hyperventilating, trying to catch my breath. I'm brought back to reality when I hear Logan say, "That's the girl I was telling you about, Sav."

Sav shouts back, "Sarah is your hooker?"

Hearing that, my breathing stops and I slide down the door and begin to cry, I hear Jordan and Kenz say in unison. "What?"

28

LOGAN

I'M CHATTING TO SAV AND MIKE, WHEN THE HAIRS on the back of my neck stand up and a feeling of excitement and calm washes over me. Shaking it off, I say, "I'll get us a round of drinks, be right back." Turning around, I see Sarah in all her beauty standing by the bar, staring intently at me. I completely zone out, not believing she's here and before I know it, she's standing right in front of me. All eyes are on us and the room goes deathly quiet. She asks me what I'm doing here, and I explain that Sav is my friend that I mentioned. I ask her what she's doing here, but before I get an answer or a kiss, she spins away from me and runs off. Leaving me standing alone in the middle of Mike and Sav's lounge room with everyone staring at me.

I'm shocked frozen and I just stand there and watch Sarah run off, tears welling in her eyes. I hear her friends by the bar yelling after her, but she slams the door on her way out. I'm so confused at her sudden departure. Sav walks over to me, nudges my arm and asks. "How do you know Sarah, Logan?"

"She's the girl I was telling you about." I know the moment it clicks for Sav and then she shouts, "Sarah is your hooker?" Immediately covering her mouth when she realises that she said that out loud...for everyone to hear.

I'm shell-shocked, all of Sarah's fears have just been revealed and I'm still standing here, stunned and all alone. My brain clicks into gear and I race outside to go after her but she's gone.

I'm walking back up the driveway when Mike, Sav, Kenzie, and her husband all come outside, confusion etched on their faces. Kenzie is the first to speak, "What the hell is going on?"

Sav and I look at each other but before we can reply, Kenzie demands, "Someone please explain why Sav thinks Sarah is a hook..." She trails off her eyes open wide, "Oh My God! You're her Logan, aren't you?" She pause and then mumbles to herself, "She mentioned you at coffee but she was very hush-hush about it all."

Looking at Kenzie, I quietly say, "Yeah, I am."

Hesitantly Kenzie asks, "H...How did you and Sarah meet?"

"In a bar."

"Don't fuck with me, Logan," she vehemently spits.

"Kenz, settle down," Jordan interjects and calmly rubs her arm.

"No, Sarah is my best friend, I knew something was up and now I want the truth." Pausing, she looks directly at me before shouting in her mum, don't fuck with me voice, "Now, Logan

Not wanting to betray Sarah, but not really have any other choice. I tell them how we met and give them the Cliff's Notes version of Sarah's life for the last few months.

"Fuck me dead, said Foreskin Fred," Mike, Kenzie, and Jordan all say in unison.

Before any of them can say anything, I add, "She was embarrassed and ashamed to tell you guys. She didn't want to add to your problems. She mentioned you had all had it tough, in one way or another, so she did it all on her own."

By this point, there are tears sliding down Kenzie's cheeks. "Ohh, Sarah, you stupid girl." She turns to Jordan and he wraps his arms around her. Mike rubs her back caringly, as Sav turns to me.

"Logan, I'm so sorry. I didn't mean to out you guys like that. You need to go find Sarah and make sure she's okay."

Kenz turns from Jordan and says, "No. I'll go. I'm her best friend and I know what she needs."

Mike says, "Wine and Jerry's?"

Logan says, "She's lucky to have you guys. She's told me all about you and I was looking forward to meeting you all. I just wish it was under nicer circumstances."

Kenz smiles and says, "Well, if Sarah and Sav both like you, you must be alright." She stretches out her hand. "I'm Kenzie and this is my husband, Jordan." She points to him over her shoulder and I shake her hand.

"As you know, I'm Logan," I say, as I shake Jordan's hand.

Turning we see Sav and Mike whispering over by the

door, they both look up and Sav says, "I'll get the ice cream and you can take a bottle of wine from here." Turning she reaches for the door handle and then looks back at me, quietly adding, "Please tell Sarah I'm really, really sorry." She opens the door and slips inside.

Mike rubs the back of his neck and says, "Sav feels really bad that she outed Sarah like that, it was just a shock."

"Tell me about it," Kenz says, as she wraps an arm around Jordan's tighter.

Sav emerges with a bag and it's rattling. "God, Sav, what are you trying to do? Get Kenz and Sarah drunk?"

"Yep, after what was exposed tonight, because of me, she needs and deserves it."

Kenz and Jordan head off to find Sarah, it kills me not to go after her, but Kenz assures me that she'll look after her. Sav, Mike, and I head back to the party. As soon as we walk inside, all chatter stops and all eyes are on us; it's awkward as all hell. Thankfully, Mike creates a distraction by shouting, "It's tequila and toast time, baby!"

He strides over to the bar, grabs a bottle of Patron and the plastic shot glasses, then proceeds to pour and hand them out, threatening anyone who tries to drink or sook out. He finally gets to Sav and me; he drapes his arm over Sav's shoulder, gives her a kiss then looks to everyone. "Sav and I want to thank you all for coming here tonight to celebrate our new cottage. Sav, you are the love of my life and I'm looking forward to our adventure together. In true us style, even our housewarming is entertaining." He winks at me. "So, a toast. To love, life, happiness, and fucking awesome tequila. Cheers, bitches!" The room erupts into a chorus of 'cheers', 'fuck yeah' and a few 'ughs' as everyone takes their shot. Someone coughs and Mike whispers not so quietly to Sav, "Pussies." Sav and I both laugh. "Shit, did you hear that? I was trying to be quiet."

"From what I know of you, Mike, quiet isn't your style."

Sav bursts out laughing. "He knows you already, Mike. Man I missed you, Loges." Pulling away from Mike she gives me a big hug and whispers, "I'm so sorry, Logan. I didn't mean to out you both like that, I feel like a big turd right now. It was such a shock that it was our Sarah that you are in love with."

"I'm not in love with her."

"Pfft. You're not fooling anyone, you totally are."

"Let's just see how she feels tomorrow before we start getting too excited." I notice that Sav sinks into herself. "Shit, Sav, I didn't mean it like that."

"No, I know. I just feel bad for Sarah, I can't imagine what she has been through and to do it all by herself." She smiles at me. "I'm glad she had you though."

"It's not your fault. It's not anyone's fault." Pausing, I add, "Look, I think I'm going to head home. I'm not really in a party mood anymore, and I want to be home in case Sarah stops by."

"I understand. Thanks for coming, Loges, and again, sorry."

"It's all good, baby girl. Want to do lunch one day this week?"

"Sounds good. Text me when you are free."

"Will do. Thanks for a great night, guys." Hugging

Sav goodbye, I shake hands with Mike, before heading outside to wait for the cab that I ordered.

Thirty minutes later, I'm climbing into bed but I can't sleep; I can't stop thinking about Sarah. I'm worried about her. Knowing Sarah, she won't answer if I call, so I send her a text.

Logan – *Hope you are okay. Thinking about you*

Immediately I get a reply.

Sarah – *I'm fine. Kenz is here. Chat tomorrow*
Sarah – *Nite nite Logan Xo*

I write and delete love you on the end of my next text several times before deciding the first time I say it will not be via text so I don't type it.

Logan – *Nite Sarah. Sweet dream gorgeous Xo*

After chatting with Sarah via text, albeit briefly, I feel confident that we will be okay. I fall into a deep sleep where I dream that Sarah and I live together and we get our happily ever after...if only it was as simple as that.

29

SARAH

Before I know it, there's banging on my front door and I just know it's Kenzie; I guess Logan told her where I live. "Sarah Bryant, you open this door right now, otherwise I'll just set up a picnic out here and drink the wine and eat the ice cream by myself...I would much rather sit on a couch and do it with you. Your choice?"

Kenz always makes me laugh, so reluctantly I get up and unlock the door. She places the bags at her feet and envelopes in me a Kenz hug; just what I need. This causes the waterworks to start and I break down in her arms. We stand in my doorway hugging until I have no more tears to cry. Sniffing, I pull away, look at Kenz and whisper, "I'm sorry I kept things from you, Kenz."

"I'm sooo mad at you right now, Sarah. But I understand AND I have wine and ice cream, so you will tell me everything from the beginning, and then we will call it even...but don't you ever keep a secret like this from me again." She looks me dead in the eyes. "Deal?" Choking back a sob, I just nod my head. She bends down, picks up the bags and walks inside. "Fuck me dead, this is where you live? Wow, Sarah, you hit the jackpot."

She walks into the kitchen while I close the door and whisper to myself, "Yeah, but I sold myself to the devil in order to get it."

"What was that?" she says.

"Nothing, just muttering to myself." Pausing, I take a deep breath. "So, ice cream or wine first?"

We both look at each other and together we say, "Wine!" Before we burst out laughing, just like we always did...in three minutes Kenz has out me at ease, and I know that she'll help me get back on track. Joining Kenz in the kitchen, she puts Jerry in the freezer and I grab two wine glasses from the cupboard. Placing them on the counter as she opens the bottle. "I really miss uncorking a wine, twisting a metal cap just isn't as exciting."

"I know, right?" I reply, smiling. Even though the biggest secret of my life was just exposed, Kenz and I are still the same. It gives me hope that this will all work out.

Over the next few hours, I fill Kenzie in on everything and I mean everything. This time I don't omit anything, like I did when we had coffee the other week.

"Holy shit, you're just like Julia Roberts except you had a threesome and work for the devil. At least you landed the hot dude." Pausing, she takes and sip before adding, "WOW, Sarah, just WOW."

"I'm not a hooker." Kenz glares at me. "Well, okay, I guess technically I am, but I can't do it anymore." Taking a sip of wine I add, "Kenz, I really like Logan."

"No shit, Sherlock, the chemistry between you two

was electric back at the party. Hell, the whole place came to a standstill watching."

"How was it after I left? I bet the rumors are flying. I heard Sav say I'm the hooker."

"Umm, yeah, there was talk, but we all went outside so no one could hear our conversation. Mike said he'd fix it, so I bet he'll get rip-roaring drunk, bring out classic Mike, and your revelation will be forgotten. The focus will be on Mike and his crazy drunk antics."

"God, I hope so. Fuck, how did my life get to this point?"

"Well, your bf..."

Smacking her in the arm, I interrupt, "Hardy har har, bitch. I don't need a reminder of what a clusterfuck my life has become. Why is it always everyone is happy and I'm on a downward, out of control spiral?"

"You're not out of control, Sarah. You are just off the beaten path and now you are back on track. First things first, you need to leave the Julia job."

"But if I do that, where will I go? What will I do?"

We are both silent thinking about what's next for me. Kenz tops ours glasses before asking, "Forgive me if I'm wrong, but don't people like you make lots of money?"

"Kenz, you can say hooker, it's fine."

"Okay, fine, don't hookers make lots of money? You should have a heap put away...unless you have secret sniff sniff habit."

"Yeah. It pays pretty well and no, no sniff sniff habit."

"Well, there you go, find somewhere to live, move out of this place, and then go from there. Hell, come and live with Jordan and me."

"I couldn't do that to you, Kenz, you guys have the girls. The last thing you need is an ex-hooker living with you."

"Sarah, you are family, and family helps each other in tough times. Hell, if you had just told me months ago, you could have moved in with us when all this happened."

"Yeah, but then I wouldn't have met Logan."

"Yes, you would have."

"How? Huh, tell me how?"

"Where were we tonight when you saw him? Mike and Sav's. You two would have eventually crossed paths and fallen hopelessly in love."

"You are ever the romantic, Kenz. I hope I get my happily ever after."

———

"You will, I feel it in my bones."

The next morning I wake up still on the couch, with a blanket over me and no Kenz. My head in pounding from the hangover from hell and the sunlight shining in is blinding. Grabbing my phone from the coffee table, I see three text messages.

Kenz – *Morning bitch. Headed home early, miss my girls & Jor. Call me when you are alive. Love your hooker face*

Logan – *Morning gorgeous. Wanna meet for coffee?*

Victoria – *Call me when you wake up. It's important*

Reading my messages, my emotions go from laughing, to happily smiling, to sighing. Heading downstairs, I head to the kitchen to put on coffee. While I'm waiting for the machine to brew my heavenly morning drink, my phone rings and the sound pierces through my brain. *UGH, why did I drink so much?*

"Good morning, Victoria."

"About time you answered. I need to see you immediately. Simon is on his way, you have five minutes."

Before I have a chance to argue, she hangs up. "Well fuck you, too," I say to the room. Picking up my mug, I place it back in the cupboard and I grab my travel mug; coffee on the go this morning it is.

Filling my mug to the brim, I screw on the lid and quickly head upstairs to get changed. Forgoing a shower, I decide to spray extra perfume and quickly redo my makeup. Slipping on a white tank and my denim overalls, I grab my Chucks and head downstairs. As I hit the bottom step, there's a knock at the door; looking at my watch I mutter, "Fuck, Simon's early."

Opening the door, I find a smiling Logan standing there with two Java Lava coffee cups. Smiling back at him, I usher him in, stepping aside. "Morning, please tell me one of them is for me?"

"Morning to you too and no, they are both mine."

My mouth drops open in shock, before I pout and push out my bottom lip, looking sweetly at him. Sitting on the bottom step, I slip on my Chucks as I continue to play the poor I 'need coffee girl.'

"Well, when you look at me like that, how can I resist?"

"You can't," I reply as I stand up and grab a coffee from him. Taking a sip, I close my eyes and enjoy the goodness that is currently dancing around on my taste buds. Placing the cup of liquid gold on the entry table next to my travel mug, I turn to Logan and wrap my arms around him. Resting my head on his chest, I lose myself in all that is Logan, the beating of his heart instantly calming me. "Sorry, I took off last night." Pausing, I look up at him. "It was just a shock seeing you there. Thanks for sending Kenzie here, it was just what I needed."

"I was just as shocked to see you too, and I'm glad that Kenz was here for you. It killed me to stay away."

"But you're here now." Wrapping my arms around his neck, I pull him down towards me and I kiss him.

He breaks our kiss and says in his deep husky voice that sends my insides crazy. "I was so worried about you, Sarah, but I'm glad to see that you're ish okay."

"Ish oaky, I like that." We wrap our arms around each other and hold each other tightly; the only sound is the beating of our hearts and the music coming from the other room. Our moment is interrupted by a knock at the door. "Shit, shit, shit," I whisper. "That's Simon, I have to go see Victoria. You can't be seen here. Hide in there." I point towards to coat cupboard. "Wait five minutes before you leave. I'll call you when I'm done."

He kisses me again before slipping into the cupboard as Simon knocks again. "Coming!" I yell.

Grabbing my coffee, I open the door to an irritated looking Simon. "Morning, Simon. Let's go." Quickly I close the door behind me, grabbing his arm, I lead us towards the elevators. He jerks his arm free as if being touched by me is horrible. The air is thick with animosity and it's really uncomfortable as we make our way to the waiting car below.

Ten minutes later, we pull up at the office. Not waiting for Simon, I open the door myself and head inside. Simon is hot on my heels, which is unusual, and he knocks on Victoria's office door and stands to the side like a bodyguard. *That's weird*, I think to myself as Victoria opens the door.

"Ohh, Sarah, what are you wearing? You look so unrefined." She shakes her head as she turns on her heel and heads behind her desk. Smirking at her disapproval, I follow her into the office. I expect Simon to follow, but he waits outside like a little lap dog.

"Sarah, I know."

Looking at her confused, I ask. "Know what?"

"I know everything about last night."

"Look, I'm sorry I got drunk with my friend but I haven't seen her in ages. It shouldn't be an issue who I associate with when I'm not at work."

"I'm not talking about her, I'm talking about Mr. DeBiers."

Oh, fuck, I'm in trouble now. "What about him?" I ask, trying to hide the fear that is currently racing though my body.

"You went to an event with him that wasn't on the books. Simon informed me."

"Mike and Sav's housewarming?" *Fucking, Simon, that traitorous bastard.* "Hang on, I went alone. Simon dropped me off and I ran into him there. He's friends with my friend's girlfriend. I haven't seen any of them since I started here, so I wasn't aware of the connection until last night."

"So, you haven't been seeing him outside of work?"

"No, I have not, last night was the first time I had seen him since he and I attended the event last week." *Oh My God! I'm totally going to get busted here.* "Victoria, that's one of your rules, I wouldn't disobey you like that. I need this job, you know that."

"But..." Before she can probe me further, her booking line rings. As always, any meeting is put on hold when that line rings. She answers in her snotty, holier than thou voice, and it grates on my nerves. Zoning out, I don't pay attention until I hear her say, "Mr. DeBiers, she will be ready at 3:00 p.m."

This piques my interest and I sit up in my seat. *Remain calm, Sarah,* I tell myself as I take a sip of coffee. Sitting there I wait for her to finish the call. "Um, Victoria, I'm off this weekend. Remember?"

"Well, Mr. DeBiers is off to the Hunter Valley on business and he needs a companion. You fly out this afternoon and will be back midweek."

"Ahhh, okay. But from memory I'm booked with Xander on Monday," I shudder as I say his name, " and also Tuesday for the hospital gala."

"I can attend in your place. Mr. DeBiers is paying a premium for this, so he trumps any bookings that you have." Pausing, she looks me up and now, shaking her head. "Now, head back to the apartment to pack. And please, dress like the lady I know you are. You and your dress sense will be the death of me."

"Yes, Victoria." Inwardly I smirk because I love getting under her skin and to be honest, I chose this outfit with this in mind.

Getting up, I bid her farewell in the posh, fake way that gives her a lady boner and skip outside to find Simon waiting for me. "Home, Simon," I say in a hoity-toity voice. He rolls his eyes at me as he walk towards the car.

Grabbing my phone, I text Logan.

Sarah – *You are a genius.*
Logan – *Yes, yes I am. See you soon*

As I climb into the car, I find myself smiling and excited for the next few days. After what happened last night, I was petrified that Logan and I would be over before we even began...if only I knew what would happen while we were away.

30

LOGAN

Sarah is constantly on my mind.

She's my last thought before I go to sleep.

She's my first thought when I wake in the morning.

I've never clicked with someone like I have with her, but I'm scared that our sneaking around is going to have serious consequences for her, deadly consequences for her. Thankfully, when her friends found out last night, the fallout wasn't anything like she or I expected, but now I'm even more determined to get her away from Victoria and Elite.

The sudden death of her friend and roommate didn't sit right with me, so I've hired someone to look into Victoria and Elite. What he has found so far is clean, too clean for my liking. What surprised me the most is that Victoria is not the only principle, there's a mystery party, why the secrecy? Trying to dig up information on him or her is proving difficult, and this revelation and lack of information is extremely concerning. For Sarah's safety, and my sanity, I need to get her out of there, and soon.

I've just finished going over the weekly report that Beth sent me when I decide that Sarah and I need to get away, just the two of us where no one knows us, and we can be us. Picking up my phone, I call Elite's booking line. Making up a bullshit last minute business meeting in the Hunter Valley, I say that I need Sarah to accompany me to and decide to tack on a few extra days just for us. Not surprising, Victoria jumped at the chance and charged me a premium, but if it means I get to spend time with Sarah, then so be it—she's worth every cent and more.

I'm just finalising everything when I get a text.

Sarah – *Can't wait for spend a few uninterrupted days away with you*

Smiling, I immediately reply.

Logan – *Me neither. No need to pack clothes **WINK***
Sarah – *You'll love what I have packed*
Sarah – *....or haven't packed **WINK***
Logan – *Can't wait. See you soon gorgeous*

Quickly finishing up, I send Beth this week's action list and leave her a voice message about my impromptu leave of absence—her reaction at my spur of the moment decision will be shock and awe. I have never done anything like this since starting LDB. Leaving the office, I race back to my penthouse, pack a bag, and head over and pick Sarah up for our getaway.

The car pulls up at her place and she's waiting on the sidewalk. My cock twitches when my eyes land on her. She's wearing a black and white, Aztec print, boob tube dress with black ballet flats. Her hair is loose and blowing in the wind, she is a vision. Stepping out of the car, I lift her into my arms and spin her around before kissing her. Pulling back, I look at her as she lifts her sunglasses onto her head and her eyes sparkle in the afternoon sunlight. "My God, Sarah, you look fucking gorgeous. I can't wait to get you alone."

She giggles, "Well, you will have to wait, not sure our fellow passengers would appreciate an X-rated show on the flight."

"What passengers? I charted a flight for us."

"What?"

"It's just you, me, the pilot, and steward. As soon as we reach altitude, you and I are initiating ourselves into the Mile High Club."

She stares at me opened-mouthed, lifting her hand, she cups my cheeks before seductively saying, "Who says I'm not already a member?" Kissing me on the lips before quickly climbing into the car, I'm now the one left standing there open-mouthed and in shock.

Turning around, I go to grab her bag but the driver has already placed it in the boot. As I climb into the car, I'm grinning from ear to ear and I'm really looking forward to the next few days.

The flight is too turbulent for us to join the Mile High Club together but we do make out like teenagers the whole way. By time we land in Newcastle, my cock is rock hard and I cannot wait to get to the accommodation and check in.

An hour later, we pull up to *Casa La Vina Villas* and check into our villa. Watching Sarah as she takes it all in is mesmerising, her face lights up as she checks the room out. When she discovers the private patio with an outdoor Jacuzzi and BBQ she squeals in excitement, I can't contain myself. Striding over to her, I wrap my arms around her and nuzzle her ear. "You are fucking gorgeous, Sarah." She grinds her sexy ass against me, my cock stiffening. "You are a minx."

"Mmhmm," she whispers as she begins to circle her hips. Spinning around she kisses me deeply, wrapping her arms around my neck, rubbing her pussy against my leg. Stepping back, she unzips the side zip of her dress, the black and white material fanning at her feet. She's left standing there in a matching pale pink strapless bra and G-string. Reaching behind her back, she unclips her bra, hooks her fingers in the side of her G, and ever so slowly removes them. Standing back up, she winks before turning around and racing out to the Jacuzzi. It's bubbling away as she climbs in and sits on the edge, facing me. Her fingers trail down her neck, circling her nipples and pinching, she closes her eyes and moans. Before lightly tracing over her stomach and sliding down her slit, inserting a finger. Opening her eyes, she looks at me and through a moans whispers, "Are you coming?" Pulling her finger out she slides it slowly up and rubs her clit in circles.

My eyes are locked on her hand between her thighs

as I quickly undress and join her in the Jacuzzi. Spinning her around, I lower myself between her thighs and nudge her fingers out of the way. Darting my tongue out, I lick her mound. Taking her clit into my mouth, I gently bite down and suck, her fingers run through my hair and she moans. Slipping a finger into her and hooking it around, I find her magic spot and wiggle. "Logan," she groans. Inserting another finger, I continue to lick and finger her until I feel her walls clench around my fingers. "I'm coming," she whisper-shouts. Her body shudders as her orgasm rips through her body. She falls into the water limply and wraps her arms around my neck, nuzzling her way up to my lips and kissing me. We kiss for a few moments until she pulls back, pushing me to sit down. She straddles my hips and impales herself on my rock hard cock. We stare intently at each other as she continues to ride me. Before long, we are both shouting each other's names as we each succumb to the intense orgasms rocking through our bodies.

Sarah climbs off me and lowers herself into the water, moaning. Even though I have just come, hearing her moan like that stirs my cock once again. Linking my fingers with hers, I settle in next to her and we stare up at the twilight sky. The silence is peaceful and in this moment, I'm happier than I have ever been. Turning my head, I look towards Sarah and smile. She looks to me, smiles, and whispers, "Thank you."

"What are you thanking me for?"

"Being you." Pausing, she swallows and sits up. "Logan, I've never felt like this with anyone before. We connect on every level. You're always on my mind. I...I think I'm falling in love with you."

Sitting up, I turn and face her, grabbing her hands I squeeze tightly. "Sarah, I know exactly what you mean. You bring out the best in me and I've never been this happy before."

She jumps out of the water and crashes her lips to mine, knocking us back under the water. We kiss underwater, only breaking the surface to breathe; kneeling together our lips are locked in the most romantic, emotion-filled kiss. Placing my hands under her ass and lifting, she wraps her legs around me, and I slowly enter the tip of my cock into her. She pulls back and slams down onto my cock. We use the buoyancy of the water to thrust back and forth, the friction building into the most intense orgasm of my life. Our bodies become one as we rock back and forth, our lips fused. Feeling her pussy walls clench around my cock, she screams as her orgasm explodes and I follow soon after.

Standing up with Sarah still wrapped around me, I carefully climb out and head inside our villa to the shower. Sitting Sarah on the vanity, I turn the shower on, and once the water is hot enough, we hop in. Soaping each other up, our hands massaging and caressing each other, it turns sexual and I take her up against the shower wall.

We separately get washed and climb into bed naked and cuddle, we both lie here content in each other's arms.

Just as Sarah falls asleep, I hear her whisper, "I love you, Logan."

Kissing her gently on the head, I whisper, "I love you, too." With a smile on my face, I drift off to sleep looking forward to the next few days.

The next few days in the Hunter Valley with Sarah are magical. We visit wineries; take a horse-drawn carriage ride, and a hot air balloon tour at sunrise, with a champagne breakfast when we land. The more time I spend with Sarah only cements my love for her. Neither of us has said it to each other directly, but each night as we drift off in each other's arms we quietly whisper it.

I'm awakened on our last day with Sarah between my legs and my cock down her throat. I have to say, that is the best way to be woken up. After she has sucked me dry, she straddles my legs, leans forward and whispers, "Morning, sexy."

Smiling up at her, I grab her by the waist and flip her onto her back. "Morning, gorgeous," I say before crashing my lips to hers, the little minx lifts her hips and rubs her pussy against my cock, bringing him back to life.

Spreading her legs wider, I nudge the tip against her pussy lips before pulling back. I do this a few times before thrusting my hips forward and impaling myself to the hilt. Her pussy is warm and inviting as I keep thrusting, each thrust becoming harder and faster. Sarah digs her nails into my back and screams my name as her body shudders beneath me.

She nudges me and I know that she wants to go on top so we roll together; she gets up on her knees and rides me. Closing her eyes, she massages and squeezes her breasts as I rub her clit. I'm just about to come when I hear her moan and she squeeze her legs against mine, together we orgasm.

Falling on top of me, she sighs. We lay there, both panting, trying to catch our breath after our morning workout. Eventually she rolls off me and we lay in each other's arms, drifting back to sleep.

After waking up, we decide to head back to our favourite winery, *Tulloch* for another tasting and then head to *Tempus Two* for lunch. The day is perfect and the best way to end our getaway together.

We had just cleaned up dinner and were soaking in the Jacuzzi together when I asked Sarah about leaving Elite...that was when it all went downhill.

"Sarah, when we get back, I want to you quit Elite."

"Logan, I told you I would but I can't right now. I'm still not back on my feet. I know it's not ideal but I have no other options."

"Let me look after you, Sarah, you're better than this."

"I'm not," she pleads

"Sarah, you are. This job isn't you, you're not a hook..." I pause; I didn't mean to say that.

She sits up and splashes water, staring at me open-mouthed and shocked. "Go on, Logan, finish that sentence. I'm a hooker, a fucking whore, a prostitute. You think that's all I do at Elite, don't you? Well, guess what, asshole..." She pauses for emphasis. "You are sleeping with a hooker. " Taking a deep breath she shouts with tears pouring down her cheeks, "You are fucking a hooker, Logan, you're just as bad as me!"

Climbing out of the Jacuzzi, she storms off, slamming her wine glass down on the table as she heads inside. I feel like a real asshole and just sit there replaying the words I just said to the woman that I love. Hating myself right now, I decide to give her a few moments to collect herself before I go apologise, but I don't get a chance to because I hear the villa front door slamming. The slam causes the patio door and windows to rock from the force of the impact. *Fuck, I've really hurt her,* I think to myself as I climb out.

Heading inside, I take a quick shower and slip into my boxers for the first time since arriving. Walking back into the living room, I see that Sarah hasn't returned so pour myself a scotch and throw it back. It burns on the way down but with the way I just spoke to Sarah, I deserve it...and more. In one conversation, I managed to ruin what has been a fantastic getaway and crush the woman who means everything to me.

A few hours later, Sarah returns but she doesn't look at me or say a word. She heads into the bedroom, slips on her nightie and climbs into bed. From the lounge room I can hear her crying and I feel like a bastard, but I'm too gutless to face her. So I stay where I am and spend the night on the sofa...not the way I wanted to end our romantic getaway.

The trip back to Brisbane was awkward to say the least. Sarah never said one word to me, she's still really angry with me and to be honest, I don't blame her. What I said to her was harsh, but I want her to be safe...and with me.

The car pulls up to her apartment and she goes

climbs out without saying anything. I know I fucked up but this silent treatment is killing me. Reaching out, I grab her wrist. "Sarah, please, I'm sorry."

She whispers, "Sorry won't cut it, you really hurt me, Logan. I...I thought you cared about me, but obviously I was wrong." With that statement she pulls her wrist free and climbs out, slamming the door in my face. Normally she would wait on the sidewalk until I was around the corner, but tonight she marched inside without looking back.

That night when I'm lying in bed and missing Sarah, I decide that if she won't do anything about it, I will. I need to take things into my own hands if I'm going to get her back.

31

VICTORIA

SARAH AND LOGAN RETURN EARLY FROM HIS extended appointment and her demeanor has changed. My senses, which have never let me down, are now on high alert; especially when he calls to request a face-to-face meeting.

The meeting with Mr. DeBiers went exactly as I thought; he wants me to let go of Sarah because he's in love with her. As I reminded him, he signed a contract to spend time with my girls, not to fall in love; this isn't *Tinder*. He tried to argue with me but I put him in his place, no one tells me what to do and as of 10:51 a.m. today, Mr. DeBiers is no longer a client at Elite.

My next meeting is with Sarah. To throw her off the scent, I treat her to an afternoon at the spa, followed by a champagne high tea. Looking over at Sarah, I see that she is relaxed and that's when I strike. "So, when did you fall in love with Mr. DeBiers?" My question takes her by surprise as she spits her champagne out in shock.

Wiping her chin, she looks at me shocked and replies, "I'm not in love with him."

"Don't lie to me, Sarah. You know I don't tolerate liars."

"Victoria, I'm not lying. I care for him but I'm not in love with him."

"He tells a different story." That stops her in her tracks, *lying little bitch,* I think to myself as I sip on my bubbly and stare at her.

"I...I...don't know how I feel about him, Victoria."

"Well, you don't have to worry. He is no longer a client at Elite. No one tells me what to do, he came in this morning demanding that you be released."

"He did what?" Her reply shocks me, I thought that they has conspired together, maybe there is hope for me to keep her yet.

"He requested that I let you go as you are both in love. I told him my contract with you is none of his business." Testing her I add, "He offered me a lot of money to buy you out."

She looks over at me but doesn't say anything, her jaw drops open in shock, eventually she asks. "What did you say?"

"I told him that I'm not in the game of selling women, well not in that way. He wasn't happy, especially when I told him he was no longer welcome here at Elite."

"Okay, but you do know that this isn't my dream. One day I will leave, and I think it will be sooner, rather than later. Now that my friends know, I need to move on." She looks down to her lap and then looks back at me. "Victoria, I think I want to leave."

Her statement shocks me. "Well, that will not be happening anytime soon, Sarah. You are my moneymaker and I refuse to let you leave."

"You can't do that, you don't own me."

"Sarah, darling, I have owned you since the night I met you at Dirty Duck. You are mine for the foreseeable future."

"I beg your pardon?"

"Enough!" I shout, "You do not speak to me like that. Sarah, I saved your pathetic ass and that ass is mine." Pausing for emphasis, I take a sip of my bubbly before adding, "Sarah, if you leave, I will ruin everything and everyone who is dear to you."

"You wouldn't." I see hesitation in her eyes.

"Just try me, Sarah. If you leave, I will drag Logan's name so far through the mud that he will never come back from it."

"But..."

"There are no buts here Sarah. You. Are. Mine. Now go get ready, you have an appointment tonight."

"Since when?"

"Since now and must I remind you not to talk back to me."

"Fine, I will stay but you have to guarantee me that Logan and everyone else will be safe."

"You have my word." I see her relax at this. "But you fuck with me in the slightest and just see what I'm capable of. You have forty minutes to be ready. Simon will pick you up and deliver you to Cyril Barnstead. You're in for quite a night."

Her head snaps towards me when she realises she is

in for a rough night. She is conflicted about staying but I can see it in her eyes, she will do anything to keep Logan and his reputation safe. If she does this tonight, I know that she will do anything and everything that I say from now on.

I now know without a doubt that she loves him and now she is mine. She will not let me take Logan down, and that's fine, because this will work to my advantage. I always win, always. However, if she screws me over, she will pay...just like the others.

32

LOGAN

My meeting with Victoria went as I had planned and now I'm worried for Sarah's safety. I have a sick feeling that I have just made her life a living hell. I've tried to call her but she's either ignoring me or busy, I'm hoping she's just ignoring me. Victoria's warning on the way out scared me.

"Mr. DeBiers, I'll warn you now, no one messes with me and lives to tell the tale. Take this warning seriously; otherwise I can make life extremely difficult for Sarah. You wouldn't want that now, would you? You are no longer welcome here or a member of Elite; now get off my property and out of my sight. Ohh, and don't think about contacting, Sarah to say goodbye, I'll pass on your regards."

Now I'm even more determined to get Sarah out of there, sooner rather than later. My PI is still looking into Victoria and Elite but so far nothing, hopefully he can help me, otherwise, I'm at a loss what to do to save the woman I love.

My thoughts are interrupted when Sav waltzes into my office. "Dude, where have you been? We had a lunch date booked and when I got here the place was locked up tighter than Fort Knox." She sits down and looks at me but her expressions changes immediately when she sees my face. I hate that she can read me like a book. "Okay, what's wrong? Or more to the point, what did you do? Your worry line is prominent."

"I don't have a worry line."

"You do, now spill?"

"I think I fucked up with Sarah. I may have called her a hooker to her face, and then I met with her boss to let her go, and I think I made things worse."

"Shit, Logan, you're a fuckwit. You majorly have fucked up."

"Thanks for the pep talk, it really helped."

"What? It's the truth, but the question is, what are we going to do to fix it?"

"You don't happen to have a time machine so I can go back and not rip Sarah to shreds."

"That I can't help with but together we will come up with a plan and get your girl back. Did all of this happen due to the party fallout?"

"Yes, no, I don't know." Looking up at her, I sadly add, "Sav, I love her so fucking much. I think I screwed up the best thing to happen to me since you hit me with your bike all those years ago."

"Well, let's fix this then. Why don't you come over tonight? I'll make Mexican and we can come up with a game plan to win her back."

"Not sure I'll be good company."

"How's that different to every other time we catch up?"

"Hardy har har, bitch." I look over at her and hesitantly ask, "Do you really think I can win her back?"

"Loges, the chemistry between you two is off this charts electric, and that's from me only seeing you two together for like four seconds. Trust me, we'll get her back. Now come on, let's go."

"Ummm, unlike you, I have work to do. I'll be over just after six. I'll bring the wine."

"Dude, we are having Mexican, it's either beer or tequila."

In unison we both say, "Or both." Immediately laughing our asses off, just like we used to, and then it all comes crashing back to me. I haven't laughed like that since Sarah and I were in the Hunter. It only makes me miss her more.

"Dude, you were thinking about her again. Weren't you?"

"Yeah, I can't stop thinking about her."

"Wow, you've got it bad." She stands up. "Okay, I'm off to start on our feast, see you just after six."

"It's a date, Sav. Have I told you how glad I am to have you back in my life?"

"Only all the time, but I am pretty kick-ass, so it's understandable." With that she walks out of my office, leaving me sitting there smiling and appreciating my best friend, but at the same time, missing the person I love with all my heart.

The afternoon drags and come 5:00 p.m., I decide to call it quits and head home. I grab a quick shower, call a cab, and head over to Sav and Mike's cottage. We all have a great night; I end up getting absolutely shitfaced on red wine and tequila. No brainstorming to win Sarah back occurred, but it was nice to let loose and get to know Mike. He's a great guy and I can see why Sav is so happy. He is perfect for her...just like Sarah is perfect for me.

33

SARAH

My fight and breakup with Logan is still weighing heavily on my mind. Actually, it's all I have been able to think about for the last ten days, five hours and thirty-four minutes—yes, I know how long it has been. Trying to forget Logan DeBiers is hard but he really hurt me with what he said, even though most if it was true. Maybe I should look at finding a way to leave; I always said I wasn't going to do it forever. Perhaps now is the time to move on. But first, I need to find a way to do so without she-devil fucking over everyone that I care about *Ohh, I don't know*, I think to myself as I climb into the shower.

Drying off after my shower, I head into my closet to get read for another appointment with Xander and Morgan; I'm not excited at all. Victoria is punishing me at the moment. She is giving me back-to-back appointments every day. I haven't had a day off since I returned from my disastrous trip with Logan; thankfully she was joking and it was cuddly, old man Cyril and not Saskawhore's freaky Cryil.

On Tuesday, she sent me on one of the more kinky appointments that Saskawhore would have loved. She knows I don't do those ones but I'm being punished, I just know it. The bitch had an evil glint in her eye when she told me about it...I'm definitely being reprimanded; at least I will have Morgan with me today. Her and I click really well and we always have fun together, even if we have to endure Xander.

Looking at my reflection in the mirror, I close my eyes and sigh deeply. *I can't do this anymore*, I think to myself as I finish putting on my mascara. Walking back into my wardrobe, I see the dress that I wore the first night I met Logan and sadly smile. I say to the room, "I miss you, Logan." Picking up the dress, I hold it tightly to my chest and I start to cry. As I slip the dress over my head, I realise that for the first time since starting at Elite, I feel like a whore; damn you Everclear for making me sing that to myself. Logan's words keep flying around my head and he's right, I am better than this.

Pursing my lips together in frustration, I remember that I forgot to put lipstick on; I head back to the bathroom and put my lippy on. As I'm blotting, I decide that tonight will be my last night at Elite. I just hope everyone doesn't hate me if Victoria goes after them. I'm ending this and Sarah 3.0 will begin. I don't care that I will be jobless or homeless because Kenz is right. I've saved enough money to get my own place, and I have a little nest egg set aside that I can use until I find my feet again. I'm Sarah Bryant and it's time to take MY life back.

I'm sitting on the end of my bed, putting my shoes on, when Morgan walks in. Her hair is piled in a messy bun on the top of her head and she's wearying a charcoal jumpsuit. Smiling at her I whistle and she does a little spin before plonking down next to me. "Ready for a fun night?" she says, but not with the usual enthusiasm she has. Ever since Angel was murdered Morgan has been quiet and reserved.

"Ready as I'll ever be," I reply, standing up I walk over to my dresser and grab my clutch. Turning back to Morgan, I stretch out my hand and she links her arm with mine, and we make our way down stairs to the waiting limo.

Morgan climbs in first and as I stare into the afternoon sky, I really wish the car was taking me to Logan, instead of to Xander. Hopefully after tonight, the next time I am in one, it will be taking me to him.

Sitting next to Morgan, the limo pulls away. She grabs the bottle of bubbly and pours two glasses as I pull out my phone and text Victoria.

Sarah – *I need to speak with you*
Sarah – *Urgently*

Her reply is immediate.

Victoria – *Tomorrow, 10am*

I shake my head at the abruptness of her reply, but really. it doesn't surprise me at all. Victoria has been off lately, nothing anyone does seems to be good enough, and the appointments seems to be getting desperate and degrading, like she's taking anybody to just bring in money. We are bordering on being whores and not the escorts that we used to be. We hardly ever attend galas and mingle with high society or celebrities at gallery openings, it's always a restaurant followed by a room in a seedy hotel. Thankfully I've become a pro, pun intended, at getting the seedy guys drunk and they pass out before anything happens. This change only cements by decision to leave.

The limo pulls up to the hotel and the concierge opens the car door for us. I nod my thanks and wait for Morgan. Linking arms again, we head inside and make our way up to Xander's suite. He opens the door after I knock and from his demeanor, and the strong smell of bourbon, I know that tonight is not going to be smooth sailing.

Morgan walks in first, kissing Xander on the cheek on her way past. Taking a deep breath, I walk into the suite and sweetly say as I quickly shuffle past him, foregoing the customary kiss, "Hey, Handsome, are you ready to go for dinner?"

He grips my wrist, pulls me towards him and plants a wet, rough kiss on my lips, before slapping me on the ass, hard, and pushing me into the suite. My pulse quickens as I make my way to the couch and take a seat next to Morgan. She's leaning forward popping open the bubbly that was in the wine bucket; *guess we aren't going out this afternoon.*

Taking a glass from Morgan, I walk over to windows and gaze at the river and traffic below. The view out the window and drink helps to calm my nerves, a little, until Xander invades my space and stands next to me. An eerie feeling envelopes the room, and all the nerves that had just disappeared return with a vengeance. He glances over at me and the look in his eyes, at this moment, tell me that this afternoon will not be pleasurable.

A wave of unease washes over my body and fear begins to build within me. Not knowing what to do, I awkwardly smile at him and wait. The silence is deafening. After a few moments, he looks between Morgan and me before snarling. "It's show time, bitches!"

He roughly squeezes my arm, pulling me closer to him, sliding his hand up my leg as he roughly bites my neck. Grabbing his wrist and squeezing with all my might, I look at him confused, "Time for what?" I say as I push away from him. Looking towards Morgan for help, I see that she has zoned out and is just sitting there sipping her bubbly, oblivious to the scene unfolding right next to her.

He ignores my question and demands, "Bed. Now, Sarah." He begins to untuck his shirt and undo his belt; he looks at me with menacing eyes and shouts. "Now!"

"No, Xander. Not like this, please?" I plead with him, his eyes are glassy due to the bourbon, but beneath the haze, I see rage simmering deep within. From the corner of my eye, I see Xander raise his hand, but before I can get out of the way he slaps me hard across the cheek. "What do you mean, no?" he sneers, his eyes darken as his shoulders tense with anger before he hits me hard across the other cheek.

Clutching my cheek, I squeak, "I said no, Xander. I'm not sleeping with you tonight...or anymore for that matter and neither is Morgan. I'm done."

"No one tells me no, especially not a hooker. Now, get your clothes off, get on the bed and spread your legs. You are done when I say you are done."

A surge of adrenaline pumps through my veins and I face him, between clenched teeth I snarl "I. Said. No." Pausing between each word, taking a deep breath I add, "We're leaving."

Turning on my heel, I make my way to the door of the hotel room, just as I'm reaching out for the door handle, my shoulder is grabbed and I'm spun around. **SLAP** "I say when you leave and you're not going anywhere, bitch." **SLAP** "Victoria said this would happen, but I told her that you weren't silly enough to fall for twat boy but looks like for the first time ever, I was wrong. I'll let you go, but not before I get what I want." **SLAP** "Now, as I said before, clothes off and on the bed."

Standing there, I'm staring at him speechless, frozen, and not able to move. Gone is the sweet and seductive Xander, standing before me is a wild beast. I'm beyond scared but I can't do this anymore. It's in this moment that I realise I want a life with Logan, and that I love him deeply; I have to get out of here, and now.

Taking another deep breath, I say. "No, I...I can't, Xander. I won't. I just can't. I'm so sorry."

"Wrong answer, Sarah." He lunges for me and

punches me in the face, grabbing me roughly; he pushes me towards Morgan. I trip on the end of the couch and my head catches the coffee table corner on my way down. Lying on my side, my vision blurs and before I pass out, I see him dragging a struggling Morgan into the bedroom.

When I come to I can hear him with Morgan in the other room. He's grunting, flesh is hitting flesh and Morgan is crying. Using the coffee table, I lift myself up and I race into the bedroom, trying to pull him off her. Grabbing his shoulder, I pull with all my might.

He stands next to the bed, his face red from exertion and he stares menacingly at me. "So, you decided to join the party, did you?" He reaches out and grabs at my dress. Quickly I step back, but I'm not fast enough. He grips the neckline and pulls, tearing my dress off, leaving me standing there in my bra and undies. A surge of adrenaline races through me body and I step forward, shoving him in the chest.

"You bitch," he spits. Pulling his arm back, he punches me in the face again before propelling me viciously into the wall. My head hits with a thud and I fall to the carpet, passing out.

I'm awakened to Morgan shaking me. Opening my eyes I see that she is naked, covered in bruises and bite marks. There is blood between her thighs and her eyes are swelling shut. "Ohh, Morgan," I manage to say before wrapping my arms around her. She winces in pain but curls into me, quietly crying.

We sit together, huddled on the floor, not saying a word to each other. When I look up next, it's dark outside and Morgan is asleep in my lap, by now her body is purple and her eye sockets are as black as the ace of spades. Gently I lift her head, and I make my way into the other room, thanking the universe that Xander is no longer here.

Picking my purse up from the floor by the door, I grab my phone and I call the one person I know who will help me without judgment. Dialing I put the phone to my ear and wait for the call to connect, they pick up on the second ring.

"Hey, bitch, I was just thinking of you."

"Help me, Kenz." I start to cry.

"Sarah, what's wrong? Where are you?"

"Morgan and I need you, Kenz, please?"

Frantically she replies, "I'm on my way. Where are you?"

Through my tears, I manage to tell her where we are. She tells me she's on her way.

Grabbing a robe, I slip it on and go back to Morgan after calling the front desk and arranging a key for Kenz. Morgan is still curled into herself, but she's awake now, as soon as she sees me she swallows deeply and then bursts into tears. Racing over to her, I gently ease her up and wrap my arms around her, whispering, "Shhhh."

"Sarah, he was a monster. I've never seen him like that before."

"I'm sorry, sooooo sorry, Morgan." Swallowing the lump building in my throat because I need to be strong for her I ask, "What happened?"

Leaning against the wall, she closes her eyes and says, "After you hit your head, he turned towards me but I couldn't move. I was frozen with fear. I...I just left you there and I sat on the couch staring at you laying there, not moving. Before I had time to process what was happening, Xander grabbed me by the wrist, squeezing tight, really tight." Morgan begins to rub her wrist absent-mindedly. "He then dragged me towards the bedroom, he turned around an threw me over this shoulder and stalked into the bedroom. I started kicking and screaming, tears pouring down my cheeks, I kept pleading with him. *'Please, Xander, don't do this; this isn't you. Please, Xander, please.'* But he ignored me; he was in his own world. His eyes glazed over and I knew in that moment that there would be no reasoning with him. When we reached the bedroom, he threw me violently face down onto the bed before straddling my hips. Roughly grinding himself on my ass, I could barley breathe or move. I began crying, he shoved me harder into the mattress, the tears wouldn't stop, Sarah. I've never been so scared in my life. With a force I have never seen before on any man, he tore my jumpsuit off me and flipped me over. I closed my eyes 'cause I couldn't look at him. I remember him growling for me to open my eyes but I wouldn't. He hit or punched me in the face so hard I felt like I was going to pass out. I opened my eyes and realised that I was only in my bra and undies, but not for long. He reached out and ripped them off my body. Leaning down, he…he bit my breasts and twisted my nipples, again I screamed out in pain. No one came, no one. I wriggled and wriggled to get free, my hands hitting at his head and body, but he just didn't stop. He kept biting and sucking my tits. Eventually he lifted his head up and he looked directly at me. I've never seen a face full of anger like that before. He slapped my face repeatedly, Sarah, I just lay there and took it. I did nothing to stop him. My head thrashed to the side, I started to see stars and everything around me faded in and out. I've never been hit that hard before in my life. Eventually, I passed out."

"Ohh, Morgan, I'm so sorry."

"That's not the end of it, Sarah."

"Fucking hell, he's a monster."

"I came to and I felt him sitting between my thighs. I heard the jiggle of his belt and the lowering of his zipper, I began to panic again when I saw his dick pop free. It was rock hard and the tip throbbing and deep purple in colour, without warning he thrust deep inside of me. The burn was unbearable. I screamed out in agony but before I could scream again; he punched me before wrapping his fingers around my throat. I couldn't breathe. Between the not breathing and the stabbing burning feeling between my legs, I passed out from the pain. When I woke up again, you were here. Sarah, he raped me." Morgan begins to cry again.

"Shhhh," I whisper. "It will be alright, I've got you now."

The door to the suite opens and Morgan freaks out; she races into the bathroom and slams the door. I'm still sitting on the carpet when I hear Kenz. "Sar, I'm here, babes, where are you?"

Hearing her voice opens the floodgates again and I begin sob. "I'm in here," I manage to say, but I'm not sure if she heard me as it came out as a jumbled mess. Looking up, I see her walking in and the look on her face confirms that I look as bad as I feel. "Ohh, Sarah, what happened?"

Hearing her makes me sob even harder, I lean my head on my knees and continue to cry. Kenz walks over to me and carefully wraps her arms around me. I shuffle and wrap my arms around her waist, pulling her closer to me, gripping her tight. I sit there, holding tightly onto my best friend and I cry; I cry like I have never cried before, I let it all out.

Movement by the door startles me and I look up into the worried eyes of Logan. "What are you doing here?"

He shuffles on his feet before leaning on the doorframe, "Kenz called me and said you were in trouble so I told her I'd meet her here."

"Well you can leave, after all, I'm nothing but a whore who deserves all that I get. Well, I guess you got your wish. Besides, I'm fine."

Leaning back against the wall, I close my eyes and whisper, "Kenz, please make him leave."

With my eyes, still closed, I feel her stand up and they move into the main room. Their voices are quiet and I can't hear what is being said, but a few moments later I hear the click of the door closing and feet shuffling back. Looking up, I see it's Logan still here and Kenz left. *Bitch*, I think to myself.

Taking a deep breath, I swallow and confidently say, "I don't want you here, Logan, I'm fine, I'm just a hook..." but I can't finish the words as I start to cry again. Logan is in front of me crouching down, he hesitantly reaches out and brushes a strand of matted hair behind my ear, and he looks deep into my eyes. "Sarah, I'm so sorry for what I said. You are none of those things, you are a fighter and I took my frustrations out on you. If I wasn't such as ass..."

I don't let him finish; I wrap my arms around him and hug him tight. His embrace calms me and is just what I need right now. No other words are needed in this moment, for now there is nothing more to be said...we can broach that elephant at another time.

34

LOGAN

When I got the call from Kenz to say that Sarah was in trouble, I didn't hesitate to help. Even though I said some horrible things to her last week, I still care deeply for her. She didn't deserve any of them, I could have handled it a hell of a lot better, but as usual, I approach things with the usual Logan DeBiers stubbornness. I just hope that I haven't lost the best person to ever come into my life.

Getting the address from Kenz, I haul ass to the hotel and I end up pacing in the foyer waiting her; the wait is nerve-racking. Hearing my name, my head snaps up and Kenz is running towards me.

"Hey, what's going on?" I ask, as she races past me towards the check-in desk.

"No idea, but after I get this key we will know." She steps to the counter and is bouncing on her feet, she looks just as agitated and worried as I am. Finally the clerk looks up.

"Can I help you?"

Kenz quickly says, "Umm, my friend is here. She said there would be a key for me. She's in room 2207."

"You must me Mackenzie, can I please see some ID before I give you the key?"

"Yep, sure." She digs in her monstrosity of a handbag and finally passes over her license.

"Thanks for that, here you go. The lifts are to your left."

She snatches the key from the clerk and we race towards the elevators. Repeatedly I punch the button, willing it to come quicker. Finally the doors open and we both race in. We reach the floor and make our way to the door, as we are standing there I start to panic that she won't want me here. I replay in my mind the horrible things that I said to her when I hear the click of the door opening.

I let Kenzie go in first, following her in, she yells out and we hear a muffled sound coming from the bedroom. Hanging back, I look around, it's a pretty nice suite, I hear Kenzie's shocked reaction from the main room and I make my way there. The bed sheets are all messed up and it looks like there is blood on them, turning towards them at the end of the bed, my heartbreaks at what I see.

Sarah is a crumbled mess, clinging to Kenzie for dear life. She is sobbing and there is nothing I can do. She looks up at me and her reaction is shock, which is quickly replaced with anger when she demands to know why I'm here. I explain and she glares at Kenzie; I feel for Kenzie in this moment. Sarah is not happy that I'm here, and asks Kenzie to make me leave.

Kenzie and I move into the main room, before she has

a chance to speak I say, "I'm not leaving, Kenz. I need to be here for her. I need to show her that I care and that I'm not the asshole I was the other day."

"Look, I don't know what happened and had I known I would not have brought you here..." I go to interrupt her but she gives me a look that says 'shut the fuck up and let me finish' so I let her continue. "But I know Sarah, deep down she wants, no, needs you here. I'm going to go but I swear, Logan, if you fuck this up you will have me to deal with. Now, go back in there and look after my best friend."

"I promise, I won't let anything happen to her, but first, we need to get her out of this room. Can you go downstairs and book another room for us, we can't stay in this one."

"Sure, no worries." She puts her hand out, and shakes her fingers, indicating she needs money. Grabbing my wallet, I give her my credit card, and before I can say anything, she is out the door.

Turning around, I head back into the bedroom. Sarah's head pops up when she hears me approaching and her face is void of any emotion. She starts talking and telling me that she doesn't want me here but I ignore her. I crouch down to her level and carefully I push a stand of hair behind her ear, cup her cheek in my hand, and I grovel. I'm only halfway through my apology when she wraps her arms around me and starts to cry again. "Thanks for coming," she sniffles into my shoulder.

The bathroom door clicks open and Sarah freezes in my arms and grips me tighter, when she sees Morgan standing there she releases her hold on me and races over to her. "Morgan, Logan and Kenz are here to help."

"I...I just want to get out of here, Sarah. I want to go home."

Before I get a chance to reply, Kenz comes into the bedroom, I didn't even hear the main door open. "Okay, I managed to get another room. I also asked them to call the police, they will direct them to the new room."

Sarah and Morgan's heads snaps up, Morgan shrieks, "Police? Why would you do that?"

Sarah turns to her and gently say, "Morgan, you've been raped and beaten, and I was attacked, we have to report this."

"No, I can't. I'm a hooker, I deserve what happens to me."

In unison, we all yell, "No!"

"Morgan, look at me, I know you don't know me, but you have to report this, regardless if you are a hooker or not." Morgan looks up to Kenz, not believing what she's saying when Sarah butts in.

"Morgan, who gives a shit what we are? You and I have been beaten black and blue that in itself deserves punishment."

Kenz interrupts me, "I know what you are going through and as much as this will be tough, you need to do this. Sarah and I will be here with you. Whoever did this, cannot not get away with this."

"I can't," she pleads, before burying her face in her hands and crying.

"Look, let's get into the new room and we can talk about this later," I say.

Standing up, I reach out for Sarah but she flinches away from me, hugging Morgan to her side and walking ahead of me. Her flinching like that was a kick in the guts, especially after the hug we just had, but I guess I can understand. Kenzie helps them towards the door but Morgan is exhausted and collapses onto Kenz. Taking a step forward, I lift her into my arms, Sarah smiles at me and it warms my heart to see her smiling again, I find myself grinning back at her. Morgan wraps her arms around my neck, but my smile falters when I feel her body shake from the sobs rippling through her body.

We head towards to lifts together, and the four of us make our way up to the new room. Settling Morgan in the bed, I head back to the lounge room, where Kenz is ordering coffee and Sarah is sitting on the lounge staring into space. "You know her well," I say to Kenz as I meet her in the kitchen.

"Yep, Sarah always says coffee or wine can fix anything. I don't think she needs wine at the moment, but I know her, that will come later. For now we drink coffee." Pausing, she looks up at me. "Thank you, Logan."

"Don't mention it. Look, I know I was a complete asshole and said some horrible things to her, but I still care deeply about her. Hopefully now, she will leave Elite and let me take care of her."

"Before she does that, we need to get her and Morgan to speak to the police. I know it's going to be tough, but I know they can both do it. They are both strong."

"I agree with you there. I'll call reception and tell them to send them up here and to not touch the other room." Pausing, I look to Kenz. "You realise she will hate us for this."

"Yeah, I do, but I don't care. Whoever did this needs to be punished, Sarah is lucky she wasn't raped, too."

From the other room, we hear the shower turn on. "Bitch," Kenzie and Sarah say in unison. Looking at one another they smile and race into the ensuite. "Are you stupid, Morgan? You're washing the evidence away. The police will need swabs and all that." I can hear Kenz yelling at Morgan.

"Kenz, don't speak to her like that. She's in shock," Sarah vehemently spits back.

"Sorry, but she's washing all the evidence away."

"I told you, I'm not talking to them," Morgan stubbornly replies.

"Well, that's too bad, they are on their way." There's a knock at the door. "Looks like they are here. Sarah, you stay here and help her. I'll go out there and you both come join us when you're ready."

Kenzie enters the room and I introduce her to the officers. We tell them that Sarah and Morgan, who are in the other room, have been beaten and we think that Morgan has also been raped. We also tell them that Morgan doesn't want to speak to them, and Sarah is also hesitant.

After ten minutes, they are both still in the other room, I excuse myself and head in there. Standing outside the bedroom door, I can hear crying and Sarah whispering to Morgan. My heart is breaking for them both right now and I don't even know this girl. I raise my hand and gently knock on the door, I hesitantly ask, "Sarah, Morgan, can I come in?"

"Yeah," they both quietly say.

Opening the door, I find them in the hotel's robes sitting on the floor, facing each other; Morgan is hugging her knees. Her hair is still damp after her shower and even though her face is swollen and purple, I can tell that she is broken. Looking towards Sarah, I smile and she smiles back at me. Even though her eye is swollen shut and her face is fifty shades of purple, she's still the most beautiful woman I have ever seen. "Sarah, is everything okay here?"

She shakes her head. "No, yes, I don't know. Logan, this mess is all my fault."

"No, sweetheart, it's not. It's my fault; I shouldn't have said the things that I did. I should have protected you."

"Can I have a hug?" she quietly asks.

"Of course you can. Can you stand or do you want me to come over there?"

"I can stand. I think." She carefully gets up, wincing in pain as she does. She takes three careful steps towards me and wraps her arms around me waist, resting her head on my chest. Gently, I wrap mine around her and rub the base of her neck with one hand and hold her close to me with the other; her shoulders begin to shake as she starts to cry again. "Shhhh," I whisper, "I've got you now."

She composes herself and looks up at me. "Logan, I really don't want to speak to the police. Please just let this go. Morgan and I were chatting and we just want to forget that any of this has happened."

"I'm sorry, Sarah. I can't. You both need to report this." Spinning her around, I hold her upper arms and rub them while I whisper, "Look at yourself, Sarah." She keeps staring at the floor so I gently place a finger under her chin and lift her head slightly; our eyes lock in the mirror. She refuses to look at herself. "Sarah, look at yourself. This needs to be dealt with, if I ever find him, he is going to look a lot worse than this."

"Logan, I can't. Please just drop it."

"Well, you tell them then." Turning my back on them I storm out of the room, kicking the bed on my way past in frustration. When I enter the lounge again, the two officers and Kenz turn to me and stop talking. "She's so stubborn. She's now refusing to talk to you or even press charges, she feels like it's all her fault."

The female officer, whose name I forget, says, "That's not uncommon in situations like this. We are happy to hang around for a bit, in case she changes her mind but while we wait, we'd like to talk to you both and get a bit more information if we can."

From the doorway we hear Sarah, "That's not necessary, I'll tell you what I can, but Morgan doesn't want to."

35

SARAH

Staring at myself on the mirror after Logan stormed out, I don't recognise the girl reflected back at me. Aside for the swelling and bruising, I'm a shell of my former self and I realise he's right; I need to do something but I'm scared.

Looking to Morgan, who is still sitting on the floor, staring into space, I decide that I will do this for us both. Walking over to her, I crouch down and gently place my hand on her knees. "Morgan, honey, I need to talk to them. I'm not going to force you to, but I really think you should."

Morgan just stares at me, shaking her head from side to side. "No, I can't. I'm sorry, Sarah." She starts to cry again.

"Hey, it's fine. No apologies necessary. You wait here and I'll hurry this along, okay?" She just nods at me before turning her head and staring out at the night sky.

Taking a deep breath, I head out to the main room. The four of them are deep in conversation about giving me time and don't hear me enter. From the doorway I say, "That's not necessary, I'll tell you what I can."

Walking slowly over to the couch, I take a seat, wincing in pain as I sit down. Four sets of eyes watch my every move. Closing my eyes, I take a deep breath. "I can't tell you much. All I know is we were here to meet him, we were going to dinner and then I'm not sure; probably back here for...umm, you know. But when we got here, he decided otherwise." Pausing, I swallow hard. "That's all I can tell you."

Logan stands up and shouts, "That's fucking bullshit, Sarah, that's not all there is!"

Kenzie grabs Logan's arm and pulls him into the kitchen, I can hear her ripping into him and it makes me smile. Officer Jones comes and sits on the coffee table. "Look, Sarah. I know this is scary, but you need to tell us a name at least."

"Xander, that's all I know. I honestly don't know his last name." Hanging my head in shame at not knowing that information.

"Thanks, Sarah. We will leave you be. We have your details and if your friend changes her mind, give us a call or if you remember anything else please call me. Here's my card." She passes me her card and I spin it in my fingers, staring into space after I say goodbye to them.

The front door clicks and I look around the room, Kenz and Logan are in the kitchen whispering to each other. All of a sudden, I smell coffee and smile.

———

While the three of us are in the lounge room chatting, Morgan sneaks out of the hotel room. How we didn't hear her leave still amazes me. I've tried calling her but her phone goes straight to voicemail. I'm really worried about her.

After Xander attacked Morgan and me, I left the apartment and moved in with Logan. Even though he said some horrible things to me, they were all true and my feelings for him are much too strong to ignore. Plus he came running when I was in trouble.

I held my ground and refused to go back the police, I just want this to be over and bringing them in will only prolong that. Kenz and Logan didn't agree with me, but eventually they stopped asking me to.

Logan has been working from the penthouse and Kenz has stopped by every day to visit. I'm thankful for their support and friendship but I just want some me time.

Ten days after the attack, I'm finally starting to feel like me again. I still have not been able to reach Morgan, and that worries me. After lunch today, Logan has to head into the office, and finally, for the first time since the incident; I'm alone. It's so peaceful being here by myself, so I curl up on the patio with a coffee and read the next book in the *Storm* series. This book is forking awesome and the craziness that has become Lexi's life is a great escape.

My peace is disturbed when my phone rings, picking it up I see that it's Victoria. Against my better judgment, I answer the phone. Walking over to the edge, I look out at the river, hoping the water will have a calming effect on me as I take this call. "Hello, Victoria."

"So you are alive."

"No thanks to Xander."

"I'm sure you're exaggerating, besides that's all in the past, dear, now when are you returning?"

"I'm not. Victoria, I'm done."

"You will be done when I say you are done. Sarah, your have twenty-four hours to get back to the apartment."

A surge of confidence flies through my body and I quickly reply, "No, Victoria. I'm not coming back and you can't make me."

"Is that really what you think?"

"I don't think, I know."

She laughs in her fake hoity-toity laugh, "You will return to the apartment. End. Of. Story." Pausing for a few moments, she adds, "You wouldn't want anything to happen to Mackenzie, Rory, Indy, or Morgan now, would you? And you definitely don't want it to get out that up and coming businessman, Logan DeBiers, uses an escort agency. Would you now, dear?"

"You wouldn't."

"Just try me, Sarah. You have twenty-three hours and fifty-seven minutes to get back to the apartment. After that time, I guarantee you that I will follow through on my previous threats. Mr. DeBiers will be splashed all over the front page of every newspaper in Australia and around the world."

Before I can reply, she hangs up on me. Dropping my phone, I slide down the wall and sit on the patio floor, my heart hammering in my chest. Hugging my knees so I'm squishing my boobs, I start to cry. The tears cascade down my cheeks, leaving mascara track marks in their wake. I thought it was too easy to get away.

My heart is breaking once again but this time I'm choosing, well, being forced, to walk away because I refuse to bring Logan down, and I will not compromise the safety of Kenz, Mac and Cheese, or Morgan. Unless I heed to Victoria's demands, she will destroy those that I care about the most and I cannot let that happen. I refuse to let them suffer due to my stupid decision.

Things were starting look up again after the attack. Moving in with Logan was perfect, all my worries were lifted and I was smiling again; really genuinely smiling. But in typical Sarah style, it's all fucked up again. Now, all because of me; his life and business are being threatened by the devil herself; unless I do this. I have to do this. To save Logan, I have to walk away, but I don't know if I'm strong enough to stay away this time.

Taking a deep breath, I stand up, head into the bedroom, and pack what few things that I have with me. Once packed, I head into the kitchen, placing my bag on the black leather breakfast barstool. Through my tears, I write a goodbye note to Logan, struggling to breathe as my heart breaks into a million tiny shards.

Logan,
I'm sorry. I can't do this with you right now. I need to find myself and I refuse to bring you down with me while I do that.
You will always be in my heart and thoughts.
Love always and forever,

Sarah

With tears pouring down my cheeks, I place the note on the island bench, next to my access card, before grabbing my bag off the stool. Turning around with my shoulders held high, I walk out the door towards the lifts and push the call button. I know this is the right thing to do, even if I'm dying on the inside. With a ding, the lift doors open and for the last time I leave the one place that I was truly happy.

The last week has been agony. I'm missing Logan with all my heart and Victoria is running me ragged. She keeps sending me out to social gatherings and galas with Xander. He's such a smarmy bastard, I can't stand to be around him, but thankfully he hasn't tried to sleep with me again. What I wouldn't give to attend a boring art gallery with Chow. The other clients are all just handsy and slimey, thankfully no hanky-panky; not even from Xander and that's frightening.

Bitchtoria is trying to break me but I refuse to let her win. I'm going to find a way out of this, and in the meantime, I'll cozy up to the devil herself until I can make my move and trust me; I will take her down.

The hardest part of all of this is missing Logan, I've been ignoring all of his calls and I've pretended not to be home when he has stopped by, but it's getting harder and harder to ignore him. There is a magnetic pull between Logan and me and it's strong, but I have to do this...for him...for us...for everyone, even if I'm miserable in the process. One of these days, I will give in and answer his call and when I do, I know I'll crumble, but I have to be strong...for now at least.

Logan was my saving grace. He came along when I was at my lowest. He made me feel happy and safe; I started smiling again, the old me was resurfacing. Soon, I'll be able to be with him again, but first I need to finish this. I need to find a way to end this and get my life back.

36

VICTORIA

That feeling of being watched is back, it has been, on and off, for the last few weeks now. I'm sure I'm being paranoid but with all that is going on anything is possible. Since Xander lost his shit with Sarah and Morgan, I keep waiting for a visit from the police but so far nothing; and that's just as frightening, if not more so.

No one has seen Morgan since the incident, but ever since Angel was found, she hasn't been herself. To be honest, for once a girl leaving has been for the best.

Business is booming again, and the cliental has returned to those worthy of being an Elite client. Sarah is booked solid for the next few days, which gives me pleasure. Since her return, she has been sad and dejected, she's become a 'yes' bot and this has pleased me immensely. I keep giving her the more hands-on appointments, waiting for her to crack; I will break her yet...just you wait. I've even sent her to galas with Xander and he has ramped up his obsession with her, similar to when she first started. She has to realise that no one tells me they are leaving. I make the rules and everyone will abide by them; regardless of whom they are.

Sarah broke not one, but two cardinal rules, don't fall in love and don't fuck with me. When that trust is broken, it's hard to win back said trust. Even though she is exceeding my expectations at the moment, I don't trust her one iota, and trust is key in any successful business.

I've just hung up from Mr. DeBiers again; he's still trying to get me to let go of Sarah. He is relentless, I will give him that but she's my moneymaker, and I will not be letting go of her anytime soon. I didn't want to go there, well, yeah, I did, this time I threatened her safety. Not that I would ever do anything to harm her, well not personally, but he doesn't need to know that. I can guarantee that nothing per se will happen to her, but accidents do happen.

I'm still confused to everyone's fascination with her, but after twenty years in this business, nothing surprises me. When she first started, she reminded me of when I became an escort, working for Esteban. I was hoping to mold her into me, possibly even passing the reins over to her one day, but now that will not happen.

Esteban, I haven't thought of him in a very long time and I can't help but smile. He was the father that I never had and he molded me into the sophisticated lady that I am today. It was a shame he passed in the manner that he did, but Alexander and I didn't need him anymore.

Simon calls to tell me he is running late, so I'm decide to wait in the bar, and I'm glad that I did. I feel his presence before I see him, looking around the bar I see him and smile. He starts making his way over to me and I start to grin, watching all the women swoon over him when he's mine, all mine. "Good evening."

"Good evening, Sir. Care to join me?"

"Why thank you." Before he sits down he kisses me deeply and I become a puddle of mud. He is the only person who makes me weak at the knees. Breaking our kiss, he winks before taking the seat next to me. Stephen comes over with a tumbler of scotch and a glass of champagne for me.

Looking over at him, I smile. "So I guess you and I have a date."

"Yes, Vicky, you and I have a date, but I'd much rather be in your office ravishing you."

"After what you recently pulled, what makes you think I want that?"

"You know you want me," he arrogantly replies but he knows me too well. "Just like every other woman in this room, you want me between your thighs."

"Don't be so crass."

"You love it when I speak dirty to you, Vicky. You want my cock buried balls deep inside that sweet cunt of yours as I pound into you, biting your tits as I choke you, summoning all sorts of pleasure."

His words cause me to clench my thighs together, my pussy throbbing with want and need. I swallow hard; he smirks smugly at me before he throws back his drink. Standing up, he puts his hand out to me. Accepting his outstretched hand, I stand up. He tugs me closer to him and smashes his lips against mine in a searing kiss.

Pulling back, he looks into my eyes and he knows he has me hooked. "The office, five minutes. You know what I like."

He shoves me towards the exit and I nearly trip on my heels, but I regain my composure and head towards the door. On my way out, I notice a man standing by the bar talking to Simon. He looks familiar but all I can currently think about is what's about to happen and the throb in my pussy.

When I get to my office, I quickly unlock the door and head over to the seating area. I'm feeling particularly naughty this evening so I defy him; I remove my undies and my undies only. I go and sit on the coffee table. Inching my skirt up, I run my finger up and down my slit, making myself wet, the need for him to ravish me increasing. Perching myself on the edge, I spread my legs wide and continue to pleasure myself, so when he enters he can see my bare, wet pussy. Leaning back on my arm, I wait.

A few moments later, the door slams open and Morgan is thrust into the room, she falls to her knees and scurries towards my desk. She is crying when he storms into the office, furiously slamming the door behind him. Quickly, I remove my finger, close my legs and jump up, thankful that I defied him tonight. "What's going on?"

"Seems we have a problem, a massive fucking problem," he snarls, before stalking over and kicking Morgan in the face, knocking her out cold. He turns to me, fuming. "I thought you took care of our problem."

"I did, I assure you that I did. She has been cooperating and being the model employee, just like in the beginning."

"Well, obviously she's been deceiving you because someone has been snooping in our affairs, Victoria, and they know everything. They know every-fucking-thing, Vicky."

37

LOGAN

Once again, Sarah is ignoring my calls. It has been seven, painfully long days with out her. I'm going out of my mind here, I need her in my life and at this point, I would do just about anything to have her safely beside me.

My PI and I are currently playing phone tag and that is pissing me off too. Earlier today, I yelled at Beth for something that I fucked up, and now I feel like a douche for doing that. Everything is falling apart at the moment, it's like I stepped on a crack, killed a black cat, and smashed a billion mirrors.

Finally, my PI and I speak. "Justin, please tell me you have something. I'm going out of my mind here."

"Logan, it's good to chat to you as well. I'm fine; thanks for asking."

"Yeah, yeah. Just tell me what you have...please?"

"WOW, you really love this girl don't you?"

"With all my heart, I need something so I can get her out of there."

"Well, today will be your lucky day. I hit the jackpot with what I've found, but before I tell you, please don't do anything stupid. These two are batshit crazy."

"What do you mean two? I thought...I don't know what I thought."

"Well, you thought wrong. She runs it with her husband, and from what I've discovered, they take anyone out who is threatening their empire or gets in their way. That girl you mentioned, Angel, she was killed by them. My guys have proof that their driver, a umm, Simon Jameson, killed and dumped her body. It looks like they have killed many more ex-employees, too. The number listed as missing is staggering. They also have a subsidiary that deals in drugs and the sex trade. Logan, you need to get your girl out of there and quick smart."

"Holy fucking shit." *What have you gotten yourself into, Sarah?* I think to myself. "I promise I'll be safe, Justin. I'm going to get my girl out of there, you can hand what you've found over to the police. I want these assholes taken down and I want them to stay down."

"Can do. Now go get your girl."

"Will do. Thanks again, Justin. I really appreciate all your help."

"Anytime, Logan, anytime."

Hanging up from Justin, I sit in my office chair and let out the breath that I didn't realise that I was holding. "Fuck, fuck, fuck," I say to myself before I grab my phone again. Dialing Sarah's number, I hope and pray that she will answer me this time. Thankfully she finally picks up on the second ring. "Hi," she shyly says. "I'm so sorr..."

Interrupting her, I forcefully ask, "Sarah, where are

you?" I feel bad for being abrupt but my main concern right now is Sarah and her safety. After what Justin told me about Victoria and her husband; I'm scared shitless.

"I'm at the apartment, Logan. I'm about to head outside and finish that *Storm* series that you recommended. I'm addicted and that Anthony dude is one crazy fucker."

"Sarah, listen to me...you need to get out of there; we have real life crazy fuckers to deal with."

"Why? What are you talking about? You're kind of scaring me, Logan."

I'm trying to get Sarah to listen to me, but I'm so worked up that I'm not explaining myself very well. She doesn't understand the danger that she is currently in. While I'm still on the phone, unsuccessfully trying to explain myself, I race down to the underground car park, jump into my car, and race over to her place, but a feeling of dread washes over me.

38

SARAH

"Sarah, you need to leave, now!" Logan shouts through the phone.

"Why? What's going on, Logan? You're kind of scaring me right now."

"You need to get out of there, Sarah. I'll be there to pick you up in five minutes."

"Logan, you're scaring me. What's going on?"

"I'm not trying to scare you, Sarah, but please, get out of there and wait downstairs for me. It's not safe for you there. Please," I beg.

"Okay, fine, I'll be downstairs in ten minutes."

"Five minutes, Sarah."

Hanging up from Logan, I race upstairs and quickly pack a bag, our conversation playing over and over in my head, but I can't really make sense of anything. All I know is that he is scared for me and wants me to leave. I trust him so, for once; I'm following his instructions. Zipping up the bag, I swing it over my shoulder; grab my handbag off the dresser and head back down the stairs. Swinging open the apartment door, I'm met with an enraged Victoria. With all her might, she pushes me back into the apartment, and in behind her walks Xander, with a frightened Morgan in his grasp. Her cheeks are stained with tears and her left eye is swollen shut and a deep shade of purple.

"Morgan!" I shout and try to get to her, but Xander shoves me hard in the chest.

"Shut the fuck up, bitch," Xander snarls before throwing Morgan towards the lounge room. Turning his attention to me, he roughly grabs me by my upper arm and drags me behind him into the room, throwing me onto the couch. His eyes are dark with rage, and in this moment, he gives me the creeps. Fear is coursing through my veins and I'm petrified.

Morgan groans in pain. Immediately I drop to the floor and crawl over to her, she's in the fetal position rocking back and forth, mumbling to herself. She flinches when I lightly touch her arm, but when she sees it's me, through her one good eye, she lifts herself up wincing in pain, wrapping her arms tightly around my neck. She starts to cry harder and I whisper, "Shhhh," as I rub her back gently.

"Ohh, how nice, slut two caring for slut one. It's such a shame that it has to end like this because you two are phenomenal together...maybe I'll get one more in before it all has to end."

From the bar, Victoria scoffs as she pops the cork on a bottle of bubbly. *How can she be drinking at a time like this?* I think to myself as she pours two glasses, handing one to Xander before placing the bottle on the coffee table next to Morgan and me. She returns to the bar, grabs her flute and raises it. "A toast. To good times and the end of Sarah Bryant."

"What?" I say.

Xander replies, "Cheers to that." They both silently salute each other before each taking a sip.

I'm sitting there stunned; I have no idea what is going on. Morgan is in a catatonic state, so I can't use her to help me get out of this. "I...I don't understand. What's this all about? I broke up with Logan, what more do you want?"

Victoria cackles as she stalks over to me, taking a seat on the coffee table edge she stares intently at me. "Well, my dear, it seems your ex-boyfriend." Air quoting ex-boyfriend, she continues, "Has been digging into Elite and me. Somehow he has discovered everything that Alexander and I have been up to, and now, you will suffer for his digging. We need to teach him a lesson." Pausing she takes a sip as Morgan moans. "Morgan here, was simply in the wrong place at the wrong time, just like Saskia, but since the demise of Angel, she has not been performing to her full potential. So it's a win/win for Elite and me to get rid of you both. We've worked too hard for it to all come crashing down now."

"Oh My God, you killed them, didn't you?" Victoria just smirks at me before taking another drink. "You killed them all," I whisper. Tears well in my eyes and I quietly ask, "Why?"

"Because we are Victoria and Alexander Chalmers. No one fucks with us, especially a little slut like you."

Morgan sits up and we both sit there open-mouthed and stunned at that revelation. Everything starts falling into place; to say I'm shocked is an understatement. "Oh My God! That explains why Xander always got special treatment from us girls, and why nothing was done when I told you that he beat the shit out of me and raped Morgan."

From behind me, Xander starts clapping, Morgan scurries towards the bar as he stands up and looks directly at me. "Ding! Ding! Ding! We have a winner. Luckily you're a better fuck than you are smart. It will be a shame that you won't be around anymore, but I can always find another cunt to fill the void. I refuse to be taken down by a slut and sloppy work." He turns around and shoots Morgan in the head, right between the eyes. She falls to the carpet, her lifeless eyes stare at me as blood pours down her face, pooling on the carpet beneath her.

A scream slips from my lips but stops when I hear another gunshot ring through the apartment. Turning my head, I see Victoria falling to the floor, landing on top of Morgan with a thud. "Bye bye, wifey, you got too cocky and this is all your fault." Staring at the dead bodies in front of me, I start screaming again. Xander lunges towards me and slaps me hard across the cheek, the butt of the gun catching my cheekbone. "Shut the fuck up, bitch." Dropping the gun next to the couch, he slaps me again and again before storming to the bar and pouring himself a scotch. Drinking it back before pouring another, he looks at me at says, "You and I have an empire to rebuild, Sarah. You and I will rule this city."

"You're a fucking crazy monster. I will never be by your side."

He doesn't say anything, he just stares and at me laughs; pouring drink after drink down his throat, muttering incoherently to himself.

Pulling my legs to my chest, I hug them tightly as I stare at Morgan and Victoria's lifeless bodies. My heart is beating so fast in my chest that it feels like it will burst through. I'm snapped back to reality when Xander crouches down in front of me and starts clicking his fingers in front of my face, I didn't even see him walk back over to me. "Hello, Earth to Sarah!" he shouts.

Shock is taking a hold of me, I start shaking my head from side to side, the tears cascading down my cheeks. "You...you killed them. Th...they're dead."

"Well, thanks for stating the obvious there. Now, if you don't want to join them with a bullet in that pretty little head of yours, I suggest you think carefully about what I said earlier. While your thinking about our future, pucker up and start sucking my cock...or better yet, bend over the back of the couch and let me fuck you. Sarah, it's our time to reign and it all begins now, just like it did with Vicky and me all those years ago when we took out Esteban."

I'm beyond frightened at the moment, I can hear Xander speaking but nothing is registering, it's all muffled. I'm snapped back to realty when my phone starts to ring. The damn Bluetooth on the *Bose* mini system connects and announces to the room, "Logan calling."

"Well, well, well, isn't that nice. Your non-boyfriend is calling my little whore. Go on; answer it. Tell him you are fine." He bends down and squeezes my cheeks roughly. "And don't fucking mention a thing about any of this...understood?"

Before I have a chance to answer, it's stops ringing and I breathe out a sigh of relief. Only for it to start ringing again. "Answer it, bitch, and put it on speaker." He looks at me before yelling, "NOW!"

Picking up my phone, I answer. "Hey, Logan."

"Sarah, where are you?"

"I'm...I'm with Morgan." As I say her name I look down at her body and my eyes well with tears. "She's turned up just after you called. She's not doing too well at the moment and she needs me. I can't leave her like this, Logan." Taking a deep breath, I add, "I'll call you when she's okay and I have her settled. Umm, Logan, I...I love you."

Xander grabs up my phone and throws it against the bar, smashing it into a million pieces. "You fucking little whore. I didn't believe Vicky when she told me that you were in love with the fucker. I just thought he was enamored with your hot little ass, like all of us are." He winks at me and I shudder. "Speaking of ass, bend over the couch now, I want to pop your ass cherry."

I'm frozen on the spot, I don't move a muscle; I'm in complete and utter shock. He wants to screw...my ass... with two dead bodies in the room, one of them being his wife. A surge of adrenaline courses through my body, I stand up and glare at him. "I'm not fucking you with your dead wife and my friend in the room. Actually, I'm never screwing again, you psychotic piece of shit."

"Like they care," he scoffs. "Now, strip off your clothes and bend over the couch." He starts stroking his cock through his pants and licking his lips, staring intently at me. "Now, bitch!" he bellows.

Swallowing hard, I look around the room for something to use as a weapon, but I'm pulled back to reality, literally, when Xander grabs me by my ponytail and throws me over the coffee table onto the couch, landing with a thud on my back. I shuffle back, trying to get away from him, but he's too strong for me. Pulling his arm back, he punches me in the stomach, knocking the wind out of me. "Ugh!" I moan as I curl into a ball to protect myself. Rolling me onto my stomach, he straddles my legs and shoves my skirt roughly up my hips, tearing my undies from my body. He frees his cock from his pants before pressing his body to mine. He whispers, "I'm go to fuck you one last time, and then I'm going to fuck you as I choke the life out of you." He licks my ear before sitting back up, I can feel his cock slide down my ass crack and it's in this moment I realise that he is going to rape me. My body tenses; fear taking me over. Closing my eyes, images of Mum, Dad, Kenz, Jordan, the girls, and Logan flash before me. I sadly smile; knowing that they will all be safe once I'm gone.

Tears pour down my face when a surge of adrenaline courses through my veins. With all my might, I wriggle and try to buck him off me. As he pushes me further into the couch, my arm drops off the side of the couch and my hand lands on his gun. My eyes fly open and I grin, gripping the butt of the gun tightly in my hand, I flick off the safety, and with all my might, I roll over and pull the trigger. The last thing I remember before passing out is the deafening sound of a gunshot.

39

LOGAN

WHEN THE LINE WITH SARAH GOES DEAD, I jump out of my car, not caring that I'm double-parked, and I race inside the building. Repeatedly, I punch the lift call button and eventually it opens. Racing in, I hit the button for her floor. The thirty second lift ride is excruciatingly slow. The elevator finally slows at her floor and when the doors open I hear a gunshot.

"Sarah!" I shout as I race towards the door.

It's locked! I take a step back and with all my might, I kick it down. The frame splinters and the door crashes into the apartment, smashing when it hits the foyer floor. Stepping over it, I race into the apartment but come to a halt when I enter the lounge room. The first person I see is Victoria slumped over a body, both of them lying in a pool of deep red blood. My heart stops, until I realise the person she's on top of has red hair, *"Thank God it's not Sarah,"* I think to myself, but then my heart breaks when I realise it's Morgan.

Looking around the room, I see a man slumped on top of a brunette, and I know that it's Sarah. Racing over to the couch, I pull him off her and I sigh in relief. I shout her name but she doesn't stir, she's covered in blood and I start to panic. Squatting down next to her, I check her body for wounds but I can't find any. Picking up her wrist, I check for a pulse and thankfully I find one. Gently I left her up and sit on the floor with her in my arms, crying in relief that she's alive. Pulling my phone from my jacket pocket, I call triple-O and tell them we need the police and an ambulance.

I've just hung up when Sarah stirs in my arms; she opens her eyes and blinks a few times. She stares up at me for a few moments before the waterworks erupt. "L... Logan," she sobs, before pushing herself up and wrapping her arms around me.

"Shhhh," I whisper, kissing her head. "I've got you now."

About twenty minutes later, I hear from the foyer. "Police"

"In here," I whisper-yell, as Sarah has passed out in my arms.

Looking up, I see two officers enter the room, followed by two ambo officers. They all pause midstep, open-mouthed and take in the scene.

"Who are you?"

"I'm Logan DeBiers and this is my girlfriend, Sarah Bryant. She needs medical attention, she keeps losing consciousness."

The ambos enter the room and one comes over to me. I lay her on the couch so he can assess her. The other ambo assesses Victoria, Morgan, and Xander, but he confirms that they are all dead.

"I'm Detective Ferguson, can you shed some light as to what happened here?"

Walking over to him, I give him as much as I know about what happened. I also tell him what my PI had discovered. They both look shocked but not completely taken by surprise. "You don't seem so shocked by what I've just said."

"I'm not. Victoria and Alexander Chalmers have been on our radar since the disappearance of Megan Hill six months ago and the recent murder of Angel Hurley piqued our interest."

"Holy shit. So Sarah is pretty lucky to be alive right now?"

"Yes, your girlfriend is extremely lucky, Mr. DeBiers. The Chalmers have been operating some very dangerous and shady endeavours but we have never been unable to nab them for anything. With the help of your PI, who I will need the details for, we should be able to close these two outstanding cases."

Before we can talk any further, the ambos are wheeling Sarah out, but she is still unconscious. "Excuse me, I need to go with her." Reaching into my pocket I hand over my business card. "Here are my details, feel free to call me anytime, but I'm sure I will see you at the hospital shortly."

———

"Thank you, we will see you when Sarah is up to chatting with us."

Sarah is admitted to hospital, but thankfully she has no major injuries, we just need to wait for her to wake up. The doctors advised that from all the excitement, if you'd call it that, her body has shutdown and needs time to recover. They said it's up to her as to when she wakes up.

After the doctors have left, I step out of her room and make a few calls. First, I call Beth and ask her to cancel everything for the rest of the week for me. Then I call Kenzie to let her know what happened, not looking forward to that call, she picks up after several rings.

"Hey, LDB, how are ya?"

"I've been better. Umm, Kenz, Sarah is in the hospital."

"What?" she bellows down the phone, deafening me. "Which hospital? I'm coming."

"She's at the Royal..."

Interrupting me she quickly says, "Be there soon," and hangs up on me.

Walking back in Sarah's room, I drag the recliner chair closer to her bed and take her tiny hand between mine. Lifting it to my lips, I place a kiss on her palm before gently placing it back on the bed and holding it tightly. "Please, Sarah, come back to me."

40

SARAH

My body feels heavy and I'm struggling to open my eyes. There's a loud noise ringing in my ears and a weight is crushing me. Suddenly the weight is gone and I can hear Logan. I manage to open my eyes. "L...Logan," I whisper as I start to cry. He wraps me in my arms and I feel safe, the heaviness takes over and once again everything goes black.

My body jolts and it feels like I'm floating. We come to a stop and I hear doors opening, metal clanking, and voices. I don't recognise any voices and I can't open my eyes. Logan, I feel and hear him but I can't open my eyes to see. Again, darkness takes over.

The next time I wake, I feel lighter than I did before and there's a constant beeping and voices. This time I hear Kenz and Logan, I try to talk but nothing comes out. I'm so tired; I drift back into blackness.

Finally my eyes open, after blinking a few times, my vision adjusts to the brightness and I glance around the room, I realise that I'm in a hospital and my body is aching. Someone next to me moves, they are holding my hand tightly and I hear them whisper, "Sarah, please come back to me."

Logan, I think to myself. "Hey," I manage to whisper; a lone tear falls down my cheek. "I'm sooooo sorry, Logan." Tears begin pouring down my face and my vision blurs. He stands up and carefully slides onto the bed and pulls me close to him. Wrapping my arm around his abdomen, I snuggle into him and cry. I must fall asleep because when I wake again the sun is just starting to rise outside and Logan is sound asleep next to me.

Looking over at him, I smile and he whispers, "Are you watching me sleep?"

"Maybe." Snuggling into his side, I breathe in his scent and it instantly calms me. Looking up at him, I hesitantly ask, "Logan, what happened?"

Before he can answer, a nurse walks into the room and asks Logan to leave so she can assess me and get me showered. He kisses me on the forehead and says he'll go get coffee and be back.

Forty minutes later, I'm freshly showered and sitting in the unflattering, itchy hospital gown when the door to my room opens. I'm hit with the amazing smell of coffee and Logan. My tummy rumbles really loud and Logan stops midstep, looking at me, and he laughs. "Well, hello to you, too."

"Hey," I manage to say, trying to pull the blanket up because I look like a mess.

"Are you cold? Let me help you." He places the coffee and bag on the bed table and helps me pull the blanket up.

"Not really but I look like shit, I don't want you to see me like this."

Looking at me, he smiles, pushes a strand of hair behind my ear, and kisses me forehead lovingly. "Sarah, you are absolutely beautiful. Black eye and all."

"I think you need your eyes tested." My tummy rumbles again.

"Well, let's get you fed and caffeinated and then we can get you out of here. I ran into the nurse, and she said you will be discharged later this morning."

My face drops when he tells me this, I don't want to go back to the apartment. Logan notices the change in my demeanor, as he places my coffee on the table he enquires. "What's wrong, Sarah? You're as white as a ghost. Do you need me to get the nurse?"

"No, I'm fine." Twirling the coffee cup in circles on the bed trolley, I look up at him and quietly whisper, "I don't want to go back to the apartment."

"Sarah, you're coming home with me. Your place is officially a crime scene." My head snaps up, tears welling in my eyes once again. "She's really gone, isn't she?"

Pushing the trolley to the end of my bed, Logan sits on the edge and pulls me into his arms. "Yes, Sarah, she's gone." He holds me tightly as I cry for both Morgan and Angel. Once I've composed myself, he fills me on in everything that the detective told him yesterday as I sip on my coffee and nibble on my carrot and walnut muffin. When we have finished our coffee and muffins, Logan climbs into bed with me and I drift off to sleep in his arms.

I awake to the sound of giggling, Logan is entertaining Indi and Rory in their pram and Kenz is staring at me. "Morning, Sleeping Beauty. How you doing?"

"Did you just Joey me?"

"Normally I would be, but at this specific moment I'm just asking how you are."

"I...I don't really know, to tell you the truth." A lump forms in my throat as I say this.

"Yep, I know that feeling, but trust me when I say, you will be fine. You are strong and you have wonderful friends to help and support you."

Kenzie's words open the floodgates and once again, I'm crying. She climbs into bed next to me and wraps me in her arms. Pulling away, I shuffle around and rest my head in her lap; she rubs my hair and lets me cry. Kenz doesn't say anything but she says everything with her actions, she's my person and I'd be lost without her.

Opening my eyes, I look up to see that I'm still lying in Kenzie's lap, she has my iPad and is reading. She notices me stirring and says, "This book is amazeballs, Sarah. This M Stratton is forking awesome, I'm totally swooning over Noah and Lexi is totally kick-ass."

"Don't let Jordan hear you say that, you know he gets jealous when you gush over fictional characters."

"Pfft, he'll get over it." Putting the iPad on the bed trolley she shuffles around, I realise her legs must be dead from me laying on them. "Sorry, your legs must be killing you from my fat head sleeping on them, but if it's any consolation, I feel much better now."

The door to the room opens and Logan walks in. "Glad to hear that you feel better." Leaning down he kisses my forehead before nodding at Kenz. He places a tray of coffees on the bed table and takes a seat on the recliner.

"Logan, you are a gem. I've been dying for a coffee but Sleeping Beauty here had me pinned to the bed." Grabbing a coffee, she moans, "God, I love coffee."

Logan and I both laugh; it feels good to laugh again. Looking between Kenz and Logan, I realise that I'm lucky to have such great people in my life. There's a knock on the door and it edges open, peeking around is Mum. She smiles at me, and when I see her, I jump off the bed and race over to her. "Mum," I say through tears as I wrap my arms around her, hugging her tightly. I feel a hand rub my back and I look up to see Dad standing there. "Daddy," I say before wrapping an arm around him, I'm enveloped on a Bryant family hug. The three of us stand there hugging, Mum and I crying, and for the first time in months, I know that everything will be fine. Mum and Dad are back in Australia, Victoria and Xander are no longer a threat, I have my best friend back, and I hope, that Logan and I can get back on track, too.

The moment is interrupted when a detective and Officer Hamilton enter my room. They ask everyone to leave so I can give my statement; I ask if Kenz can stay, I don't think I can do it by myself. Mum, Dad, and Logan exit my room, as the door is closing, I hear Logan introducing himself to Mum and Dad, and once again I find myself smiling.

After the door closes, Officer Hamilton is the first to speak, "Kenzie, it's nice to see you again, and for once, I'm not here to speak to you."

"Shocking I know. We missed you at Mike's house-warming the other week."

"Yeah, I was on night duty. I heard it...." A throat clearing interrupts our conversation. "Sorry, this here is Detective Ferguson, he is the lead on this case. He has been following Victoria and Alexander "Xander" Chalmers for quite a while now. Sarah, he has a few questions for you, are you up for answering them?"

Nodding my head. "Umm, yeah, I think so."

For the next forty minutes I recall everything from the moment I met Victoria at The Dirty Duck up until yesterday. I omitted the names of clients because I don't want to get any of the nice ones in trouble, but I'm pretty sure they will have the names from the books. No surprises that 'Sleazy Simon' rolled over and spilled his guts about all the dirty work that he did for the Chalmers over the years that he worked for them.

After the detective and officer leave, Mum, Dad, and Logan come back in and they are all laughing. Seeing them together like that gives me a warm and tingly feeling inside. Josh never had that kind of relationship with my parents and here's Logan joking around, and he's only known them for less than an hour.

Kenz nudges me and winks; I swear that girl knows exactly what I'm thinking. She and I are grinning and giggling at each other, just like we used to when we were thirteen when Mum says, "What are you two giggling like schoolgirls over?"

"Nothing," we both say at the same time and this cracks us up. While we are still laughing the nurse comes in, and says that morning visiting hours are over, and that they can came back for this evening's hours. They take turns hugging me bye and they all leave, Logan hangs back and sits on the edge of my bed. Leaning forward he rests his forehead against mine and whispers, "I'm so glad that you are safe. When I heard that gunshot, my heart literally stopped beating, and then when I saw all the blood and you not moving, I thought I'd lost you. Sarah, you mean the world to me, and when you are released from here you are moving in with me, no questions, no objections, it's just happening."

"Okay," I whisper.

"Sarah, I mean it you are mov...hang on, did you just say yes?"

"Yes, Logan, yes..."

Kenz comes back into the room and squeals. "Oh My God, you two are getting married?"

Both our heads snap towards her, Logan's face pales, and I quickly say, "Fuck no." Logan looks at me, "Sorry, but no, not getting married; just moving in together."

Logan whispers, "Yet!" I hear it and butterflies appear in my stomach at that thought, and I can't help but grin. This year has been rough but finally I'm on my way to getting my happily ever after.

41

SARAH

...7 months later

Sitting on the plane, I still have on the eye mask that Logan has made me wear since we left home earlier this morning. Home: I love that Logan and I have a home together. There was a time when I thought I'd lost him forever, but fate was on our side, and we are now together, I'm over the moon happy...wearing a blindfold on a plane; never thought I'd say that in a sentence. I'm sure that I got some weird looks as we walked together through the airport, but to be honest, as much as I'm complaining and being obnoxious, the not knowing where we are going is really exciting.

All of a sudden, I feel Logan fiddling with the blindfold and he slips it off, blinking a few times, my eyes adjust to the light. I look over to see Logan staring at me with a huge grin on his face. "Hi," I manage to squeak.

"Hi yourself." He winks at me, before handing me a glass of bubbly. "A toast," he says, raising his glass. "To us and our happily ever after." He winks at me again, as our glasses gently touch and we each take a sip.

"So, why are we finally getting out happily ever after, again? You know, I got mine when you and I moved in together."

"Happily ever afters are forever, Sarah, and our forever is just beginning. Therefore there will be many, many special occasions to add to our happily ever after, and I'm pretty sure that this one will top moving in together." He palms my cheeks and rubs my jawline with his thumb as he says this. Closing my eyes, I lean into his hand, enjoying the moment. Gently, Logan turns my head towards the window and then I see it...sparkling azure blue water and white sandy beaches below.

Snapping my head towards him, I excitedly ask, "Are we?" Turning my head back towards the window, I lean forward. " Seriously, are we heading to Bora Bora?"

"Surprise," he says.

Turning to face him, I undo my seatbelt and jump into his lap, smashing my lips to his as I throw my arms around his neck. He wraps his arms around my waist and everything around us fades away; I'm lost in this kiss and Logan. We are brought back to reality by the airhostess clearing her throat. "Excuse me, the captain has turned the seatbelt sign back on as we are about to land. Can I get you to hop back into your seat and buckle up please?"

"Yeah. Umm, sorry. Sure," I say, as my cheeks turn fifty shades of pink and I hop back into my seat. Logan just sits there laughing at my embarrassment and me. "Shut up, butthead."

"Butthead, wow, bringing out the big guns there, pinky."

"Shut up, or you won't get any sex tonight."

"Pfft, like you could not want a piece of this?" He sits there with an unsexy smug look on his face, roaming his finger up and down his body.

I can't help it and I burst out laughing. "Dream on, buddy, dream on."

"Okay, let's make a deal. You will be begging me for sex later this evening and when you do, you have to do ANYTHING that I say."

"And when I don't beg for sex?"

"Whatever you want."

"Ummm, you and me, spa day, the works."

Without hesitating, not missing a beat, he stretches out his hand and confidently says, "Deal." I'm kind of scared with how easy he agreed to this but I'm so winning this bet.

"Deal. My vag is closed for the next twenty-four hours."

"We'll see."

I'm scared….I'm excited…I'm so going to win this…I hope…

42

LOGAN

I'm so winning this bet, and by the end of the day, Sarah will be beneath me screaming my name in pleasure. This will be the easiest bet I have ever won...but I do hold an ace up my sleeve that is a kind of an unfair advantage, but all's fair in love and war.

Keeping this secret and surprise from Sarah has been killing me, we don't have secrets—well, except this one and one other, but really it's not a secret, it's just an omission of something. Thankfully, I now only have one omission that I'm hiding, and it's even better than the Bora Bora surprise...less than twelve hours to go.

Once we have cleared customs, someone from *St. Regis Bora Bora* meets us and we have a short private boat ride to the resort. The look on Sarah's face is priceless, she is so excited and happy; she's beaming. Her hair is blowing in the wind on the transfer; she has never looked more beautiful. She must sense me staring at her because she looks towards me. "What?" she asks.

"Nothing, you just look absolutely fucking gorgeous right now, Sarah."

Her cheeks tinge pink and the corner of her lips lift up in a smirk, she gives me an emphatic cheesy smile. "You don't look too bad yourself, Mr. DeBiers. Play you cards right and you might get lucky." She lifts her eyebrows in a seductive way before realising her mistake, quickly adding, "In twenty-four hours you'll get lucky."

"We'll see," I say before pulling her closer to me and holding her tightly as the boat glides across the crystal clear water. Just the feel of her in my arms has my cock twitching...*It's going to be a long twenty-four hours if she holds up her end of the bargain*, I think to myself, but I'll have her begging for me before that time, mark my word.

"Fuck me, this is stunning, Logan. I've always wanted to come here but this, this is, magical...I'm speechless."

"That'd be a first." That comments garners me a smack in the ribs and a scowl. I wink and Sarah can't contain her smile and the corner of her lips lifts slightly. I'm mesmerised by her beauty and it's in this moment that I know, Sarah is the one for me and this trip will be perfect.

We disembark the boat and make our way to check in. Lacing my fingers with Sarah's, we head inside reception; she lightly squeezes my hand. Tugging her closer, I place my arm over her shoulder and she wraps her arm around my waist; we fit together perfectly. As we approach the reception desk we are warmly welcomed. "Mr. and Mrs. DeBiers, welcome to the St. Regis Bora Bora."

"Ohh, we're not married," Sarah quickly says, my

heart deflates at how quickly she shut him down, but inside I'm saying, *yet*.

"My apologies, ma'am." A laugh erupts from me because I know how much Sarah despises being called ma'am.

"Please don't call me ma'am either, Sarah will be fine."

"Duly noted, Sarah. I hope you had an uneventful journey here?"

"It was smooth sailing. It's absolutely gorgeous here, I can't wait to explore."

"Yes, we are very lucky, but I'm afraid your exploring will have to wait, Sarah. We have you booked into *Miri Miri* for a pampering package."

Sarah inquisitively looks towards me. "Surprise." I say, with a smile.

"Logan, what have you done?"

"Nothing, I just wanted you to have a little pampering so you'd be relaxed for our holiday." She jumps towards me, wrapping her arms around my neck and plastering a kiss on my lips. Gripping her tightly, I kiss her back, coaxing her lips open as I slip my tongue into her mouth. *What I would give to sink myself balls deep inside of her right now,* I think to myself. Lowering her down, I lean my forehead against hers and whisper, "Sarah, I love you and if you keep kissing me like that I'm going to explode in my pants. Now, go to the spa and I'll meet up with you later this afternoon."

"But what will you do?"

"Sarah, we are in paradise, I'm pretty sure I can find something to keep me out of trouble. To be honest, I just want to relax so I think I'll laze at our villa and read that Stratton lady's book you keep raving about."

"The *Storm* series? Or *Fade to Black*?"

"The Black one, I finished the Storm one on the plane. She writes seriously messed up characters but it's like crack, I'm addicted."

"Told you, You'll love *Fade to Black* and Devon **SIGH**." Pausing, she winks at me. "Okay, well I'll meet up with you later?"

"It's a date."

Sarah kisses me on the cheek and then heads off with the lady from the spa, who appeared while we were chatting. Turning towards the desk, the clerk, Jonathan says, "Mr. DeBiers, I hope we didn't ruin your surprise."

"No, Jonathan, it's fine, she still doesn't know anything, just the way it's meant to be. Is everything set for this evening?"

"Yes, Mr. DeBiers everything is ready for 7:00 p.m. this evening and the others are all here, too."

"Great. Perfect. It's all falling into place and please, call me Logan."

In a little over five hours there will be no more secrets and Sarah will be getting the surprise of her life. I always thought I'd be nervous when I came to this point in my life but there are no nerves whatsoever, I'm excited for tonight and this next adventure.

The room attendant has just left and the villa phone rings. "Hello."

"Hey, everyone is here and we are all settled into our McMansion, seriously, Logan, this place is amazeballs."

"I'm glad, she still has no idea."

"She is either going to be pissed, or too shocked to say anything."

Together we both say, "And then pissed."

"Logan, you are perfect for her, and I'm so glad to be here and help you arrange all of this."

"Thanks, I appreciate it. Now, go chillax in your McMansion and I'll see you later this arvo."

"Sounds good to me. Later, dude."

After hanging up, I grab an ice-cold beer, my iPad, and head out to the deck, hoping to relax but I'm so nervous and excited that I can't concentrate. Grabbing another beer, I sit down on one of the outdoor lounges and look out at the view. It is magical here and the perfect place to make Sarah my wife.

43
———

SARAH

Oh My God, I have never been so relaxed in my entire life. I thought the spa that she-devil took us to was amazing, but the ladies here at *Miri Miri* are angels sent from heaven, with magical hands that know what they are doing. For a brief moment, I become sad at the loss of Angel and Morgan, but I tell myself that they are now happy and free.

I'm enjoying myself in the private wellness area, relaxing back in the spa, enjoying the tranquility, and a sneaky glass of bubbly when one of the staff comes out with an envelope for me. He places it on the sun lounger. "No rush, but this was waiting for you. Can I get you anything else, Ms. Bryant?"

"I'm fine, thank you. What time do I have to be leaving?"

"This area has been reserved for you for the rest of the afternoon. Please don't hesitate to ask if you need anything." He smiles before turning around and heading back inside the spa.

Resting my head back, I close my eyes to relax, but the note is eating at me so I climb out, wrap one of the fluffy white towels around me, and sit down. Picking up the card, I flick it open and I immediately recognise the handwriting. I smile as I begin to read.

My dearest Sarah,
You are the light of my life and I hope, as you are reading this, that you are relaxed and glowing. Please do me the honour of joining me this evening at 6:30 p.m. for a night that I hope you will never forget. When you are ready, head inside where your hair and makeup will be done and a dress is waiting for you.
I can't wait to see you
L

Holding the card to my chest, my smile deepens; I'm so excited to see what Logan has planned for me this evening. Looking at the time, I decide that I have enough time for one more dip before I have to head inside. Just as I've immersed myself in the water, another attendant comes back out with another glass of bubbly and a fruit platter. She places it next to me, not saying anything but her face is beaming; like I'm missing something but before I can ask she heads back inside.

I've finished the bubbly and fruit so I decide to head inside and get ready. When I walk in, the room goes silent, everyone is looking at me smiling; it's really weird. Someone claps their hands and then it's all go go go. I'm shuffled into the bathroom to have a shower; the *Clarins* products used here are divine. Stepping out of the shower, I dry off and lather my body in moisturiser before slipping on my robe once again. Walking out, I see a gorgeous, Grecian-style, ivory dress with gold embellishments hanging up and a purple and silver box sitting on the table next to it. Heading over, I lift the lid and inside is a pair of gold sandals, which match the dress perfectly, and an exquisite black and nude *Victoria Secret* bra and matching undies set. Reaching out, I run my fingers over the ultra soft material, a lone tear falls down my cheek; I never thought I would be this happy. The last seven months I have been happier than I have ever been and that's all because of meeting Logan.

Wiping the tear away, I carefully grab the bra and undies and slip into them. Pulling the robe back on, I head back out into the adjoining room and set up is a hair and makeup stand. "Please take a seat and we will begin," the lady says to me, gesturing towards the chair.

Smiling, I skip over to the chair and sit down. Another glass of bubbly is handed to me and as I sit here staring at myself in the mirror the ladies get to work; first my hair is done into a loose half up-half down style and curled, a crown of baby's breath is pinned in place. *I look like a Grecian goddess,* I think to myself. Then it's time for my makeup, the lady either has been warned I'm not really a makeup kind of girl, or she is just good at her job. She doesn't do a lot, but somehow my eyes pop; using a mixture of greys and pinks she gives me a smokey, sultry look that doesn't look over the top. My blush is light and my lips look amazing, the colour is perfect and looks like it's one of mine from home. Logan obviously had this delivered to them while I was being pampered. Once they are finished, I sit there staring at myself in the mirror, I haven't felt like this happy, relaxed version of Sarah in a long time. Looking towards the makeup artist, I say. "Thank you, I wish I could do my makeup like this."

"Your welcome. Now let's get you dressed, I hear there is a man waiting for you."

When she mentions Logan butterflies appear in my stomach, much like the first night met him, and I smile like the cat that got the canary. Even though Logan and I met unconventionally, I'm glad to have him in my life. Standing up, I walk over to the dress, and with the help of the spa staff, we slip it over my head and it fits like a glove. Finally, I slip on the gold sandals, completing my ensemble. Straightening up, all of the spa ladies are grinning and murmuring. Spinning around, I look in the mirror and my mouth drops open in shock. "I...I look like a bride."

"You look stunning, Sarah." Spinning around, I see Logan standing in the doorway with his hands in his pockets. He's wearing charcoal slacks, a white linen shirt, with the top buttons undone, and a suit jacket hugs his shoulders. "Logan!" I breathlessly say. I'm lost for words right in this moment. Looking around, I realise that everyone has left and it's just Logan and me, the heat radiating between us would be enough to melt steel. "You're early."

"I couldn't wait any longer to see you." He strides over to me, placing a gentle kiss on my cheek, sparking something deep inside of me. I feel lost when he pulls away but my cheek is tingling from where his lips just were. Reaching out, he grabs each of my hands, holding them tightly to his chest. "Sarah, you came into my life when I least expected it. We've been on an amazing journey together already, and I can't wait for our next adventure together." He lifts our clasped hands and kisses them, letting go, he bends down on one knee and I gasp. "Sarah Bryant, will you do me the honour of becoming my wife tonight?"

I'm frozen, my heart rapidly beating in my chest. Inside my head I'm screaming *YES! YES! YES!* but nothing is coming out. Logan squeezes my hands and I realise that he's talking to me. "Sarah, Sarah, are you okay?"

Shaking my head, I finally manage to say, 'Yes, yes, yes." Squatting down, I place my palms gently on his cheeks and kiss him. He breaks our kiss and slips on a white gold, princess cut diamond onto my finger. Staring at it, my mouth drops open at the ring. "Logan, this is, wow. It's simple yet stunning." Wrapping my arms around his neck, I kiss him again; this one is more passionate than the last. Pulling my head back, I ask, "Tonight?"

He laughs, "Surprise." Logan runs his palms softly up and down my arms. "Tonight, Sarah, I want you to become my wife tonight."

Open-mouthed I just stare at him, and without an ounce of hesitation, I quickly reply. "Okay, let's do it. Logan, I love you with all my heart, and I would be honoured to become Mrs. Logan tonight, but you have to promise me one thing?"

"Sarah, I would do just about anything for you to become Mrs. Logan, as you put it, tonight."

"We have to have another ceremony when we get home so our family and friends can be there."

"Anything for you. Now, let's go get married."

Standing up, I wrap my arms around his neck and kiss him again. "Let's do this." Grabbing his hand, I lead us to the doorway; opening it we walk down the hall into the waiting area of the spa. When we enter the staff all start clapping and whistling. Logan pulls me into his side, and I wrap my arm around his waist, and once again I'm beaming.

A man, in a chauffer's uniform, steps forward. "Mr. DeBiers, Ms. Bryant, your chariot awaits."

Logan and I link fingers as we walk out to the waiting golf buggy; the driver whisks us away, towards my happily ever after. We stop suddenly and Logan turns towards me, lifting the blindfold from the plane out of his pocket, he's smirking at me again. "Seriously?"

"Seriously. Now turn around so I can place this over your eyes."

"Fine," I huff. "Don't mess my hair or you die," I add with a smile, spinning around, but deep down I'm excited to see the next surprise. Logan ties the blindfold in place and then we are off again. Once again, the buggy stops, I feel Logan climb out and I'm left sitting here blindfolded. I can hear the waves gently crashing ashore. I smile, when I feel Logan grab my hand and escort me off the buggy. The ground sinks beneath my feet and I realise that we are on the beach. He pulls on my hand, halting me in my tracks, leaning forward he whispers, "Surprise." Lifting off the blindfold, I blink at the light and take in the view before me.

My mouth drops open in shock. "Fuck me," I declare, covering my mouth with my hand at my faux pas. Before me are my family and all our friends. Turning towards Logan, my eyes well with tears. "Logan," I manage to squeak out as the first tear falls.

"You like?" he hesitantly asks.

"More like, love." Shaking my head, my eyes continue to scan the scene before me. To the left is a large round table, set with candles and light pink roses, obviously for the reception. Down by the water is a timber arbor with white chiffon flapping in the wind and decorated with light pink flowers and greenery. "This is stunning, Logan." Turning to face him, I grab his hand and squeeze it. "I'm speechless."

Amanda, the celebrant from Kenzie and Jordan's interrupts us. "Are you ready?" she asks.

"Absolutely," I quickly reply. Logan leans over and kisses my cheek before walking down to the arbor by the water, leaving me standing there with Amanda. Kenzie and Dad appear, I can't hold back at tears anymore and the floodgates open. Kenz races over to me and wraps her arms around me. "Shhhh." Rubbing my back, she adds, "Surprise."

Laughing at her, I pull back. "You are a bitch, a totally big bitch, but you're my bitch sista and I love you for this." Dad steps towards us and he smiles at me. "Daddy," I manage to say before I start crying again. He envelopes me in a dad hug and it calms me immediately.

"Hey, munchkin," he says. "You've got a good one

there." He nods his head towards Logan, and I look to where he nodded and smile.

"I sure do."

"Let's get this show on the road," Kenz says.

Amanda and I have a quick chat so I know what's going on. I nod to everything that she is saying but I'm not really listening. I'm staring at Logan...my fiancé...my soon-to-be husband "I'm ready." Looking towards the sky I shout at the top of my lungs in excitement "I'm getting married." Everyone laughs. Logan smiles and winks at me, I know this is meant to be and it couldn't be more perfect.

Amanda heads towards Logan, Sav takes her spot next to Logan as his best man, and I have Kenz by my side, just like I was beside her on her special day. *A Thousand Years* by Christina Perri begins to play and that's Kenzie's cue. She heads down the aisle and Dad links his arm with mine. "You look beautiful and your mum and I are so proud of you."

"Thanks, Daddy," I choke out. Taking a deep breath Dad and I head down the aisle. My eyes are locked on Logan, my face is beaming, my eyes blurry with tears, and I realise that I am about to marry the man of my dreams in paradise.

Dad and I stop before Logan; he kisses me on the cheek, hands me over to Logan, does the manly hand-shake, one-arm hug thing and then he takes a seat next to Mum. Her face is streaked with mascara but she's smil-ing, she blows me a kiss before burrowing into Dad's side. Handing my bouquet to Kenz, I then turn and face Logan. Amanda begins to speak and I wink at Logan, everything around me fades away. As usual, I'm lost in everything that is Logan. I'm snapped back to reality when Logan squeezes my hands and clears his throat. "Sarah, you came into my life when I thought I had everything, but the more time I spent with you, I realised that I wasn't truly happy until I met you. We've been through so much together already, but I wouldn't change a thing because it led to this point in time. Sarah, I promise to always have wine and Jerry whenever you need it, but most of all, I'll always be here when you need me. Sarah, I love you with all my heart and soul."

Swallowing the lump that formed in my throat, I clear it and take a deep breath. "Logan, this is hard 'cause I've literally have twenty minutes to wrap my head around being engaged and now getting married." Looking out at everyone, I sternly say, "And you all are on my shit list for keeping this from me, but that can wait." Looking back to Logan, I wink. "Okay, sorry, here goes. Logan, you are everything that I dreamed and hoped for when I was a little girl and this is perfect." Flicking my hand around at everything, I wipe a tear before gripping Logan's hands again. "I never wanted this big 'look at me wedding' and this, this is beyond my wildest dreams. Logan, you are not only my partner but you are also my friend. You give me the strength and courage to go after my dreams, and when we get back, not only will we be starting a life as Mr. and Mrs. Logan; we will be starting a whole new chapter together. I can't wait for the next phase in our life. I love you, Logan."

Stepping forward, he dips me back and kisses me

deeply. Everyone cheers and Amanda says, "Not yet, Logan."

"Oops, I just couldn't wait."

"Two minutes, I promise," Amanda says. "Logan and Sarah, you have chosen today to become one, and with these rings that you are about to exchange, they symbolise your love and life together. Logan, please repeat after me. With this ring, I marry you and bind my life to yours. It is a symbol of my eternal love, my everlasting friendship, and the promise of all my tomorrows."

Logan slips on a white gold band onto my fingers and repeats the vows; rubbing my finger after slipping the ring on, I begin to cry. It's now my turn, I slip the ring on his finger and through my tears I repeat the vows.

"Logan and Sarah, today you have joined your hearts and love with not only each but also your family and friends. It is with great pleasure that I officially declare you husband and wife. Logan, again, you can kiss your bride."

Logan lifts his hands, encases my cheeks, and kisses me. My eyes close, my leg lifts and I quietly moan into our first official kiss. We rest our foreheads together as everyone around us cheers. "Wife, moan like that again and I won't be held responsible for what I do in front of our guests."

"Husband, don't make promises you can't keep." Before he can reply, I crash my lips against his and he dips me back, our lips not separating; everyone around us cheers and hollers again. Flipping me back up, Kenz hands me my bouquet. Logan takes my hand, our fingers entwine and I throw my arm up in the air in celebration of our nuptials and smile. Millions of bubbles appear around us, Indi and Rory giggle excitedly and chase the bubbles down the aisle. Jordan apologises and chases after them, scooping them up in his arms, so they can reach the higher bubbles.

Logan and I make our way down the aisle and over to Amanda. A table has been set up in the middle of a love heart made out of different shades of pink rose petals, and we sign the registry and pose for a few photos. The rest of the guests make their way to the table and Logan and I head down the beach for a few more photos.

We are walking along the beach, hand in hand as the sun begins to set; the orange orb of the sun is encased in purples, oranges, reds, and pinks—it's magnificent. Logan pauses and wraps his arms around me, "I love you, Mrs. DeBiers."

"I love you too, Mr. DeBiers." Dipping me down again, he kisses me deeply just as the sun dips below the horizon, leaving in its wake millions of tiny stars shimmering in the midnight black sky. "We better get to our reception, I need to yell at a few people."

"Save the yelling for tomorrow, wife. For today, let's just enjoy it."

"Fine, but how the fuck did you pull this off?"

"I'm awesome," he says with a cocky grin on his face.

"Yes, you are awesome, husband. Now let's get to our reception so I can take you back to our room and lose our bet." I pull on his hand and start walking back to everyone.

"I like the way you think, wife." Winking at me, he

adds, "My wedding present to you is a null and void on said bet."

"My hero, but I'm still getting sex, right?" I say, he stops suddenly and laughs, he pulls me into him and kisses me again.

"Sarah, I will be by your side for the rest of your life, anytime day or night that you need me; I will be there." My eyes light up at this, hand in hand, we silently continue the walk towards our wedding reception.

Jordan notices us first, clears his throat and declares, "Welcome Mr. and Mrs. Logan DeBiers." Everyone turns towards us and they start clapping and cheering. Indy and Rory toddle over to me and I drop to my knees to cuddle them. "Don't you two look lovely in your sauce covered dresses." They giggle before poking Logan's leg and running towards the water, Jordan chasing after them yelling for them to stop.

Standing up, I turn around and laugh at seeing Jordan trying to stop the girls from going for a swim. Kenz taps my arm and whisper-shouts, "That will be you soon, missus," before running down to the waterline and helping Jordan. I stand there watching the four of them splash around; I'm so happy that Kenz finally got her happily ever after.

Logan comes over and hands me a glass of champagne. "Here's to you wife."

"Why thank you, husband." Raising my glass, I look towards my husband. *I love saying that.* "To us."

He clinks his beer mug against my glass. "To us." He hooks his arm around me as we watch the McRoberts family splash around.

The rest of the night is spent mingling with our family and friends. I don't think I've stopped smiling, this is the happiest I have ever been, and it's all to do with my now husband. Sometimes life throws you a curve ball, but what I've learned is, it's how you swing and deal with it that makes you the person you are. I'm pretty sure that I've hit the home run.

EPILOGUE

Once again I have a goddam blindfold on. "Seriously, Logan, this blindfolding thing is getting old."

"I promise this will be the last time...in public anyway, in the bedroom, it stays."

My panties dampen when I think about the blindfold and what Logan and I did in paradise on our wedding night. "Fine, it can stay in the bedroom ONLY after this." Putting a lot of emphasis on the word 'only,' but truth be told, I'd go and do anything with Logan, blindfold and all.

He opens a door and carefully ushers me inside, taking a few steps forward, he tugs on my hand to stop me. He lifts up the blindfold and I'm standing at the entrance of an empty brick room, but on the wall is a sign. "What's this, Logan?"

"This is yours, Sarah."

"Are you shitting me?"

"No, I'm not shitting you. This is your bar, Sarah. This is my wedding gift to you."

"You bought me a fucking bar, seriously?"

"Seriously. A few months ago you mentioned that you wanted to open a wine bar one day, and one day is now."

"Fuck me dead, said Foreskin Fred, did you seriously buy me a bar?"

"Look at me, Sarah." Turning toward him, my breath catches. My husband is gorgeous and he just bought me a bar, a fucking bar. "Sarah, this is all yours, well ours, but yours. I want you to be happy and I know that this." Waving his hand around the room. "This has been your dream, and as your husband, it's my responsibility to make your dreams come true."

Throwing myself into him, he catches me and I wrap my legs around him, placing quick kisses all over him. "Thank you, thank you, thank you. You are the best husband ever, and when we get home tonight, you can do anything you want to me."

Pulling his head back so he can look directly into my eyes, "Anything?" he asks.

Leaning forward, I whisper in his ear. "Any-fucking-thing that you want. Now, husband, take me home so you can have you way with me and then I have a wine bar to open."

"Well, when you put it like that, let's go."

With myself still wrapped around him, Logan heads outside and hails a cab, directing him back to our penthouse. We could have walked because it's only a few blocks away but we have more pressing matters to attend to. The cab pulls up a few minutes later, Logan throws a twenty at the cabbie, pulls me out, and drags me inside.

Before the lift doors have closed, Logan is pushing me

towards the sidewall. His hands explore my body, squeezing and kneading my breasts through my shirt. A moan escapes my lips, closing my eyes, my head lolls back; Logan takes the opportunity and kisses his way up my neck. Our lips crashing together, he plunges his tongue deep into my mouth before nipping on my bottom lip. The lift doors open, he grabs my ass and lifts me up, I wrap my legs around him, my skirt bunching up around my waist. Not breaking contact, our lips are fused together as we make our way to the penthouse door. Without dropping me, he manages to get the door unlocked and open, striding inside; he kicks it shut with his foot.

Once inside, I rip my shirt off, pearl buttons flying everywhere, tinkering across the floor. Logan spins around and slams me up against the front door; his dick is already hard and is rubbing against my clit through my satin purple undies, invoking all sorts of pleasure and moans from me. "Logan," I whisper as he pulls back, lowering his zipper and shoving his pants and boxer briefs down. His cock springs free and the tip is glistening with precum. I lick my lips and my eyes heat with carnal hunger. He grips the side of my undies and tears them off me, sliding his finger through my wetness, up my slit and circling around on my clit. "Fuck me now," I whisper. With a thrust of his hips, his cock is deep inside of me. We both grunt as he continues to pound into me, my head banging on the door, but I don't care. The pleasure coursing through my veins in this moment is all-consuming. My orgasm begins to build, and when Logan slips a hand between us and begins to rub my clit, I detonate like a rocket; I launch off into ecstasy and scream his name, riding out this pleasure explosion. As I'm coming back to earth, I feel his cock harden and his body shudders as he releases his seed.

We stay locked in each other's arms, me still pinned to the front door, our breathing laboured, hearts erratically beating. Our foreheads resting together, opening my eyes, I see Logan staring at me. "Wow," is all I manage to say. Kissing Logan on the top of his nose, he smiles at me as he lowers me down, my legs still jelly like after such as intense orgasm. He pulls up his pants before grabbing my hand; he pulls me into our room and head towards the shower. Leaning in, I turn the shower on before spinning towards him. I look up at him and silently unbutton his shirt. As I push it off his shoulders, I lean forward and place tender kisses over his chest and up his neck. Once his shirt is off, I push his pants and boxer briefs down; he steps out, kicking them to the side. Stepping back, I remove my skirt and heels. Turning around I step into the shower, Logan follows me in. We begin to soap each other up, staring at each other, still not speaking.

Once we are all washed, I wrap my arms around him. "Thank you, husband."

"You are most welcome, wife. Now let me take you to bed and show you, slowly this time, just how much I love you."

"That's perfectly alright with me." Kissing him on the cheek, I turn off the water. We climb out of the shower and quickly dry off, before falling into bed together.

For the rest of the night, we show each other repeatedly how much we love one another. In the early hours of the morning, we fall asleep in each other's arms and it's the most relaxing sleep I've ever had.

...*Six weeks later*

I'm currently standing in the middle of my recently finished and fully stocked wine bar, and I could not be happier. Today is the grand opening of Wine Not. The last month has been bedlam trying to get the bar up and running, but when your husband, *I still love saying that*, owns a development company, things get done quickly, very quickly. Considering how fast he got it all done, I think he's been planning this for a while.

Sensing him before I see him, I turn around to see him walking towards me. He's dressed in dark denim jeans and an olive green button-up shirt; he's looking just as sexy as the first night I met him and I smile. "How you doing, wifey?"

"I'm nervous as all hell. What if no one turns up?" Biting my lip as my nerves continue to build.

"Sarah, have you looked outside? There's a line down the block waiting to get in and the reservation book is full for the next week. This is going to be the hottest place in town."

Taking a deep breath, I smile, kiss Logan quickly, take another deep breath, and say. "Let's do this."

Walking towards to front doors, I open them to a round of applause. I smile in embarrassment but deep inside I'm ecstatic with the reaction I just received. First in line is Kenz, no surprises there, with Jordan, Mike, and

Sav next to her. Just behind them is Mum and Dad, having the six of them here, seven if you include Logan, makes me so over the moon happy that I don't have to hide what I do for a living anymore.

"Welcome, everyone. Wine Not is officially open!" I excitedly shout.

Another round of applause and cheers erupts from the crowd. I step aside to let everyone in, hugging and kissing my family and friends on their way past. The staff quickly jumps into action and assign people to their tables or the bar.

Opening night goes by in a blur, I think it went well but I'm currently floating on cloud nine—I have my own wine bar, thanks to my husband and I'm finally living the dream. For a while there I was lost, alone, and heading down a dangerous path, but under not so conventional circumstance, I met a wonderful man who put me back together. He made me whole again, and now Sarah DeBiers nee Bryant is going to have a winetabolous life with the man of my dreams and a plus one...shhhh!

2ND EPILOGUE

Wine Not has been open for three weeks now, and we are just as busy now as we were in opening week; Logan was right, this place is the hottest new bar to open. It's a Sunday afternoon and everyone is here for a catch up. After we all reunited, we agreed to a monthly catch up and it rotates as to which couple hosts. This month I'm excited to host because it will be my first one at Wine Not.

Mike and Sav are the first to arrive; he has his arm draped around her shoulders and she snuggles in close to him. They are deliriously happy, smiling and laughing—no doubt Mike said something really inappropriate that is somehow funny. In all the years I've known Mike, I don't think I have ever seen him this happy, and who would have thought his happiness would come in the form of my husband's childhood best friend, Sav—it's such a small world.

Next to arrive is the McRoberts clan. Indy and Rory come racing in with a frazzled looking Jordan and Kenz close behind. I hear Jordan telling Kenz that they are getting faster and faster and they need those backpack lead thingies and Kenz snaps, "We are not putting our girls on leads, that's just wrong." And they head towards Mike and Sav, who are sitting at the bar. From where I'm standing, I giggle to myself and think that will be Logan and I soon; I can't help but smile and I subconsciously rub my tummy.

Walking over to the twins, I squat down and they both jump into my arms and hug me at the same time, knocking me on my butt and they fall on top of me. The three of us giggle, and then I panic that I may have hurt the baby, so I sit up and place them between my legs, and we start to play with the dollies that they bought with them.

My skin prickles and I look towards to door, and in walks my sexy as sin husband. He's dressed in his denim jeans that hug his ass perfectly and my favourite charcoal, short-sleeved, button-up shirt. He sees me on the floor with the girls, winks and heads towards to bar and everyone else.

After a few moments, I stand up and head over to join everyone. Kenz hugs me hello and I turn and snuggle into Logan's side, He places a gentle kiss on my forehead and I melt into him. Kenz passes Sav a glass of wine and then hands me one, *SHIT*, I think to myself. She grabs another glass and hands it to me. "Umm, not for me, thanks."

"Pfft, when have you ever turned down a wine?" Pausing, her mouth drops open. "Fuck, you're up the duff!" she exclaims, "Aren't you?"

I've never been one to lie or hide anything—well except for before but that was different, so my face begins to burn and turn red. I look up towards Logan and quietly say, "Surprise." Logan immediately wraps his arms around me and spins us around, pressing his lips against mine and kissing me. When he places me down, he looks me in the eyes. "Really?"

"Really, Really."

From the bar, I hear Mike say, "Did they just quote *Shrek* to each other?"

In unison Sav and Kenz say, "Shut up, Mike." Jordan laughs and Kenz smacks him in the stomach.

"I'm nine weeks along." Watching Logan, I can see his mind ticking and then it clicks. Nodding I say, "Yep, the night that you gave me the keys to this place is when peanut here was conceived."

"I love you, Sarah DeBiers. You are going to be the best mum."

"I love you, Logan DeBiers. You are going to be the best dad."

Logan pulls me in close and kisses me deeply. I forget where we are and I kiss him back. It isn't until we hear hollering and whistles that we turn towards the bar and to the beaming faces of our friends. We pull apart and walk over to them, the girls envelop me in hugs and the boys do their manly shake/hug thing.

Mike clears his throat. "Well, while we are celebrating, umm, Sav and I are getting married. I asked her to be my ball and chain forever." Sav whacks him in the stomach and he grunts. "I mean lovely wife," he says through clenched teeth.

Kenz says, "Looks like it's a double celebration then."

"Nothing you want to celebrate, Kenz?" I ask.

"How about we celebrate friendship, family, and love."

Everyone grabs their drinks and we all toast to friendship, family, and love. Our glasses all chink together and we all fall into easy conversation: drinking, eating, and enjoying each other's company. The six of us have a winetabolous night together and it feels so good.

Finally, I'm content and happy in life. I'm married to a wonderful man, we both have successful businesses, we are expecting out first baby, and all of our nearest and dearest are living life to the fullest. Life could not be any better; we all got our happily ever after.

THE END !!!

CHAPTER 1
Kenzie

For the first time in what feels like forever, I'm awake before the girls. With a smile on my face, I quickly strip off my PJ pants, undies, and singlet and cozy up to Jordan. He's facing away from me, so I press my breasts against his back and drape my arm over him, snaking my palm down to his cock. I grip it tight and gently begin to stroke him, as I nuzzle along his neck and up to his ear. His body stirs and he effortlessly rolls onto his back. He gropes my ass and lifts me so I'm straddling him. Gripping my cheeks, he pulls me down and secures his mouth against mine. Circling my hips, I begin to grind myself on his now stiff cock. Wrapping his arms around me tightly, we continue to kiss. Lifting up, I position his rock hard cock at my entrance and lower myself down, his length filling me completely. I moan into his mouth as we begin to thrust together. Sitting up and resting on my knees, I continue to ride him as he plays with my breasts. "I'm close," I whisper as I continue to slide up and down his cock. He lowers his hand and squeezes my clit, the pressure sets me off and instantly my insides explode. My orgasm ripples through my body. As I'm coming back to Earth, I feel Jordan tense beneath me. Knowing he's close, I begin to ride him faster, my pussy walls tightening around him. "Ennfff. Ahhhh!" Jordan groans, as his orgasm releases inside of me.

When his body stills, I roll off him and we both lie their panting. Our breathing returns to normal when we roll onto our sides to face each other. "Morning," I whisper.

"Good morning, indeed," Jordan says with a smile. "That is by far the second best way to wake up."

Smiling, I ask, "And what's the first?"

"Your lips wrapped around my cock."

Smirking at him, I cheekily reply, "Duly noted for next time."

Before I can reply, he leans towards me, runs his fingers through my hair, cups my head, and brings his lips towards mine. We kiss passionately and just as I'm ready to mount him again, the girls giggling on the baby monitor interrupts us. Jordan breaks our kiss and whispers, "Man, they have impeccable timing."

"Mmhmm," is all I say, as I flop back on the bed and grin. After listening to the girls for a few moments, I look towards my husband and smile. "I'll get them if you start breakfast." Looking at the alarm clock on the bedside table, I add, "We will need to leave here by 8:15, at the latest."

"I can't believe Mike is getting married today. Who would have thought?"

"I always knew he'd get his happily ever after. If anyone deserves it, it's Mike. He's found the yin to his yang with Sav."

"I could insert a really inappropriate Mike joke here, but I'm a responsible dad and all that shit, so I will just lie here and do this." He leans over and takes my nipple into his mouth and gently bites down and sucks before letting it pop out of his mouth. He winks at me as he does the same to my other breast.

"Fuck it," I say, I push Jordan back onto the bed and straddle him before I impale myself on his cock. He sits us up and wraps his arms tightly around me as we rock back and forth vigorously. My lips crash against his and before we know it, we are both tumbling over the orgasmic cliff, screaming our release into each other's mouth.

Pulling back, I look deep into my husband eyes and huskily whisper, "I love you, Jordan McRoberts."

"I love you too, Kenzie McRoberts."

Reluctantly I climb off Jordan; I would love nothing more than to stay in bed with him all day, but today is a special day, one that will go down in history.

The Final Shot is now available.

ACKNOWLEDGMENTS

For the last two books I have always started off thanking my husband but this time the first person I want to thank is **Scarlet Wolfe**. Thank you for being my sounding board when I was lost and ready to delete it all. You gave me the encouragement to go on when I felt flat and sucky. On that Friday when we chatted, it gave me the kick I needed to make the changes to this book and now I have something that I am extremely proud of. I'm glad to have you on my team

Now, I can thank my hubby, **Troy**. For encouraging me to keep doing this and allowing me to go on this authoring journey. Your encouragement and love means the world to me. The last book released on our anniversary and I didn't even mention that so to cover all bases, Happy Anniversary, Happy Birthday, Happy Father's Day, Merry Christmas and Happy New Year. Love you long-time husband. And I cannot forget, my munchkins,

Piper and **Kade**. You two drive me crazy at times but you also provide me much entertainment and encouragement. I love you both to the moon and back.

My beta readers – Amy, Lyssa, Amanda, Crissy, Heather, Megan and Beth; thank you for taking the time to read Wine Not and picking up on my undies error and giving me advice on how to end the series on a high note. Thank you from the bottom of my heart for all your support and encouragement. Love you ladies, like I love wine; hard!

To those who work behind the scenes to take my little Word doc, and turn it into something amazing, thank you doesn't seem adequate. Without the following ladies, I would be lost and not have something amazing. My editor, **Karen Hrdlicka** (Barren Acres Editing); my cover designer and **Tash Drake** (Outlined with Love Designs). A special thanks to the following authors for giving me guidance and support on a daily basis; **Anita Gillham, BJ Harvey, Scarlet Wolfe, Ruby Rowe, M Stratton, Michelle Dare, Jodi Perry, Rebecca Rohman** and **Angel Justice.**

M Stratton, thank you for letting me reference your forking awesome series. You are not only a fellow author, but you are also a friend and I am grateful to have you in my life. I look forward to the day that the troublesome trio meets in real life; it will be forking amazeballs PS.

Her works can be found online and I highly recommend M Stratton

Thank you to the following book buddies for offering to be Escorts within Wine Not...your enthusiasm to be Escorts was awesome...and kind of scary.

PS. Sorry to the ones of you who died #Sorry-NotSorry

THE FINAL SHOT PLAYLIST

FML – Godsmack
Red Red Wine – UB40
Sunsets – Powderfinger
Pony – Ginuwine
Beautiful – Christina Aguilera
Just A Girl – No Doubt
Unconditionally – Katy Perry
Dancing in the Dark – Amy Macdonald
Faded – Alan Walker
Poker Face – Lady Gaga
You Make me Feel Like a Whore – Everclear
Just Dance – Lady Gaga
Sweet Dreams (Are Made of This) – Eurhythmics
Primadona Girl - Martina & The Band
Fuel – Metallica
Bleeding Love – Leona Lewis
Come Fly With Me – Frank Sinatra
Bad Things – Jace Everett
Down Under – Men at Work

I Don't Wanna Live Forever – ZAYN feat, Taylor Swift

Bad Intentions – Digital Daggers

Wannabe – Spice Girls

Untouchable – Garbage

Down in Flames – Daughter Jack

I'm Gonna Be (500 miles) – The Proclaimers

Fly Me to the Moon – Frank Sinatra

What a Wonderful World – Louis Armstrong

Dream a Little Dream of Me – Ella Fitzgerald

Just the Way You Are – Bruno Mars

It's Not Over – Daughtry

Need You Now – Lady Antebellum

Oh, Pretty Woman – Roy Orbison

Make War – From First to Last

Crawling – Linkin Park

Rolling in the Deep – Adele

You're the One that I Want – Film Musical Orchestra (Grease)

A Girl Like You - Edwyn Collins

Bitch – Meredith Brooks

Question Everything – Five Finger Death Punch

A Thousand Years – Christina Perri

Nothing Else Matters (Instrumental version) – Apocalyptica

Tomorrow – Silverchair

This playlist can be found on Spotify.

ABOUT THE AUTHOR

DL Gallie is from Queensland, Australia, but she's lived in many different places all over the world, including the UK and Canada. She currently resides in Central Queensland with her husband and two munchkins. She and her husband have been together since she was sixteen, and although they drive each other crazy at times, she couldn't imagine her life without him.

Shortly after her son was born, DL began reading again. With encouragement from her husband, she picked up the pen and started writing, and now the voices in her head won't shut up.

DL enjoys listening to music, drinking white wine in the summer, red wine in the winter, and beer all year round. She's also never been known to turn down a cocktail, especially a margarita.